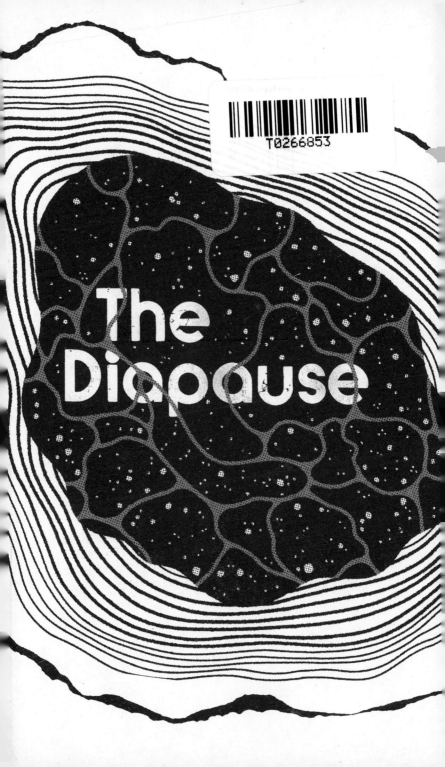

The Diapause

The Diapause

Andrew Forbes

Invisible Publishing
Halifax | Fredericton | Picton

Library and Archives Canada Cataloguing in Publication
Title: The diapause / Andrew Forbes.
Names: Forbes, Andrew, 1976- author.
Identifiers: Canadiana (print) 20240368991
            Canadiana (ebook) 20240369017
            ISBN 9781778430503 (softcover)
            ISBN 9781778430510 (EPUB)
Subjects: LCGFT: Novels.

Classification: LCC PS8611.O7213 D53 2024 | DDC C813/.6—dc23

Edited by Bryan Ibeas
Cover and interior design by Megan Fildes | Typeset in Laurentian
With thanks to type designer Rod McDonald

Invisible Publishing is committed to protecting our natural environment. As part of our efforts, both the cover and interior of this book are printed on acid-free 100% post-consumer recycled fibres.

Printed and bound in Canada.

Invisible Publishing | Halifax, Fredericton, & Picton
www.invisiblepublishing.com

Published with the generous assistance of the Canada Council for the Arts, the Ontario Arts Council, and the Government of Canada.

 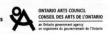

To my mother, Mary Uldene MacKinnon
(1942–2022)

"Mama, here comes midnight
with the dead moon in its jaws"

—"FAREWELL TRANSMISSION,"
SONGS: OHIA

PART I: TUMBLERS

WHEN I WAS JUST SHY of ten years old, my parents threw a New Year's party and invited everyone they knew.

We lived in Peterborough's south end in a cramped, leaning two-storey brick row house they'd been renting for years. Opposite the house, across narrow Albert Street, was a twelve-foot hurricane fence topped with barbed wire. Beyond that, stretching for two hundred metres in either direction, stood the imposing brick wall of the old General Electric plant, a mostly abandoned campus of buildings constructed throughout the late nineteenth and twentieth centuries. Our home faced a section of wall that was three storeys high, a dark reddish brown, and free of windows. There were once windows in it, but they'd been blocked up with the same colour of brick. Several large doors or gates had also been closed off that way. There were no openings across the whole blank expanse.

The row houses were put up shortly after the factory opened to house its employees and their families—six thousand workers at its height. But that had been long ago, and by the time we lived there only a shadow of that massive operation remained. The rest of the jobs had been shifted to Mexico and China, gradual rounds of layoffs sweeping through Peterborough's workers across the decades like erosion, until just one unit remained, hidden in one building in one corner of the giant complex, the rest abandoned and fenced off. The walls across from our house were silent and still. There was never any activity.

I saw that long wall, stretching across my entire field of vision, as the ruin of something ancient and fantastic, its bricked-over windows witnesses to astonishing events that would change to suit the stories in my head. Great wars, the invention of time-travelling machines, complex secret government programs. I dreamed of exploring the ruins, like Frank Hardy would have done, with a heavy flashlight and a pocket knife and a brother. What we might find there was secondary, really, to the feeling of potential discovery, and to the excitement, warmth, and happiness of fraternal conspiracy.

But I had no siblings. It was just me, my mother, and my father.

At our New Year's party, I wandered room to room feeling ambassadorial, welcoming people on behalf of our little tripartite unit. The small rooms overflowed with people waiting for midnight; neighbours and friends spilled across our thrift store furniture, crowded around our chipped birch veneer kitchen table. Some of my school friends were there with their parents. Around a firepit in our small, tightly fenced, and stone-paved backyard, adults sat in camp chairs, drinking from bottles, smoking cigarettes, passing joints, singing, laughing. It was an unusually mild patch of weather, I remember, and the relative warmth— right around freezing—coupled with the overfed fire, the flames gorging on old lumber, cardboard, magazines, and a stool with a broken leg, made the yard a popular spot.

In the poorly lit rooms, I found some people I knew and more I didn't. Once I felt I'd seen everyone there was to see, I stayed near the TV, which was streaming all of the Pirates of the Caribbean movies in succession. My closest friend, Max, was there for a while, but long before midnight his mother, hair to her waist, cheeks red, appeared next to where we were sprawled before the TV, holding his black and neon-green winter coat by its empty shoulders. She gave it a shake, like you would a towel with sand on it, and said, "There you are, Maxie. Time to get going." Max stood and she slid the parka over one arm and then the other.

"See you at school," I said to Max.

"Yeah," he said, and then they were out the door.

At a few minutes to midnight Dad came and found me. He was exuberant and loose. Mom called this version of my father "sweetly drunk." He said, "Gabey, buddy, come on outside! We're just about to start the countdown!"

"Okay," I said, standing, looking for the remote to pause the movie.

"Do you need a coat?" he said. "Naw, no, you'll be fine. Let's go, come on."

The fire, contained in a ring of bricks, had died down to coals. More people had moved outside, so we all had to stand very close to one another. My mother stood at the centre of the crowd's densest point, her phone in her ungloved hand showing a live stream of the ball descending over Times Square. My father hoisted me onto his shoulders—a fraught and momentarily terrifying action as I swayed forward, feeling his neck muscles strain to hold me upright, his arms struggling to situate me just right, seated up there, my legs over his shoulders, feet squeezing his sides. I could smell faintly alcoholic fumes rising from him, and the acrylic warmth of his toque. Once I was safely up there someone handed him a bottle of spumante, which he held by the neck and shook back and forth to make sure it was good and bubbly. Adults with lax focus milled around us, and those kids not held aloft stuck their chins high to try to see Mom's screen, or to find some fresh air. Dad peeled the gold foil off the neck of the bottle and began unwinding the wire cage over the cork as the countdown hit ten, and everyone in the yard—perhaps two dozen people in all—began to chant raggedly along. A woman I did not know stood next to us wearing shiny silver glasses that spelled *2020*. She shook with excitement.

Our count was a second or two ahead of New York's, but we decided to stick with it, eager maybe to start the new year with all its promise. Some shouted *Happy New Year!* just after one, but others said zero first. Dad worked the cork an extra second or two before it rocketed skyward with a lovely popping noise. I felt its small percussive escape on my face. Everyone whooped and Dad began pouring wine into disposable red cups. When the bottle was nearly empty, he tipped it up to slurp its last drops, tilting his head back and giving me a sudden jolt of fear that I'd go down. "Easy," he said, patting my knee. "I've got you."

As people cheered and clapped and kissed, Mom waded through bodies to stand before Dad and me. She reached up and patted my head and said, "Happy New Year, baby," and then she held my father's face in her hands and kissed his mouth. "Happy, happy," she said.

◄

There are no days like those days. Shredded cheese and ketchup on my hot dogs. Fruit punch through a plastic straw. I broke a tooth on a popcorn kernel and got to stay home for four days drinking milkshakes. Smell of diesel fumes as we idled in highway traffic. Marvel movie marathons with Dad, when I'd fall asleep before the first film ended. Cigarette smoke and grilling steak. I called the big orange jug of Tide laundry sauce. We played a game we called kitchen hockey, scrambling on our knees, wooden spoons for sticks, swatting a roll of masking tape. Mom read to me at night, windows open, a light breeze and the sound of passing cars. I once found a dead dove and hid it under the front porch, trying to spare myself from a shame I couldn't define.

I loved road trips, Netflix, potato chips, spending my Christmas money at the dollar store. At my ninth birthday party, Mom's hair caught fire when she leaned over the cake, and my father, standing opposite her, led her away by the elbow and doused the flames with store-brand root beer from a two-litre bottle. Then they laughed. I hadn't known what was happening, so it never occurred to me to be alarmed. Most of what my parents did was inscrutable to me; adults were an alien species.

We were a small family with few living relatives. My father's father—always called Papa—had died when I was three, and left his fishing shack to Dad.

It was a simple wooden structure on the shore of a weedy little bay of a pretty, though unremarkable, Ontario lake. The cabin wasn't insulated and hadn't been well cared for since my father inherited it. The small parcel of land on which it sat was overgrown. The landscape was rocky and forested, the southernmost incursion of the Boreal Shield ecozone. Pull up a map of the area and marvel at the number of lakes, most of which—in that part of the world, at that point in time—were used recreationally. There were few other buildings evident and the nearest town was twenty minutes away by car, but it wasn't uncommon to see boaters on Papa's lake, nor to hear hunters' rifles.

There were, and remain, thousands of shacks just like it in Ontario, and there was nothing particularly special about this one except that it had come into my parents' possession. We used it sparingly in the summer for fishing or swimming, but I don't think my folks ever had much interest in staying there.

—

A few days after the New Year's party, my parents spontaneously decided we should drive up to the cottage. There was no warning, no long-term plan. It was as though someone had called Dad and said, *Art, get your kid up here quick, the ice is great*, and so we grabbed our skates, jumped in the car, and were gone.

We drove two hours north out of Peterborough and turned off the highway, bumped down the narrow dirt fire road and stopped at the end of it, where the cabin, with its peaked metal roof and cedar siding painted brown, sat in the midst of the forest, seemingly miniature below the enormous trees.

It was a bright, sharp, freezing day in early January. There was no snow, but the ground was hard, and winter sunlight fell through the trunks and branches. We did not go inside the cabin, where there was no heat—only a cold stove—and no running water. We walked instead over the hard ground and frozen needles and leaves, weaving between the trees, down to the dock, where I sat and took off my boots, legs dangling over the edge. The lake had frozen quickly, and it was perfectly flat.

Dad had a black nylon hockey bag over his shoulder, and he swung it down next to me and unzipped its great silver zipper, the large teeth purring their lovely sound as they parted. He removed my second-hand black-and-white Bauers, bought at the skate exchange in Peterborough, and began to loosen the laces. He worked the right one onto my foot and braced its blade against his thigh.

"Go ahead, push," he said, but I was afraid that I would hurt him, or cut his jeans. "Don't worry," he said. "I'm fine. Push."

I did, and he leaned against my straightened leg, too, and after some struggle my foot popped into place. He moved closer, placed the skate between his knees, and tied it up very tight, his fingers turning red in the cold.

"Other foot," he said, then cupped his hands to his mouth and blew into them.

We repeated the exercise, and then he placed a black helmet on my head and buckled its strap beneath my chin as I winced, certain it would pinch my skin, but it didn't. Then he pulled my coat's hood over the helmet and patted my head.

"That wind's got teeth," he said.

"Claws," my mother said. "We used to say a cold wind had claws." She was on the dock next to me tying up her own skates—clean white figure skates—and rewinding her cream and fawn-brown scarf around her neck, her light brown hair spilling over it like waves. Then, as I sat in stillness, watching, she walked on her blades away from the dock and began to test the ice with a few slow, smooth turns and a quick balletic spin.

"Mom!"

"I took lessons until I was fifteen," she said. Her cheeks were in high colour, her lips pink, teeth gleaming in the cold air. "Mrs. Swift, who'd once been with the Ice Capades."

"Ice Capades?" I asked.

"Professional skaters," she said.

"Like Disney On Ice," said Dad, who was lacing up his own scuffed black CCM Tacks, their laces mismatched, one yellow, one white with black hashes. When he tied off the second double knot he stood and pushed off, and we all made our way out across the bay toward the open lake.

The sun was low and reflected blindingly off the surface. The wind whistled into my hood, the plastic of the helmet cold against my head. The ice was smooth as glass, and clear enough in some places that we could see through to the black water below, which sent a jolt of fear through me. I was not a strong skater, but I could stay on my feet most of the time, taking short, choppy steps, my arms out from my sides as counterbalance, like a tightrope walker. I did my best to keep up with my parents, and they took turns wheeling around to skate by my side while the other went on ahead.

When we were clear of the narrows at the head of the bay, they left me for a moment, speeding together in parallel course before crossing one another's path, my mother light and graceful on her figure skates, my father hunched and bent, all the power in his knees and back because he had learned to skate while playing hockey. They whooped and laughed, the wind throwing Mom's long hair out behind her. I watched my parents experiencing a rare moment of pure animal joy, flying at great speed across the frozen lake, free of impediments and appointments.

"Yee-hee!" my father cried, and I took it as permission for me to do likewise, a hint that certain rules had been suspended. There were no people around, no one to censure us.

Before long my back began to hurt, and Mom said her toes were cold, so we turned and headed back into the bay and over to Papa's dock. Dad placed his hands under my arms and lifted me up onto it, then began untying my skates. Once I had my boots on again, Mom dug a Thermos and three red plastic cups from the hockey bag, and poured us each a hot chocolate. I tilted mine toward my lips slowly and blew. The steam rose into my eyes, and condensation collected on my eyelashes.

As we drove home, I rested my head against the car's window and felt the uneven road buzz in my skull and jaw, cushioned by my knit hat. The sky became flat and opaque as clouds rolled in, or we rolled into them. It quickly grew dark. Snow began to fall in streaks and tracers in our headlights, zipping and bending in a way that Dad said looked like time travel. "We're making the jump to hyperspace," he said.

The first case in Canada was reported in late January, in Toronto, ninety minutes down the road from Peterborough. They closed the schools in March. The stores and restaurants, the sporting venues, the libraries, the theatres.

At Mom's insistence I tried to keep up with online math lessons and reading. I sat at the kitchen table each morning, opened a laptop, and logged in for attendance. But I wasn't suited for learning that way, and I'd soon drift away. I missed Max, and art class, and the chocolate-dipped granola bars Dad put in my school lunches.

Furloughed, unusable, Mom and Dad kicked around the house, trying to find a routine. We shied away from anyone outside our household. Avoided parks and sidewalks. The infection rate continued to climb, its curve on the ubiquitous graph refusing to flatten. Dad obsessed over local case counts, rising death numbers, overwhelmed emergency departments. He had nothing to do but pickle himself in news.

Mom came home from picking up groceries with a tickle in her throat, so we sat in our idling car for two hours in the parking lot of an arena. We snaked toward the front of a line, and when our turn came we rolled down our windows so a nursing student could use comically oversized Q-tips to probe our frontal lobes via our nostrils. Three days later my parents got an email confirming we were not infected. In the interval between test and result, it was expected that we would not risk any circumstances that might spread infection. Like so many of the improvised systems that had sprung up, it was imperfect, but it was what we had.

In May, when we could finally leave the windows open in the evenings, my parents began to talk about relocating to the cabin. A change of scenery, a new bunker in which to shelter for a matter of weeks while things, we stupidly hoped, sorted themselves out. I think it was only meant to be a temporary arrangement—but it would be wrong to say my parents had anything resembling a plan. Like everyone else, they were only waiting on the next piece of information, the next development, the next finding. The future was a moving target.

We finally left one morning in June. Mom locked the front door and Dad started the Honda, put it into gear. We didn't talk at all. I sat behind Mom and looked out the window.

Two police cruisers idled on a vacant lot, pointed in opposite directions, driver's-side doors edged close. The officers inside wore white masks over the lower halves of their faces and sat in quiet conference through the cars' open windows. One nodded, put her cruiser in gear, eased it out.

A masked family of four stood on the patchy lawn of a retirement home holding balloons and a brightly decorated sign, marker on bristol board, while inside, seated in a chair near the window, a white-haired woman waved distantly in response.

In the parking lot of the concrete and glass hospital, a temporary structure of corrugated aluminum had been erected, its entrance cloaked in tenting, doctors and nurses in masks, face shields, full protective garments.

The parks and schoolyards were vacant. Masked people lined up outside a grocery store, spaced at six-foot intervals. Others exited the grocery store, carts piled high with rolls of toilet paper. Above the entrance a banner flapped: *ALL LANES OPEN.*

As we sped past the park by the river, I caught a glimpse, far off, of a massive old willow, shaggy and round, its leaves blowing as if in slow motion. It was so grand and permanent seeming. Each time I saw it I thought, *What strange things are trees.*

Before long we were out of the city—Peterborough was not large then—flung out by our fear that life was closing in around us, making infection inevitable. The cabin was for me a wild, unknown place, and I foresaw great adventure. And I was happy, after three months of lockdown, to be going anywhere.

We needled northward into the trees and the green and pink granite of the Kawartha Lakes. The highway narrowed.

◆

Papa had been a high school math and woodworking teacher. He collected duck decoys, cheered for the Leafs, and divorced my grandmother when my father was sixteen. When they split, they sold the family house in Peterborough. She moved to Toronto, where she was from, and he stuffed himself and his ducks into a two-bedroom condo that was walking distance from the high school. The mortgage had been paid off, so Papa used his share of the sale proceeds to buy an unserviced lot just north of Maynooth, at the end of a fire road, on the shore of a mid-sized lake. Over several years he put up the cabin and garage, plus an outhouse, a woodshed, and a canoe rack of thick, lathe-turned cedar with mortise and tenon joinery. The cabin became his retreat. He would spend his summer weekends there fishing, sitting on his screened porch, and tinkering. Once retired he would stay for longer stretches, until a hip replacement slowed him down and made his trips to the lake less frequent.

He and my grandmother had a matching pair of pastel-rose armchairs at their old house. She'd wanted nothing to do with any of the furniture, nor really with any remnant of their life together, so Papa kept both chairs. Eventually, he moved one to the cabin. The other he kept in his condo, and it was in its overstuffed embrace that Dad found him unresponsive one Sunday afternoon, a Steelers-versus-Patriots game flickering on the television. Papa hadn't really liked football, my father told me, but would watch it if he couldn't find anything else on TV.

There was no TV at the cabin. It was a spartan place, consisting of one large, simply appointed room with a queen-sized bed; a sitting area; and at the far end, opposite the door, a small kitchen with a sink, an old, wheezing refrigerator, a stove, and wooden cabinets and drawers beneath an aqua-coloured linoleum countertop. Over the stove and next to the refrigerator were three rows of shelving, stocked with non-perishables, pots, and dishes. In the corner sat the squat black wood stove, its stovepipe extending straight upward into the ceiling. Between the kitchen and the sitting area there stretched a long, sturdy pine table that Papa had made himself.

In the sitting area there was a red-and-yellow plaid chesterfield, a small oak side table, and Papa's armchair. Both the chesterfield and the armchair faced the lake, which could be sensed as an openness and a play of light through a wall of windows. A sliding glass door gave onto the narrow screened porch, which was barely deep enough to squeeze by if a second person was sitting in one of the four chairs lined up out there. The cabin was on the northern edge of the bay, so it had a southern exposure, and the sun would stream right into the porch and the wall of windows behind it.

Along the wall farthest from the lake, behind the chesterfield and armchair, there was a long, skinny storage corridor, separated from the room by thin wood panelling. It was accessible through a door at the far end, near the main door. At the other end, by the kitchen, was tucked a small bathroom with a toilet; a pedestal sink; a crooked, veined mirror; and a claustrophobic shower stall.

The walls throughout were bare studs painted brown, and the back of the plywood cladding to which the cedar siding was affixed. There was no insulation, and the electrical wiring was visible in its flexible metal conduit. The ceiling was peaked, with lines of perfectly uniform pine slats held in place by thick wooden rafters, painted the same dull brown. There was precisely one adornment: on the wood-panelled wall that concealed the storage space there was tacked, with four push-pins, a linen tea towel printed with an image of a bagpiper and the words and music to "Amazing Grace." It had been my grandmother's, but just where it came from and why Papa chose to hang it there post-divorce, I can't say.

The cabin sat atop large boulders of granite and leaning columns of stacked cinder block. Tucked beneath, in a crevice between rocks, the loud, quivering pump stood upon a rotting wooden scaffold, pulling water from the lake through a long PVC hose that snaked along the ground down to a spot fifteen feet offshore, where the foot valve was tied with rusted wire into a plastic milk crate and weighed down with fist-sized rocks. For the roughly seven months between the thaw and the freeze-up, this set-up would provide the kitchen and bathroom faucets, the rusty showerhead, and one outdoor spigot with slightly brownish running water, unsafe for drinking but used for washing bodies and dishes.

To the north and east of the cabin, tucked beneath thicker coverage, was the garage and workshop that Papa built, with large barn doors and a cool concrete floor. To the northwest of the cabin, in a little swale of trillium and poison ivy, stood the outhouse, pitched at an almost comical angle so that when you sat inside, it was necessary to brace your right arm against the wall to avoid sliding off the seat. In a bright clearing near the lake's edge rested the cedar crib that cradled the sixteen-foot blue fibreglass canoe.

Everything in this scene huddled beneath tall and sturdy oaks, beeches, maples, a few ironwood trees, and, by the water, a pair of ancient, towering white pines. On the ground, held within the shifting green light that heat, sun, and chlorophyll combine to create, there grew cleavers, poison ivy, Solomon's seal, trilliums, columbines, and ferns. Near the shore and in the mucky shallows were cattails, water soldiers, arrowheads. In the slow water beyond, water lilies' yellow bulbs and white blossoms bobbed above their flat green pads, broad as turkey platters. Further back, away from the lake, where Dad had parked the car at the fire road's widened end, there was a clearing of sorts. It was lined with giant boulders that seemed to have been dropped there, and between them sumac, buckthorn, and a few showy elderberry bushes that in late June were in white, fragrant blossom. The air was alive with mosquitoes, flies, midges, moths, cicadas, paper wasps, yellow jackets, and monarchs.

❦

When we made the trip it didn't seem to me there would be anything dire or unusual about our stay. It felt like we were on a sort of vacation. We'd live there for a while, have some fun in the water, get sunburns. Then we'd go home. But the number of supplies with which we arrived should have told me otherwise.

Mom had bought everything she could imagine we'd need before we'd left. She was our designated shopper, and had been since the lockdown began. She knew something about my father's character, about how he'd been mainlining the warnings and protocols, about the particular nature of his insomnia, the shortness of his patience, his proneness to anxiety. When she brought the groceries home, it was Dad who used disinfecting wipes to clean the packages, and who washed all the produce piece by piece. I don't imagine it was necessary for them to have a conversation about assigning roles once isolation began. I think my father was self-aware enough to accept his position from the jump.

Before we left, Mom must have spent all of the government emergency cheque on food, great quantities of it. She went to Costco, followed by her regular grocery store, and bought all the family packs, the large boxes, the two-litre containers. She bought four eighteen-litre jugs of spring water. When she returned home she stuffed the refrigerator and piled bags and boxes of non-perishables near the door where we left them overnight, except the water jugs, which she left in the car—two in the trunk and two in the back seat. In the morning we carted everything back out to the car. We also jammed bags of clothes—shopping bags, garbage bags, my school backpack—and boxes of books and board games and anything else we might need over the course of an indefinite stay.

We drove the two hours north on fairly quiet roads beneath an overcast sky that soon gave way to rain, pummelling sheets of it thudding the windshield and roof, spraying up from the black road into the undercarriage, vibrating in my feet. When finally we arrived at the head of the fire road, I felt a dread sense of oppression, fear, boredom, and inconvenience. The road looked to me impassable, slick and muddy, large puddles everywhere. Dad stopped the car and we sat idling, the rain drumming the roof.

He lowered his window and reached his arm around—the sleeve of his red plaid shirt already rolled up, as his sleeves always were—and rubbed at a spot on the windshield that the wiper was missing. My mother lowered her window too, pressing the small button on her door until the glass was halfway down, and she extended her arm straight out into the air. The radio was on but I couldn't hear it over the sound of the rain. Her arm was getting wet up to the shoulder, but she didn't seem to mind. She wiggled her fingers and made a fist, released it. On my face I felt the finest spray drifting in from her open window. The air was rank and heavy. She closed her window and my father closed his, and then he began driving very slowly.

We jostled in and out of ruts and potholes. The road was gravel in some spots, hard-packed dirt in others. Roots strained their way above the surface and back into it. In places Dad had to slalom his way around fallen tree limbs. The car's axles groaned beneath the weight. On the seat next to me, bags and boxes of groceries and supplies shook and tottered, and the water jugs sloshed. A cantaloupe spilled out of a bag. I palmed the strange rough texture of its sandy-grey husk, and thought that it must be what the skin of an elephant felt like. The forest on either side of us grew thicker, more wild. There was an opening, where there were no trees, only grasses and cattails, that I later came to know was a wetland, and where the rank smell was heavier.

When Dad at last eased the car to a stop at the end of the road, it looked like nowhere I had ever been. I did not recognize it for its orientation nor for the way the grey, watery light fell through the trees. The cabin, not visible from the road, seemed to be nowhere nearby. I thought there was some mistake. But Dad did in fact say, "Here we are," and I looked through the rain-spattered windows to see if I could identify something familiar.

The rain intensified, and my parents came to a wordless agreement to stay in the car until the storm let up. Mom put her bare feet up on the dash, and Dad turned up the radio, though I still could not make out the song. Perhaps he couldn't either, because after a moment he shut it off, and we sat quietly, each of us looking out a different window, waiting.

When the noise subsided, my mother swung her feet down, slipped her shoes back on, and opened her door, sticking her arm out once again. "Good a time as any," she said. I opened my door, too, and stood, feeling only a weak, warm drizzle on my face and arms.

Dad opened the trunk and filled my arms with bags and boxes. "Can you take a little more? Sure you can. Here." We walked single file like a train of pack animals down the narrow path, beneath the dripping trees, toward the cabin that was there after all, looking sad and neglected, but in some way permanent in its place, as though it had passed a test and so the forest would allow it to remain. Dad dropped his load on the small, overburdened step and worked the key in the lock for a moment before the door fell open, releasing stale, unmoving air. We tracked mud and wet leaves inside, a little puddle forming at our feet. Dad wiped his shoes on the shaggy sisal rug and pressed his palm against the big rocker switch on the wall panel near the door. The old refrigerator sputtered reluctantly to life, and the lamp next to the chesterfield blinked on.

We placed our armloads on the floor and on the bed, and then Dad and I trudged back out to the car for another load while Mom stayed behind and began to find a place for each thing. It was overwhelming. Boxes and bags. Cereal and coffee, sugar, cabbage. Clothes. Two cases of beer. A sleeping bag. Two boxes of books, one for me and one for them. A family-sized bottle of shampoo with a pump lid. Oranges. Bananas. Potato chips.

Mom stocked the groaning fridge. Milk, cheese, eggs, cold meat. Dad pulled a dangling chain, and an overhead fan coated in dust lazily began to turn. The rain intensified once more. The cabin smelled strongly of dampness and still, sour air. I hadn't imagined feeling this way—flat, un-thrilled. When they'd told me we were heading up to the cabin I'd dreamed only of sunny days full of adventure, but the lifeless afternoon and the practicalities of relocation seemed to me about the worst combination of circum-stances. I did my best to stay small, curling up in Papa's armchair, as my parents stocked the fridge and freezer, the shelves, the musty drawers. After a while, Mom, likely sensing my frame of mind, called me over and put me to work running things to places she called out. She knew that I liked to feel useful, in some way instrumental to the opera-tion of this small machine, our family.

I was a quiet, inward child. Sometimes I asked questions, sometimes I laughed, but my default was to remain silent and watchful. I lived my life afraid to be called upon, but obedient when I was. I did not always feel resilient enough to be in the world; I thought I lacked armour. If this was true, I was fine with it. I didn't mind being soft or delicate—I only wished not to appear that way to others, including my father. With my mother, however, it was different. I couldn't deceive her—she knew me too well. My father was inattentive enough that it sufficed to pretend.

Perhaps an hour went by as we organized and stashed all our things. It might have been two. When we were done the rain had stopped and the sun had begun to shine. Thick drops of water fell from the trees when the wind stirred them, and the light turned liquid and golden. There circu-lated among us a feeling of ease—or among them, certainly, and I was open enough to absorb it, or ape it. They both opened bottles of beer, and we sat unspeaking on folding lawn chairs in the small screened porch, watching the late afternoon sun on the water, through the trees. My parents exchanged smiles and nods, as though we had achieved some manner of milestone. There was a feeling of safety— one I didn't realize had been lacking until that point, but that I would recognize in the future for its absence.

—◆—

I am the only child of Katherine Reynolds—Kat—and Arthur David Ward—Art. She sometimes called him Artie.

By that summer they were both in their late thirties: Mom was thirty-nine, and Dad would turn thirty-seven at the end of July. Though there is no concrete proof, I have nevertheless always believed my existence to be acciden-tal—or, more charitably, *unexpected*. I wasn't the plan. They both had creative interests they likely would have preferred to pursue, probably hadn't envisioned life with a child—especially not a fragile boy who represented all the most brittle aspects of both their personalities. My father found it difficult to be out in the world. He was anxious and silent in the company of most people other than Mom and me, and I can see the shadow of that in me. Mom was more outgoing and had a bigger personality, but she was quick to be stung and slow to forget—both traits I share.

Physically, I inherited my mother's pale, burn-prone skin, my father's bad joints. I have his dark brown hair and her freckles. He gave me the acne that was just beginning to bloom that summer, and she passed along her weak eyes. I am very much the middle point between the two of them.

They met in university, where they were both studying what Papa called the unemployable arts. Dad, born and raised in Peterborough, landed at Trent University—a fifteen-minute drive from the 1970s bungalow he'd grown up in—because it was the easiest and cheapest post-secondary option. Mom had grown up in Eastern Ontario, in a small town that's since been absorbed into Ottawa's sprawl.

She never took me there, but she described it to me like this: Small families living in cold, empty homes, suffering through interminable winter nights, having Canadian arguments in Canadian kitchens. The wind whistling death down desolate Main Street. The sub shop sitting dark next to the Red & White store which was itself just closing up, its bottles of ginger ale and its bags of Cheezies, its urn of stale coffee, its packs of John Player Specials, its discount VHS tapes, all unavailable until morning. The temperature would continue to drop until sunrise, the coyotes raising a chorus somewhere not all that far away, and if you forgot to plug in the block heater, good luck starting the truck up in the morning. The fathers packed stubbies of beer in their lunch boxes, and the children all smoked cigarettes and tortured animals.

Kat had few fond memories of the place, and couldn't wait to escape it, which was how she found herself at Trent. She met Artie in a second-year Canadian art history class, and by third year she convinced him to move out of his father's house to share an apartment on Dublin Street with a shifting collection of roommates.

They both graduated, Dad just barely, and he began delivering pizzas and making lattes while she got a master's in women's studies. She started teachers' college but quit midway through her first year. Dad was still touring the service sector—property maintenance, house painting, waiting tables, and, eventually, bartending—but had begun throwing paint at large rectangles of plywood in what spare time he had. He read French theory and watched Japanese films. Mom participated in knitting circles and joined the Friends of the Public Library. She baked, both for us and for her friends, as well as for any cause requiring that funds be raised. She went to council meetings and marched as an ally.

They rented a series of lopsided or listing apartments and rundown houses across the river in East City, and in the south end of town. They worked in bars and restaurants, attended concerts of friends' bands. Mom sewed some of her own clothes, thrifted the rest. Dad quit smoking, took it up again, quit. They gave up gluten, meat, chocolate, processed foods, caffeine, and alcohol, then welcomed all of these things back into their lives one by one. They drove second-hand cars, avoided Toronto. Dad's favourite albums were by Radiohead. Mom lit candles the night Leonard Cohen died.

Dad gave up painting shortly after I was born, and started watching hockey, I think in part because it seemed to him a fatherly thing to do. It was something he hadn't done very often—not since he was a boy, when he and Papa would watch the CBC broadcast each Saturday night.

By the time I could walk, Dad had wandered tentatively back toward art, deciding that he was a collagist. He repurposed many of the plywood sheets he'd painted, plastering them with magazine pages, newsprint, and other assorted media. To my knowledge he sold exactly one of these, to a bar on Hunter Street that held monthly meat draws and hosted open mic poetry nights. The rest of his pieces would remain stacked against the wall of the dingy, dusty basement of our house back in Peterborough. In time, several of them developed mould and salt stains, sitting as they did atop seams in the rough, ancient concrete that became furred and spiky with white crystals. My father knew this slow-motion damage was taking place but did nothing to save his work.

At the moment the world stopped turning he was deep into his coupon phase—he'd recently completed a piece made almost entirely of Tide laundry detergent coupons he'd collected from neighbours' flyer inserts very early one morning. It was, he explained to me, a critique on the notion of cleanliness, as well as—like all his work—an attack on capitalism. I understand that he thought of himself as a product of mid-twentieth-century avant-gardism, shaped by the invisible girding of geopolitical tension, zine culture, and punk and noise bands, and was having some trouble reconciling himself with the demise of all that. The lines had shifted, his heroes' relevance had dried up, and his targets had been supplanted by greater evils. I think he also held on to a small bit of guilt over the fact that, while his grandfather was a coal miner in Cape Breton who drew his last, laboured breath at fifty, and Papa was a high school teacher, he, Art, lacked stable employment for most of his adult life. The point where that guilt met his stated position on the ills of capitalism was probably just one of the many sites of conflict within him.

I believe my mother harboured a similar internal struggle: whereas she hated housework, chafed at routine, and generally disliked working for others, her maternal grandmother had crawled out of Lodz on her stomach and fled the continent on a boat to Halifax, then trained to Ottawa to invent a new life. Kat's parents, Ottawans both, were civil servants, components of the great bureaucratic mechanism, the underlying goal of which was stability and the avoidance of the sort of chaos that had brought half her family to Canada to begin with.

When I came unexpectedly into being, Kat and Artie bowed to necessity and took up steady, if varied, work:

Mom in a knitting shop that ran crafting classes and work-shops, and Dad managing a series of bars and restaurants including, briefly, a floating tiki bar that toured Little Lake and moored at the marina next to the Holiday Inn. After the tiki boat's failure, one of the decorative masks took up permanent residence in our basement, leaning against the wall near his paintings—a silent, somewhat sinister totemic presence that served to remind Art of his track record of insolvency.

I think my parents had expected a very different future for themselves and for the world. After having spent their young lives in the 1980s and 1990s, they emerged from the torturous gauntlet of the twentieth century only to find the new one full of fresh horrors. I would sometimes catch them, when they were watching television or reading on their phones, looking momentarily dazed and overcome by news or events.

By the time I was born, their routines, their curious little habits, and their beliefs had already hardened into bed-rock. It's to their credit that those beliefs were tolerant and reasonably progressive—Black and Indigenous lives mattered to them, and love was love, and they put signs in our windows stating as much—but when confronted with the suggestion that something they held dear deserved recon-sideration, they bristled and bucked.

Still, I think they were basically decent people, and they managed to remain in love with one another. Certain mornings seemed to find them adrift on a refound youth, feeling beyond custodial responsibility, beholden only to whim. On those days I'd be recast as an odd friend, a third, an enthusiastic but always slow to comprehend tag-along. Those were strange days, days that suspended me between joy and annoyance. I wanted my parents to be happy, of course, and enjoyed the spectacle of their exuberance, but I resented the implication that all of this would be their constant state if it weren't for my presence.

Even on normal days, they had a life together that predated me, one filled with their customs and tics. Many were disrupted when I came along, but it was always clear to me that I would have to adapt to the ones that persisted.

Now in his thirty-seventh year, Dad was holding on to the last physical vestiges of his youth. He was just over six feet tall, lean, knobby and knuckly, hard, even with his small beer gut, and his brown hair had begun greying at the temples and nape. He had thick, bulbous veins running down his thin arms and into his hands. He wore cut-off jeans all that summer, and beat-up running shoes. He had a collection of short-sleeved plaid shirts—in red, blue, and green—that he swapped out each day. In the colder months he would wear long-sleeved flannel shirts, with the sleeves rolled up to the elbows. When we swam, he did so in his cut-offs, and stood at the water's edge unbuttoning one or another of those shirts, then hanging it from the branch of a tree or balling it up and tossing it in the canoe. When we returned to the cabin he would pin it to the clothesline—which ran off the corner of the porch and down toward the water— where the shirt would flap and wave, and he would change into another, and by the next morning the first shirt would be ready to wear again.

Mom was fuller and softer, with milky skin and wavy auburn hair. She was a half a foot shorter than Dad but her hair was big and gave her a few additional inches, especially on humid days. She had a big smile and a huge laugh. She dressed simply—jeans, sundresses, logo-less T-shirts, sometimes one of Dad's old plaid shirts.

She was an organizer by nature and tried to impose order and simplicity on things that sprawled and spilled over, as did most anything that Art touched. If she had a motto, my father joked, it was *Paint it white*. She painted everything white—*It's just cleaner*, she would say. *Airy* was another word she used.

As we sat in the screened porch in the late afternoon with the trees drip-drying, I could not have told you the state of their marriage. It didn't occur to me to question it. I was ten years old. I had no idea what knit them together, or what threatened to unstitch them. It was beyond me, when this all began, to consider their relationship violable. They were my parents—both the sky arching over me and the ground under my feet. I assumed they would persist forever.

Mom, slung over her chair, nearly sideways, her feet up on Dad's knee. Him running his hand over her ankle, resting it there in a gesture both tender and possessive. The light tilting through the trees at greater and greater angles, growing sweeter and sweeter.

Mom spoke after many minutes of silence. "I have some pork chops for dinner," she said. "What time do we want to eat?"

I can't account for why some memories stand out more vividly than others. I can reinhabit this moment endlessly, with startling accuracy.

"Let me cook tonight," Dad said. "I feel like it's my turn. I want to."

They were equitable that way, each cooking as often as the other. There were dishes he prepared that were beyond what she could produce, and vice versa. He made lasagnas, spending all day in the kitchen, the sauce, the layers. Meats done slowly, painstakingly, on the barbecue, or in a low oven. Sharp, vinegary salads that I loved. Mom baked bread, quiches with bacon that I ate in great quantities whenever she made them. Her pancakes were better than Dad's, and she made my birthday cakes from scratch.

"Let me do a salad, then," said Mom.

"Oh, good, yes," he said.

We all sat quietly a few minutes more in the late-afternoon light, the air warm and soft. A faint breeze rose, and fish started to trouble the surface of the bay. My parents went into the woefully inadequate kitchen and began to weave around one another while they laughed and prepared dinner. Dad played music on his phone, stuck it into a big ceramic mug to amplify it, and they sang along. I think it was Bob Dylan. When they were finished we ate at the sturdy pine table that was the colour of honey and as smooth as a new gym floor.

I went to bed that night on the musty chesterfield with its loud, too-firm springs and its chintzy brocade upholstery. My sleeping bag had a red plaid interior and a blue nylon shell, and my pillow was lumpy and uneven. Cool, sweet air poured gently over my face through the open windows, and I could hear the croaking of bullfrogs and high whine of crickets, the trees' soft static. There was a small bit of light from the lamp on the side table next to Papa's chair. Mom was in that chair doing a crossword on yellowed newsprint, and my father sat in a kitchen chair quietly watching her, a bottle of beer in his fist and a glass of Jack Daniel's nearby. I fell asleep while she murmured clues to him and he offered possible responses.

"Something's wrong over here in this corner," she said, tapping the pencil on the folded-over page.

"I'm stumped," Dad said.

The ghostly, plaintive sound of a loon woke me. I blinked, rubbed my eyes, then sat up on the groaning, creaking chesterfield. Out the windows the air over the lake, through the trees, was gauzy.

"Yeah, that's not gonna work," my mother was saying. She and Dad were awake in their bed, sitting propped up against the wall with their pillows behind their backs. They had been quietly conspiring.

"What's not?" I asked.

"These sleeping arrangements," she said.

"You kept us awake half the night on that thing," Dad said. "Every time you moved those springs would make so much damn noise."

"Every time you so much as breathed."

"Where else can I sleep?"

"On the floor," Mom said.

"Outside, under the stars," Dad said, "or in the garage with the mice."

"No!"

"We could anchor the canoe out in the middle of the lake," Mom said, "and he could sleep there."

"That could work. Just don't roll over too much, bud."

"No," I said. "The mosquitoes!"

"Oh, Gabey," Mom said, sensing my alarm. "Love, we wouldn't make you do any of that."

"Then what'll we do?"

"We'll figure something out," said Dad.

"Maybe earplugs for us," Mom said as she threw back the heavy blue knit bedcover and swung her legs out of bed, stretched her arms above her head. "Coffee," she said. Dad grunted in approval.

She walked on her toes over to the old GE stove, turned on an element, and pulled a green enamel coffee pot and a small white kettle off a shelf. She tore the stopper off the open water container and tilted it toward the floor, holding the kettle beneath its spout. Water sloshed into the kettle and onto the floor. She righted the jug and placed the kettle on the element, which had turned orange-red with heat. Then she opened the three-pound can of ground coffee, tore off the foil seal, and spooned grounds into a paper filter in a black plastic cone that she nestled atop the green coffee pot. When the water boiled she began slowly pouring it into the wide top of the cone in slow, circular movements. Now and then she would set the kettle down to let the water seep through the grounds and the filter before dripping into the coffee pot. She would watch intently, then pick up the kettle and pour some more. The cabin filled with the smell of hot coffee.

Dad opened a giant purple box of Raisin Bran, then took three mismatched bowls from a shelf and three spoons from the top drawer. When Mom was done pouring water over the grounds, she stepped over to the fridge and opened its door—the machine sighing in protest of its own age—then took out a carton of milk and a jug of orange juice. We ate.

After breakfast we dressed and went outside. Dad strode past me toward the garage, and I hurried after him to see what help I could offer.

Dad unlocked the padlock and swung open the garage's large, heavy doors. Inside, it was dusty and cluttered, and smelled of old oil. Dad found a switch near the doors, and two rows of fluorescent tubes blinked to life overhead, il-luminating the windowless space with a cold light. There were stacks of lumber on the floor, and shelves lining one side and the back wall. Along the third side, on my left, was a long, heavy workbench, above which were shelves and nooks packed with tools, hardware, and odd bits, all stored in old fruit bins, wooden cartons, cardboard boxes, glass jars, coffee tins, and plastic ice cream tubs. There was an outboard motor, a small electric snow blower, and a lawn mower with its guts splayed around it. There were orange life jackets hanging from nails along the face of the shelves. There were instruction manuals, magazines, and crossword puzzles that had been cut from newspapers and paper-clipped together. There were garden tools and canoe paddles. There were spiderwebs and mouse droppings.

Dad began browsing the shelves and boxes and cartons. I had the sense that interesting things lay among all that stuff, waiting for me to discover them, to build something out of them, but the idea of making order of the mess was too much for me just then. I turned around so that my back was to my father, and I faced out from the garage. I stood exactly where the polished concrete floor ended and the dirt and gravel and pine mulch began, and I tilted my head back to look at patches of sky through the treetops.

It was my habit to look at the sky for some clue as to how to feel. In that moment, spying a few discreet smearings of cloud amid the deep, deep blue of a June morning, I won-dered: *Is the blue of the summer sky the same as the blue of a winter sky?* And: *Is the heavy purple of the rain cloud the same purple as the incoming front bearing snow? And if not, why not?*

"Let's see if we can make some sense of this," Dad said to me, and I turned to face him. His hands were on his hips, and he was looking at me as though I might have some sug-gestion, because he was clearly overwhelmed too. Though he'd suggested he was about to spring into action, he was standing still, daunted by the job's complexity.

Mom came up the path from the cabin and walked into the garage. She nodded at my father and me and then began scanning the shelves and walls. "Jeez," she said, "look at all this." She took a pair of cream-coloured leather work gloves out of a cardboard box and a set of pruning shears off a nail over the workbench. "You guys knock yourselves out in here. I'm going to go tame the wilderness."

"Sounds good," Dad said, audibly deflated. I think that for a fraction of a second, when Mom appeared, he had the hope that she would take control, as she often did, and tell him where to start. But then she strode off and left him to the mess that his father had made.

All I know about my father's relationship with Papa comes from what Dad told me, which isn't all that much. I've seen photos of them together, of course—my father as a baby in Papa's rough hands, my father as a young boy being thrown into the air while Papa laughs and squints, standing up to his chest in a swimming pool. And I've seen one home video, from a trip to Colonial Williamsburg, Virginia, when Dad was about eleven or twelve, in which he and Papa take turns narrating their visit. I remember one brief scene, which must have been shot by my grand-mother, where Papa and my father pretend to run toward each other in slow motion across a cobblestoned space and then, when they meet, to bowl one another over, a bit inspired by the Three Stooges. Papa is bent low, and Dad's shoulder knocks Papa's straw hat off. They both spill to the ground eventually and begin laughing, while my grand-mother says, "Okay, you goofs, that's enough."

So I know there was humour between them, but I don't know how much, or what filled the time when it was absent. And in the lee of all that, with Papa dead and my father reaching the middle of his life, there was only this massive collection of collections, most of which would never be useful to us.

Dad paced back and forth, scanning the shelves. He picked items up at random and beheld them, turned them over, weighing their value, or sometimes just trying to determine their purpose. He returned each item to its spot and kept browsing.

The cabin was not his place. He'd had no interest in it until he inherited it, and even then I believe he and Mom considered selling it. My father hadn't grown up with the cabin in his life—it didn't represent his childhood. It was his father's mid-life, post-divorce hideaway, and it carried the faintest aroma of loneliness and desperation. It hadn't been filled with children's voices; there had been no birth-day parties in it. By the time Papa built it Dad was deep into his teens, and one of his myriad acts of rebellion was to scorn his father's cabin. He once told me he'd never gone fishing there with Papa. At the age I was then, I couldn't imagine turning down an opportunity to go fishing with my father. But I understood one's teenage years to be an age of unreason when everything was suddenly upended and nothing made sense at all. I could not yet feel those years coming, but I'd seen them play out in others, and I was a little bit terrified of the prospect.

My father, standing in the garage, exhaled heavily. "Okay," he said. "Might as well jump right in. What the hell, right?"

He began an inventory of the stacked lumber. He found a notepad and a thick pencil, and with a tape measure from Papa's red metal toolbox he had me measure the wood and call out to him the dimensions and quantity of each. He wrote them all down, saying, "Good, good," as I named them.

Next he zeroed in on the shelf of fasteners, the small cardboard boxes of nails, and the large plastic bins of screws. He didn't put these on his list, but he sampled each one, picking out a sample nail or screw, checking its length and type of head. "Good, good," he said.

Then he came to the large, black Yamaha outboard motor. It was propped on two short pieces of lumber which rested at either end on aluminum sawhorses. It smelled thickly of gas and oil, and a small black puddle lay directly beneath it on the cool concrete floor.

"Does it work?" I asked.

"No idea," he said, running one hand over the top of it and gripping the handle of the pull cord, trying twice to pull it, gently, but it refused to move. "Likely not? It's been here so long."

"Could you get it to work?"

"Well. I, uh. No. Almost definitely no."

He opened the fuel cap and peered inside, sniffing the remnants of the oil and gas mixture. He thumbed the red rubber primer bulb. "We could probably get something for it," he finally declared.

He handed me a push broom and told me to sweep the floor out. "Put it all out there," he said, pointing to the open double doors, so I began to corral the old sawdust and wood shavings, the mouse droppings, and other debris out onto the ground where, I supposed, rain would eventually carry it away. He found a whisk broom and started clearing cobwebs out of corners and from among the rafters.

Mom came back glowing; the heat was rising. She'd used the shears to cut back encroaching branches and to trim tall grasses on the path from the road to the front door. "Seen a rake?" she asked.

"Hanging there," Dad said, pointing to a row of hooks along the back wall, suspended from which were two rakes, two shovels, and a pair of post hole diggers with one handle broken off.

Mom retrieved a rusty rake and carried it back outside, where she began to clear leaves and pine needles from the places we were most likely to walk. She would later collect all of this and begin sweeping it onto a fragment of green nylon tarp, which she would drag into the woods and dump in a discreet spot so that it could eventually disappear into the forest floor.

We had a lunch of peanut butter and jam sandwiches with glasses of milk on the dock. Mom had trimmed all the weeds that had been growing up through the gaps between the planks, and Dad said he'd soon see about fixing the dock's structure—the way it leaned toward the water and dipped in the middle.

Water bugs scampered over the surface of the bay, and the air was calm. I could see the brown-and-green world below the surface, slow, thick, and tangled. Fish darted. The midday sun beat down on the middle of the bay, but around the edges the deep shady greenness made a different world. The air felt bottled. One of the big white pines sheltered us, and the buzzing of crickets rose and fell, rose and fell.

When we'd finished eating, Dad put his plate and cup aside and lay down on the dock, and then Mom lay down and rested her head on his stomach. I did the same on hers, so that we were a human zigzag. My feet were near the edge, hanging just over the water. Dad's breathing slowed, and I became sleepy as Mom ran her fingers softly through my hair. I drifted off, and I think she did too.

We were so lucky to be there, given everything behind us. A haze of pollen drifted through the hot air, and we napped beneath a tree. Nothing was troubling us.

We awoke when my father said, as though finishing a sentence he'd started earlier, "Yeah, my back hurts." I jolted awake, and beneath my head I felt Mom tighten her core muscles and then relax, as though stretching. I don't know how much time had passed. The sun was still high overhead, the lake still, but the air felt hotter.

"You get the glasses," Mom said to me. "I'll bring the plates."

Together, with Dad carrying the white plastic milk pitcher, we walked up to the cabin where I hoped we would go back to sleep, but instead Mom asked me to wash the dishes, which I did, and she dried them. Dad stood in the middle of the room looking at the ceiling, then started walking over to walls and placing his hand on the studs and posts.

"Kat," he said, "what about if we gave Gabe his own floor?"

"What's that?"

"For him to sleep. Like, a little spot."

"I can't see it," she said. "Like, we raise the roof?"

"No, nothing like that. I don't know if it would work. I need to think on it some more."

That afternoon we used rags, a mop, and buckets of lemon cleaner to scrub the whole place out. Dad cleared cobwebs using a very loud Kenmore vacuum cleaner that had been in the storage corridor. I mopped sections of the linoleum floor. Mom Windexed windows and washed the walls. The breeze came up off the water in the afternoon and moved through the cabin, and everything looked and smelled fresher.

Spending our first full day in our new residence of indeterminate duration was luring me toward accepting a new, seductive normalcy. It felt as though we were establishing the patterns that would carry us through the summer.

At four o'clock, Mom said, "Quitting time." I followed them down to the lakeside, Mom in her blue one-piece with white polka dots, Dad in cut-offs, and me in my red trunks. We stepped gingerly over rocks, twigs, pine needles. Dad carried a broom. He and Mom flipped the canoe off the cradle and onto the ground, and then he began sweeping out webs and leaves. Spiders scampered for safety.

"Ah, shit, get them all," Mom said to Dad. "Excuse me. Please get 'em all, though. There's one, don't miss that one."

When he was done to her satisfaction, he nosed the canoe into the water and we each picked up a paddle from the four that had been tucked beneath the boat on the crib. Dad held the gunwale near the back and Mom stepped in, then stuck her paddle into the very shallow water, steadying the canoe while I stepped in.

"Hold the sides," she said, looking back at me over her shoulder. "You have to hold on to the sides as you sit."

When I was settled cross-legged on the bottom, Dad pushed us off the shore and walked the canoe out until it was floating freely and the water was over his knees. He laid his paddle across the canoe, placed his left hand halfway along it, and swung his left leg up, then eased back onto the seat and pulled his right leg in, and we were underway.

We paddled—or rather they did. I tried to match their pace but found it to be more tiring than I'd guessed it would be, so I slowed to the point that I was dipping my paddle into the water every fifth stroke or so and wasn't contributing to our forward progress, only feeling the strength of the water and the power of my parents' more practised paddling. They propelled us west through tall weeds and around boulders—glacial erratics standing up to their shoulders in the shallow water, shelves of the lake bed mossed green and slick just below the surface—and out through the narrows at the end of the bay. We swung south, Dad holding his paddle deep in the water as the nose of the canoe rotated while Mom kept a steady rhythm up front, and we glided through a narrow passage between the shore and a small barren island of lichen-furred pink granite. The lake opened up a bit, and the bottom dropped away as we continued south, a heavily treed island on our right, steep rock to the left topped by stunted, twisted cedar. A marshy inlet lay on our port side, at the head of which was a dilapidated duck blind with bits of tar paper flapping from beneath its planks. Trailing off into the water was a chain that someone must once have used to secure their canoe as they sat for hours waiting for flocks of waterfowl to cloud the early morning sky. We turned back to the east.

I looked over my right shoulder toward the largest, most open part of the lake, and the sun glinted off the water and blinded me, so that when I turned back around to face what was now coming into view it took a moment for my eyes to readjust.

"The cliff," said Dad.

All I saw at first were brown dots floating in an orange field. My vision returned bit by bit, and I saw what he meant. It was an imposingly tall and sheer rock—all of one piece, or so it appeared. There were three or four hardy Jack pines clinging to it, and patches of scruffy white and lush green moss, but otherwise it was just rock, smooth and prehistoric, remnant of the Earth's very formation. One side of it sloped gently enough into the water that you could paddle a canoe right up onto it, while the other side shot upward thirty feet over black water, where even the weeds could not reach the surface.

"What do you think of that, Gabey?" Dad had begun paddling harder and faster as we neared it.

"It's huge," I said. "So big."

"Wanna jump off it?" he asked as we advanced jerkily toward it.

"No," I said, quickly.

"It's so fun," he said.

"But you don't have to," Mom added.

Before landing, Dad steered the canoe just beyond the highest part of the rock and then turned us sharply back toward it, so that in a moment we were bobbing at its base, or where it met the water—looking down I could not tell how much further it went. The water appeared bottomless.

"People jump off that?"

"Yup. It's a blast. It used to be the only thing I liked about coming to the cabin."

I could only vaguely imagine it: my father, seventeen, long-haired, impossibly lean, browned from his summer landscaping job, probably wearing cut-offs instead of trunks even then, howling and braying and launching himself off the rock into the air directly over where we now floated, daring himself to perform a suite of acrobatics and misdeeds against gravity and good sense, perfecting different angles of entry, his yelps swallowed up by the splash and then his ears filling with bubbles and wash, slicing down, then regaining buoyancy, racing upward toward a shaft of sunlight until he breached, shouting and crowing about his own ballsiness to whoever he'd come with, probably a buddy or maybe a girl, still standing up top, watching, shaking their head, both likely as not drunk, or high, or soon to be.

They paddled us slowly around the side, where the slope was gentler, and soon there was a soft scraping as we slid into a shallow, silty berth. Mom put her paddle on the rock and eased herself out on the dry side, then held her hand out to me and helped me onto land. Dad once again laid his paddle across the gunwale and put his weight in the middle and stepped carefully out into the shallow water. He walked up the dry rock, taking the long yellow nylon cord that had been coiled up at the nose of the boat near Mom's feet with him to pull the canoe partially out of the water. Then he tied the rope to a root protruding from a fissure in the rock fifteen feet away. The front of the canoe began to drip dry, while the back rose and fell very slightly in the water.

We walked up the slope toward the peak, Dad ahead, then me, and Mom just behind. The rock radiated heat. It was hot on the bottom of my bare feet, and I could feel it on my legs. I followed until Dad reached the lip of the drop, at which point I stopped and looked up at him with my arms folded around myself.

"Come on," he said. "Take a look."

My head felt so heavy that I feared if I leaned over to look I would lose my balance and tip headfirst over the edge and into the black water below. I tiptoed to a spot just behind Dad and watched him very carefully, afraid that he might grab me.

"I'm here," he said. "You won't fall."

I eased my weight forward on my left foot until I could see the drop. I was terrified.

"Like this," Dad said, grinning, and then he took two long strides, threw his arms out in front of himself, and hurled his body into space. About halfway down he brought his arms to his sides and pointed his toes, and then the surface of the water exploded as he slid into it.

"Oh, Artie."

When he came up again he shook his head like a wet dog does and let out a whoop that echoed down the lake. "How did you like that?" he shouted up to me.

"It was good," I said.

He swam in a choppy breaststroke over to the base of the great rock, kicking his legs like a frog, pale and murky under the water. He grinned, hauled himself out of the water on a slippery spot. "I spent a year among the cliff divers of Rio de Janeiro," he said. "They taught me everything."

I looked at Mom. She smiled and said only, "I hear Brazil is beautiful."

My father told stories, many of which were completely outlandish, and others based on small nodules of truth. I didn't always believe him, but I wanted to, and sometimes I made the conscious decision to do so. Mom seemed to feel that belief in fantastic things was of more value to a child than knowing the full truth. She played along, careful not to craft an outright lie herself.

"But that wasn't a dive," I said. "You just jumped. More like a fall."

"In Rio they dive into waters seventy or eighty or two hundred feet deep," he said, standing down by the water's edge and searching the face of the rock for a climbable path back up to the top. "This isn't deep enough. The results could be fatal."

"How deep is it here?" I asked, leaning forward over my feet, trying to keep my weight back from the edge. The water looked awfully deep to me.

"I don't know," he said, "but I'll try and find out on my next jump."

"I'm going to guess fifteen or twenty feet," said Mom, standing at a much lower point on the rock's gentle slope. "I don't see any rocks or outcrops down there."

"There's nothing," confirmed Dad.

"Good," she said, and then in the next breath she was in the air, pointed like an arrow at the green-black water, and then entering it with a very small splash.

"She's showing off," shouted Dad, and I laughed. He'd managed to scrabble and climb back to the top and was standing behind me. He put his hands on my shoulders and said, "How are we going to get you in there?"

I shook and wriggled away from his hands and, crouching, backed through his legs. "We're not," I said. "I don't need to."

"Oh, no," he said, seeing my discomfort. "I would never make you jump!"

Mom was treading water further out into the lake and could see us up at the top. "Come down to the bottom," she said to me. "Come down over here and you can just slip in."

She swam over toward that end of the rock, and I began clambering down to meet her.

"What about there?" she asked. "Can you jump from there?"

"No," I said, "too high." I was a slight child, bony, my chest concave. I was not clumsy, but I was awkward at that age.

"Okay, come down here and you can just fall in."

I stood on a spot of rock just at the water's edge. Below the waterline it was covered with soft green moss. My mother stood in water up to her chest just a few feet away. "Jump in," she said, but I was afraid the water would feel too cold, and of what my feet might find on the bottom.

"Go on," said Dad from high up the rock.

"I will," I said, but I stood longer still, unable to will myself to move.

"The water's nice," Mom said.

"Okay, I'm going," I said, though I didn't mean it.

A breeze riffled the surface, and the trees on the opposite shore shivered. A chill raced over my skin, and I wrapped my arms around myself. Mom waved her arms back and forth, her fingers touching the water. The granite was hard under my feet. There was a very tall tree directly across from me, a super-canopy pine. A cloud passed before the sun, and the top of that tallest tree fell into shadow while everything else remained brilliantly lit. I wondered just how long I would have to stand in the same spot in order to see that happen again. All of the variables were so flimsy: the size and density and precise location of the cloud, the angle of the sun, the height of the tree, the soil in which it grew.

"Jump," Dad said. "You can do it, just jump."

I leapt timidly, really just falling forward, and brought my knees to my chest. When I broke the surface, I felt the coppery water in my nose. I squeezed my eyes shut and heard the bubbles. For a fraction of a second I was cold, but then the water felt soft and warm. I paddled my arms and legs, and my head emerged into the air. My parents were both applauding.

"Good, Gabe, good," Mom said.

I spun my legs and churned with my arms.

"Relax," she said. "Relax."

"Okay," I said, nearly out of breath.

"Do you remember how to starfish?" she said, recalling one of the earliest exercises in the lessons I'd taken at the YMCA.

"Yes."

"Okay, lie flat, look at the sky. Look at that white cloud." Dad careened out over the water, whooping again, and landed with a great splash. "There's your dad. Show him how you can float."

I leaned my head back and extended my limbs, then took a big chest full of air. The water creeped up to my ears and over my scalp. I stuck my chin into the sky.

"You remember." She was standing near me, and though I could not feel them I knew her arms were just beneath me, waiting to help if I needed it. I could hear her breathing.

I opened my eyes and the brightness stung them. When they adjusted, I saw the deep blueness and the lightness of the lone puffy cloud, the only one in the sky, with thin wisps trailing off in the wind up there. My ears were submerged then. There was no sound but my own breath and the beating of my heart. Out of the corner of my eye, still fixed on the sky, I could just see the top of Mom's head.

Dad came over—I could sense his splashing and feel his voice on my skin. He appeared in the periphery of my vision, smiling and laughing, just as I felt his arms beneath me, hauling me up like a trawler net. He squeezed me to his chest and I laughed.

We swam a while longer, with Dad executing more of his jumps—cannonballs, twists, pencil dives—while Mom found a spot lower down the rock that she liked to dive from, and she made more clean, elegant leaps, her body assuming the qualities of an arrow, barely troubling the water. Then, with the sun getting lower and incrementally less scorching, Mom said it was time we got back and made dinner, so we dried for a few minutes on the rock before Dad untied the canoe. We took turns crouching uneasily into it, then launched.

On the way back I sat hugging my knees in the middle of the canoe while they paddled. The water was choppier than it had been, and our bow lifted and slapped several times until we slid into the bay, which was more sheltered and calmer.

We ate spaghetti and a simple salad. Dad let me cut the tomatoes and cucumber. It felt good that they were beginning to trust me with a knife. As we lingered over our empty plates, the sun sparkled off the bay and the wind eased. Birds called.

"What were you saying earlier, Artie?" Mom said.

"Earlier?"

"About Gabe sleeping upstairs?"

"Right," he said. "Okay, so, I think we should build a loft for him."

"Where would we do that?" Mom asked.

Dad turned in his chair and pointed up to the ceiling at the far end of the cabin, above where their bed stood.

"Right above there," he said.

Mom was having some trouble picturing it. "So, a sleeping loft?"

"We could put a mattress down, and he'd climb up a ladder to get there. It'd be a spot of his very own."

I couldn't see this, either, but I liked the sound of it. I knew to keep quiet as they discussed it, though, that anything I said could tilt the decision, could make the very fragile magic dissipate.

"Okay," said Mom, still clearly skeptical. "How would we do that?"

"It looks to me like everything we need is in the garage. I think Papa was planning to build a bigger deck or something before he died. It's all up there. We made a list," he said, nodding toward me, and I nodded back, still afraid to speak aloud.

Mom looked at me. "Gabe, what do you think?"

I still couldn't picture what he was describing, thought it might have to do with building a turret or a vertical addition to the cabin, but I didn't want this possibility to pass me by, so I nodded again.

"Okay, so, but, describe this to me," Mom said.

"It would be tucked in under the rafters. Like a little shelf almost." This changed the picture in my mind, shrunk the scale.

"How big?" I finally said. I didn't fear tight spaces, but I was concerned about getting stuck.

"It would be about four feet by eight feet." He'd pushed his chair back from the table and stood, and was now walking over to the spot in question, gesturing above his head, painting a picture in the air. "Put a little railing along the edge so you don't roll off in the middle of the night. It would slope down over you, the ceiling, so you'd have lots of room for your head, put a little reading light up, and then it would get narrower as you went down."

He went to the little table next to Papa's chair and picked up the pencil Mom had used for the crossword puzzle along with a crumpled yellow piece of newsprint. He smoothed the paper on the table, and in the margin, next to a bridge column, he drew the shape of the cabin in profile. "Here's the house," he said. "Over here"—drawing a quick rectangle whose lines did not quite meet—"is our bed. And up here"—he drew a line out toward the rafters' apex—"would be your loft. Put a ladder here"—extending out toward the kitchen and the far end of the room—"and there you go. It would be easy. And you could get off that awful couch."

"It's so loud," I said.

"I know it is."

"And it smells old."

"We'll stash it in the garage and eventually get rid of it."

"Can I paint all of this white?" Mom asked, making it sound like her sole condition for granting the project approval.

"Oh, of course," Dad said.

"Like, everything," she said, making a little circle with her head. "Freshen this whole place up."

"Absolutely," Dad said. "I love it."

Mom climbed into the white Honda early the next morning with several masks, a pair of blue latex gloves, a list, a pencil, and a bottle of hand sanitizer, all of which she placed on the passenger seat. The sun had yet to top the trees. Dad and I stood nervously in the driveway as she closed the door, pulled her seatbelt across her chest, lowered her window, and waved.

"Bye," she said. "Be good. Don't worry. See you this afternoon."

As she pulled away, my father exhaled heavily, unable to hide his concern. Of the three of us, only she had been in a store since the winter, undertaking a simple errand that had assumed the ominous weight of ceremony.

She was only going to hit a few places, she'd said, and stop by the house for her paintbrushes, but even these simple acts had become inescapably fraught.

"Damn it," Dad said as the car disappeared down the road. "I wish she didn't have to go." He seemed genuinely pained, if not afraid, of her re-immersion into the tainted world of city life and exhaling people and single-file lineups outside stores, motion-activated hand sanitizer dispensers, and conversations through cloth masks and Plexiglas shields.

I was uneasy, too. I had the feeling that the city was a hand that, once tickled by her presence, would close around her and prevent her return. And that without her, Dad and I would be lost.

We were each so preoccupied with our own quiet suffering that morning that Dad forgot to make me lunch. I found some crackers and ate them on the dock, and I snuck a chocolate chip granola bar out of the cabinet. I swallowed it nearly whole while kneeling in a spot in the woods that I was sure was invisible from the cabin or garage. I buried the wrapper beneath a rock.

It wasn't until the long trough of the hot afternoon that we heard her car coming back up the road. I was trying to lean two sticks together and get them to stand up, and Dad was tinkering aimlessly in the garage. When I sprinted up the path, he met me outside the garage doors and we stood watching the bend in the road where the car soon appeared, Mom's left arm extended out the driver's-side window, waving.

I knew that before I could hug her she would have to spend a long time at the sink with a bottle of hand soap, but the desire to hold her, to physically confirm her return, was overwhelming as she pulled up and opened her door, so I twisted the ball of my right foot into the ground until I had created a small crater.

"Hi, guys," she said. "Miss me?"

"Yes," I shouted, and Dad laughed and said that he did, too.

We carted the groceries from the car to the cabin, and put Mom's painting supplies and a large plastic bucket of white paint in the garage. Mom scrubbed herself at the kitchen sink and threw away her gloves and mask, and then Dad washed the produce with bottled water and wiped the boxes with disinfectant. I put on my trunks while they finished, then Mom put on her polka-dot swimsuit and we walked down to the canoe. It was earlier in the day than we had made it our custom to swim, but Mom's safe return to us after hours away was cause for minor celebration, so we spent longer in the water, under a high, dry sun, splashing and joking, Dad in his cut-offs cannonballing off the cliff's tallest point, me starfishing in the warm water, squinting up into the sky, awed by the high-piled clouds' marvellous architecture.

That night we made a fire on one of the flat rocks near the road and sat around it in woven plastic folding chairs. I found good long, straight, thin sticks that Mom whittled to fine points, and we used them to roast hot dogs, which were spicy and juicy in their thick, soft buns with squirts of mustard and ketchup. Then Mom surprised me with a bag of marshmallows that she'd bought that day, and we roasted those and ate them for dessert. I had a dozen. As the fire died down to soft red coals, we leaned back and looked at the stars, which were bright and close. An owl hooted somewhere nearby. I fell asleep in my folding chair, and someone, probably Dad, carried me to the springy chesterfield and tucked me in without waking me.

I awoke later that night when Mom placed her hand on my forehead and then touched her own cheek. She must have thought she had not woken me, or that I had gone immediately back to sleep, because she said nothing to me—instead she went to the bathroom and dug in the little leatherette satchel where she kept her few items of makeup, as well as painkillers, a brush, and so on, and took out a digital thermometer. She removed its cap, pressed a button on its flank which made it beep, and placed its silver tip beneath her tongue. Then she stood in the bathroom doorway in the cone of light from the bulb over the sink, her hands on her hips, for what seemed a long while, until there was a muffled beeping from the little unit. She took it out, looked at its display, and pressed the button again to put it to sleep. She walked to the kitchen counter, picked up the kettle, which still carried water, though it had gone cold, and moved to the sink where she poured the water over the tip of the thermometer. She put the kettle down, wiped the thermometer on the hem of her tank top, and stood for a moment looking out the pitch-black window. She returned the thermometer to her satchel, turned off the bathroom light, and shuffled past me in the dark on her way back to bed.

Early the next morning Dad stood in the middle of the room snapping a measuring tape and surveying the ceiling and walls. Mom made the coffee and we ate cereal, then she began to get her painting supplies ready, spreading an old, paint-spattered sheet on the floor, arraying her brushes and a roller across it. She opened the big plastic bucket of white paint and stirred it vigorously with a thin piece of scrap lumber, counting to one hundred before slowly pulling the stick out and laying it across the lid of the bucket. She dipped a thick brush into the white liquid—it looked like glue—and pressed it against the rim of the bucket. She lifted the brush carefully, turned to the wall nearest her, and slapped it wetly onto the plywood. She painted without caution. "This floor," she said to herself and to us. "Who cares if I get paint on it?"

Dad measured, noted, drew on a pad of paper. He went to the garage and set up two metal sawhorses just outside the door, ran an extension cord from a jiggly socket, and plugged in Papa's old circular saw. "He used this to build the cabin," Dad said, looking at me through a pair of thick safety glasses, suggesting that I should view the saw as some manner of relic.

He measured and marked a long plank of wood lain across the sawhorses with a thick, red pencil, then used a metal square to draw a line across it. He asked me to hold the far end of the wood, but made me look away when he began cutting, because I didn't have safety glasses of my own. The whine of the saw surprised me with its volume and violence. The sound bounced around inside my head, and I felt the board judder as the blade bit into it. The end of it fell with a thud to the ground. The saw slowed and stopped, and I opened my eyes when Dad said, "Okay."

I helped him carry the piece into the cabin. It was eight feet long. We laid it down on the floor next to the bed, and went back out to the garage to cut some more pieces.

When we had three more eight-foot boards, a four-footer, and a long, square post cut and carried down to the cabin, Dad said it was time to put it all together. He used large spiral nails to fix one of the eight-foot planks to the cabin's beam, above the windows. Into that he nailed a four-foot board, at the end, halfway into the room. I held the tall square post in place while he nailed the four-footer into that, and he ran a second eight-foot board to the post, where it met the shorter piece. He had his box, and inside of that, at sixteen-inch intervals, he ran the other two eight-foot pieces, until the inside of the box was well supported.

This work took all morning. By lunchtime we had a rectangular frame built about seven and a half feet above the floor, where my parents' bed was, and extending halfway out into the room, ending at the midway point, directly below the vaulted ceiling's apex.

Mom had been painting the kitchen cabinets but stopped at noon to make sandwiches. We ate on the screened porch and then went right back to work. In the garage again, Dad cut long slats of six-inch-wide decking into four-foot lengths. When we had sixteen of these, we began ferrying them down to the cabin. Dad found a box of small nails, and with a standing ladder, he began to lay them across the rectangle. When he had them all arranged and felt certain the whole construction was more or less square, he started tacking the decking down onto the frame with small, bright finishing nails.

By afternoon, my loft was nearly finished. It still needed a ladder, though, and Mom said I wouldn't be sleeping up there until the railing and ladder were done, all of it was painted white, and the paint was dry.

Then we put away Papa's tools because it was time to go swimming.

Later that afternoon, when we paddled out of the bay and into the open lake's expanse, we were met with a stiff wind that whipped the surface into a strong chop. We paddled straight into it for a while, then turned to the south so that it met our canoe broadside. I sat lower in the boat to keep from feeling that I would fall out. Mom twisted and shifted her weight with each wave; behind me, Dad, still caked in sawdust and sweat, used his paddle to keep us moving in a straight line. I tried to imagine where my parents had learned to paddle a canoe. Had they been taught, or were they born with the knowledge? And if the latter, why didn't I come into the world possessing it?

The cliff stood in calmer water. We landed without trouble and tied the canoe to the usual cedar root, then scrambled over the great rock to its edge. I went down to its lowest point. From a spot a little higher, Mom arched her back, pointed her arms and dove gracefully, cutting the water cleanly. Dad climbed all the way to the topmost point. He took three steps back, then charged ahead, launching himself off and into space. I stood hugging myself, my toes only inches above the water, and watched him fall for what seemed an impossibly long interval. He hollered on his way down, his arms outstretched, but a few feet above the water he fell silent, hunched his shoulders up toward his ears, and brought his arms to his sides. When he hit the water his right leg was extended, the foot pointed down, while his left was a little bent, preparing to absorb the impact. The splash was terrific. And then he came up, rinsed clean of the day's grime.

Mom, who had surfaced a short ways away, turned to me and said, "Okay, Gabe, your turn."

I had resolved not to dither on this day. It was a resolution I'd made to myself while lying in bed at night. I had decided that I wanted to be someone who did not dither. I would be decisive. This was my first opportunity since that conversation with myself to put decisiveness into action.

I pointed my arms straight up, my hands clasped, and I fell forward off the rock, landing flatly with a splat. But I was in the water. I had not dithered.

The water felt noticeably warmer than it had the previous day, soft and welcoming. We were in high summer. The air was heavy and thick with dust and pollen.

Mom swam over to me as I treaded water, and Dad was making his way over, too, using his inefficient breaststroke. When he arrived we had a wordless, smiling moment of unity, of solidity and togetherness. Mom smiled most broadly, her face bobbing on little waves, her eyes crinkling against the bright sun. Dad, his hair plastered to his forehead, smiled more slowly, as though he'd come to the feeling only after seeing it on her face. I grinned between gulps of air, my neck craned to avoid swallowing water.

I felt it—felt that we were fortunate, and safe, and that an insulating kind of love enveloped me. I knew that we were here, in the lake, at Papa's cabin, largely for my sake. This was the safety in isolation that my parents had decided was necessary for us, for me.

Mom saw that I was tiring, my gulping for air growing increasingly desperate, so she said to me, "Starfish, honey. Go starfish."

I lay back and stopped kicking, and as I floated I found I could relax somewhat and catch my breath. I felt my father next to me then. He said, "Climb on," so I rolled over and climbed on his back, holding his shoulders with my hands. Dad bucked and dug beneath me, and he began swimming back toward the rock, dipping below the surface but never deep enough to pull me under. When we were on the first shelf of rock, he turned and stood, sloughing me off. I fell with a laugh, and then I gingerly put my feet down, bracing for a sting or the unwanted grip of plant life. But there was only smooth, solid rock, and I stood to my full height, the water lapping at my sternum.

"Do you open your eyes down there?" he asked me.

"Down there?"

"When you're underwater."

"No," I said. "It would hurt my eyes."

"It wouldn't," he said. "Try it. My eyes are open the whole time I'm under. It's beautiful."

"Really?"

"Come on," he said. "Come here." I waded to him. He was crouching so that the water was at his shoulders, and as I neared he took me in his arms. "You just put your face in," he said, "and open them."

I began to sink into the water and got as far as allowing it to reach my chin, but then I stiffened and straightened up. "Mom said it's bad for your eyes."

"In a pool, sure. At the Y. Those chemicals are strong and can make your eyes red and sore. But not this. This is just a lake. This water is nice."

I trusted my father, so I began to ease down into the lake, and when the water had reached my mouth I turned my face downward, still with my eyes closed. The water crept up my scalp and into my ears. Dad had his hand on my back to reassure me, and Mom had swum over to us. Her presence was an encouragement.

I opened my eyes. It was not a natural thing for me to do—I had to fight my impulses. But I did it. I felt the coolness against my eyeballs, but no pain, and I was elated. The world below was indistinct and amorphous. There were no clean lines, but there were colours, and gradations of light. I could see my own limbs, bright and pale in the greenish-brown water. The rock was brilliant yellow beneath my feet. I exhaled, and the bubbles exploded out and up in a white rush.

I had only known water to deprive my senses before, but now I felt capable of seeing the entire world in a new way. It was a prebirth sensation, an amniotic cradling, but with a sudden awareness of life existing within a new set of dimensions. I stood up, whipping my head backward. "It's amazing down there," I said.

Mom and Dad smiled at one another.

"See," Dad said, "I told you. I wouldn't lie."

I was emboldened. I crouched and pushed off, out into the deep water, needling my way toward the middle of the channel, looking down the whole way. The colours darkened as the bottom dropped away and receded into blackness. Nearer to my face, though, the colours persisted. Light green plants reached up in soft, waving squiggles, and white bubbles danced. I thrashed my arms above me, into the air, and back down through the water below in great arcs, and I was afloat on an effervescence of my own making.

As a blue dusk fell on July 1, Mom lit sparklers with a long barbecue lighter that she held to their tips until they flared to life with a sound like the sharp intake of breath. The chemical fumes stung my nostrils, and white sparks pricked as they showered onto my wrists. I held a sparkler in each hand and waved them with straight arms, far away from my head.

My parents were not overtly patriotic people, but something had Mom and Dad feeling differently this particular Canada Day. We had no flags to wave, but we did dress in red and white and wave sparklers in the gathering dark. I shook mine high while they spit and crackled. Mom stood facing the lake and sang "O Canada." Maybe it was just an excuse for a little party; there had been very few during that strange year. Maybe this was a different sort of pride: the fun kind, the kind we displayed when we cheered for Sidney Crosby and poured maple syrup on pancakes, and not the kind anyone ever enforced with a rifle. I hoped it meant that we were happy to be from such a beautiful country— that the land was what mattered.

My sparklers extinguished themselves, leaving only hazy nebulae of smoke in the still air. Dad planted four more in the soft, damp earth near the water, and Mom handed him the long, pistol-like lighter, which he used to bring them to life one after another. We stood watching their shower of sparks against the water, which shone like molten lead in the last light of the setting sun. The air was thick and hot, full of life and rot and sulphur. As the sparklers spat and hissed and then quieted themselves, the bullfrogs began their nightly chorus. Dad picked up the spent metal rods and dipped them into the lake to make sure they were out, and then we went up to the screened porch, because the mosquitoes were bad on windless evenings such as this.

We sat in the dark, just a warm glow through the trees and a softness where the lake lay, my parents drinking in silence, beer for Mom and Alberta Premium rye whisky on ice for Dad, poured from its large plastic bottle. I sipped a can of ginger ale, which was a treat. We heard booms at one point, and Dad said that someone somewhere must be lighting off fireworks, but we couldn't see anything; only the bang and its slight echo found its way to us. I tried to listen for more but could hear only bullfrogs and crickets, and then my own heartbeat in my ears, and then nothing. At some point I was moved, quite unconscious, to the chesterfield, where I awoke the next morning.

That was my final night on that terrible piece of furniture. The paint on my loft's planks and rails, which Mom had laid on in two thick coats, had dried slowly in the summer humidity and remained tacky. Dad had spent part of the afternoon building a ladder—really a very steep set of stairs, like you'd find on a ship—and Mom had painted that, too, as it lay on the floor in the garage. I would have to wait to use my new space. Standing below it, I'd said, "It looks like a baby's crib," and as soon as I'd said it I regretted making it sound as though I was upset by that, because what I'd meant was that it looked safe and comfortable.

"That's your cubby, your own little space," Mom said in reply, and I touched her hand.

"I could climb up there without the ladder," I said, eyeing my parents' bed, the window frames, and the little cross-struts running between the studs on the wall. I wasn't actually sure I could do it, but I wanted to be able to, and I wanted to try.

"How about we wait for the ladder to be ready?" Mom said.

The following night all of my mother's white paint was dry, and Dad installed the ladder, bolting it to the sturdy railings of my little box. I said goodnight early, the light still in the west, through the trees, and climbed the steps to my personal platform.

It was like being toy-sized and being put away on a shelf. The wooden rafters ran above me and down close to my feet. The space was tight but felt secure, like an indoor tree house. Mom had laid down a foam mattress with bedding and a pillow. Against the wall, in a nook between two studs, she had piled a dozen of my books, Hardy Boys and Nancy Drew, and there was a string of white lights pinned along one rafter. I flicked the switch on the battery pack, and the loft was warmly aglow. The big window at the ceiling's apex, above the screened porch, was not too far from my head. If I craned my neck, I could see treetops and a small patch of open sky. From the open windows below, I heard my parents' soft voices between long stretches of silence, as they sat in the cooling, bugless air of the screened porch.

There was enough light to read by. I lay on my stomach, propped on my elbows, and opened *The House on the Cliff.* Frank and Joe Hardy were watching over Barmet Bay, keeping an eye out for smugglers. A warm breeze drifted through our cabin.

"How is it?" Dad called.

"It's nice," I said. "I like it a lot."

"It's all yours, buddy," Mom said.

I'd read this book a dozen times, but it was one of my favourites. *"We've stumbled onto something important,"* *Frank Hardy said. "That may be the smugglers' cove."* I read for an hour or more, and below me Mom and Dad sat and drank their drinks and chipped away at a crossword puzzle. I'd have read all night if they'd have let me, and if I could have stayed awake.

I'd come late to reading. I knew kids my age who were reading novels when I was still struggling to print my name. I had only learned to read the summer before this one—I was reluctant, thinking it a kind of magic trick or display of extreme intelligence—but once the awareness fell into my head, it was miraculous. The world opened up so wonderfully. I found excitement and wonder in black text on a white page.

I had a very distinct image in my head of Bayport, where Frank and Joe Hardy lived, and of their house, and of Bayport High, and of the area around Barmet Bay, a bright, clean, windswept place of wooden docks and American regattas and homes with white clapboard siding. I read more modern books, too—about talking animals, and clever imperilled orphan children, and mystical teenage descendants of Greek gods engaged in secret wars in New York City—and I enjoyed them, but none felt as homelike as the Hardy Boys books, which also stemmed from my wish to have a younger brother, someone I could shepherd and show the world and play with and tease. I had read all the Hardy Boys books at least twice, and would read them again and again. Mom knew that, which was why, when hastily packing, she'd cleaned them off a shelf and stacked them in a box, along with the Nancy Drew books, about which I felt similarly, though somewhat less passionately. Nancy occupied the same safe, deducible universe as Frank and Joe, but I didn't want to comb my hair like the image on the front of her books.

"Gabey," Mom finally said, and I knew what was coming next, "did you brush your teeth?"

"Yes," I lied, hoping to squeeze in a few more minutes of reading.

"Are you sure? I don't remember you being in there."

"Maybe I forgot," I said with a sigh. I laid my open book down on my pillow, its already-cracked spine splayed, threw aside my covers, scampered down the ladder, and went into the washroom to brush my teeth. When I was done, I went through the open screen door to the porch and squeezed between my parents' chairs and the large screens that looked out over the lake. I hugged my father, standing between his knees and letting him wrap his long arms around me.

"Sleep well, Gabriel Joseph," he said. Then he pulled his legs in to let me pass.

I moved next to Mom and I hugged her. She said, "Come on," and walked me back past Dad and inside. The screen door slapped behind us as we went to the base of the ladder. She came up after me to see that I was tucked securely in, her head and shoulders just above the lip of my loft.

"Can I read more?"

She closed her eyes and shook her head. "Time to call it a day, I think," she said. "Switch off your light. Your book will still be here tomorrow." I handed her the book, and she looked at the page I'd marked. "Page 108," she said. "'A Startling Discovery.' That's your chapter. Can you remember that?"

"I think so," I said, clicking off the little white lights.

"Okay. Go to sleep. Goodnight, sweet boy." She tucked the book into the corner, near the others lined up between the white-painted wooden studs.

"Night, Mom. Love you."

"Love you, too."

She went back down the ladder and out to the porch, where she sat down again. We were all quiet. I made a game of seeing how slowly I could breathe, and I lay on my back listening to the calls of loons. It had grown fully dark and I could no longer see through the trees, but if I lay in a very particular way I could twist my face upward and see a handful of stars in a small patch of sky among the darkened treetops.

My parents sat in the darkness, talking now, very quietly at first. I could not make out their words initially, but in time their voices rose. They began speaking sharply, as if challenging one another.

"How long will that be?" my mother was saying. "How long is long enough?"

"We don't know. Nobody knows that."

"That's not very helpful, is it."

"We need to be ready to stick it out. Be ready for the long haul."

"The long haul," said Mom.

Dad was silent for a moment.

"Yeah," he said.

"Long haul," she said again. "We can't long-haul here. We're not those people. You think we're those people, but we're really, really not. And this place isn't the place."

"It's gonna have to be. Everything depends on us. This is our survival we're talking about."

"The world isn't ending."

"I'm not so sure about that. Look at your news feed."

"Well, we're gonna have to go back to it. We can't cut ourselves off forever. Maybe I should bring you with me next time I go into town so you can see that people still, like, exist. They're running. Walking their dogs. Eating hamburgers. I'll show you." She said this tenderly, with humour.

"No thank you."

"Oh, come on," she said, trying not to allow the conversation to escalate, though likely aware that it would. "Can we not panic? I didn't realize there was a survivalist in you that was so eager to break out. I don't know what comes next, but I'm pretty sure it isn't subsistence living in an abandoned shack for the rest of our lives."

"Survivalist? As in someone willing to do what it takes to survive, to keep his family alive? Guilty, I guess. But you know what, my love? You might appreciate it when the numbers really start to climb and you're here warm and safe next to the fire and Gabe's sound asleep, all tucked up."

"Fuck's sake," Mom breathed, then she said something muffled, probably because she was covering her face with her hands, which was something she did when she was too frustrated to continue a conversation. They both fell quiet then, just the sound of one or the other of them moving their chair, or placing their empty glass or beer bottle on the floor next to them. When they spoke again after a few moments, their voices were softer, and I could no longer make out what they said. Anger had passed, or had been resubmerged.

I heard Dad come inside and go to the fridge for more beers. He twisted the caps off and the bottles hissed. I rolled onto my stomach so that I could watch him, and I saw him pull a liquor bottle from the shelf and open it and take a long drink before replacing it. Then he picked up the two bottles of beer and went to the screen door, which slapped softly shut—he stuck his rump out so that it would bump against him first and then catch more quietly. The night pulsed gently with humidity and hidden life, and I shut my eyes.

⟨ ⟩

There was a tree stump next to the path that ran from the cabin's door down to the lakeshore. It was not thick—only eight or ten inches across—but it was sturdy, a maple that Papa had shorn cleanly off with a chainsaw, and it came up to my nose. It had likely been damaged by the wind, or fallen prey to a fungus and been beset by woodpeckers, so Papa, worrying perhaps that it would fall and damage his canoe, or worse, the cabin, had taken it down pre-emptively.

The middle was hollowed out, a perfect dark, empty cylinder ringed by wood. If I stood on my toes I could look down into it, but it was impossible for me to see how deep the cavity extended. All the way to the ground? Deeper? After rain it became my habit to check to see if the hole had filled with water. One afternoon, a heavy thunderstorm blew through. When it cleared, I peered over the edge into the void and saw that the water had come nearly to the top. I stared at the water, smelling its coppery richness, and when my eyes had adjusted to its darkness I saw that there were tiny, strange shapes spiralling, twisting, and flipping through it, all the way down as far as I could see. They were pale, and small enough that I could have fit several on the tip of my finger. They jerked and jumped with hidden energies, movements at once spastic and balletic, wriggling snakelike or dancing rhythmically, and some just tumbling end over end through the water.

Of course I assumed that I'd discovered a previously unknown form of life, something primordial and basic that had managed to escape human attention, unnoticed by people too busy and preoccupied to look closely at a tree stump filled with rainwater. I imagined that only I was slow, patient, and observant enough to see these fidgeters, as I called them. They were entertaining themselves in a constrained environment, in my mind. Fidgeting. Releasing the ecstatic energy in their tiny noodle-like bodies.

I thought I should spend time observing the fidgeters' behaviour before announcing my discovery to the world. That was what scientists and researchers did. And it was also true that I didn't want to share them. The fidgeters were mine. The stump was mine. Anything deemed useless by adults I considered to belong to me. These little dancers were no different.

The afternoon moved around me. Mom painted—she had worked her way along the long back wall and was now whiting out the area around their bed—and Dad was still organizing the garage. The sun shone down through the trees in a shimmering green heat. I stood at the stump, resting my chin on it, watching the strange little noodles.

The next morning the water inside the stump was lower, but the fidgeters were still there, dancing. I wondered if they'd done so all night, twisting, flipping in the dark water, or if they'd slept, hanging motionless as the air and water cooled, until daybreak. In my loft that night I put down my book—I'd moved on to another Hardy Boys adventure, *The Mystery of Cabin Island*; I never read them in order because it did not seem important to do so—and switched off my lamp. I lay on my back with my eyes shut tightly and pictured the moving shapes of the fidgeters swimming in my eyes, small animated commas in perpetual motion.

They were my first thought on waking the next morning, and as soon as I was released from the breakfast table I went out to see them. The water was gone. I stood looking in the cavity, where nothing moved, and around at the trees, which were dry and only barely stirred by the wind, trying to determine where the fidgeters could have gone with no water in their home. It had drained away, or evaporated, or been taken somehow. Had they disappeared with it, or were they hidden down there at the bottom of the dead tree, waiting for a refill?

That day was hot and remained dry, but in the coming days the sky turned dark and there was less colour in the air, and when finally the clouds split and released a great gurgling rain, the stump filled again. As soon as it stopped, I put on my shoes and ran down to see.

The water appeared clean, free of debris. Nothing moved, only the falling of drops from the trees when the wind shook their branches. I watched for a long time but did not see the fidgeters. I kept watch much of the day, but there was no change.

At ten I wasn't too old to believe that I had some psychic control over the unfoldings of the natural world. That night, I pictured again the squiggling forms suspended in water, and I asked whatever nameless, shapeless being held office over such affairs—because we did not believe in God, but I still thought someone ought to be in charge—to file the requisite forms and perform the appropriate rites.

When I woke up, the sun was shining, sharp and golden from where it had risen over a soft incline. The air was already heavy and hot. It took all the reserve I could summon not to run out in my pyjamas and bare feet. I ate my cereal as quickly as I could and raced out to the stump, nursing a sense of both excitement and dread, worried that my hoping had not been earnest enough.

Peeking over the lip and into the narrow trunk, I saw first only the blinding reflection of the sun, but when I shielded the hole with my hand and allowed my eyes to adjust, I saw them there again, twisting and flipping.

I had to consider the possibility that the worms came in the rain—that they fell from the sky, and that if they landed in the right sort of place, like the open maw of the sawed-off maple, they would slowly shake themselves to life. There were other possibilities, too: the one that seemed most likely to me was that they lived inside the wood, and simply loved to swim—for there absolutely was joy in their movement—so that when the opportunity was presented to them they seized it, making enthusiastic use of the sudden and temporary appearance of a body of water that was free of predators and that was, for them, unimaginably enormous, and which only gradually disappeared over the course of a few days. Did time seem longer to them? I thought it probable, everything being scaled in accordance with their size.

And then the cabin door opened. My father stepped out in his cut-offs and a thin cotton shirt, unbuttoned to the middle of his chest. He was wearing his white running shoes and holding a white coffee mug, and in his other hand he held his phone, which he'd been reading as he pushed through the door. He paused on the threshold and slid the phone into his back pocket while the door slowly swung shut behind him. He grimaced, but as he squinted into the sun he saw me and twisted his face into a smile.

"Things are going to hell out there," he said. "What do you think, Gabey? Do you miss the city?"

"Not really," I said.

"No." He turned his head slowly, surveying the forest and the little bit of lake he could see from where he stood. "Look at this. I don't think we're doing too bad here, are we?"

"No," I said. "I guess not."

"What are you up to this morning?" he said.

"Nothing, really," I said, trying to surreptitiously position myself between him and my tree stump.

"You been playing at that stump for a few days," he said. "Something special about it?"

"No, just an old tree," I said, protecting my discovery. I needed more time to observe the fidgeters before announcing their existence. I had to be an authority on their life cycle and habits. I had to understand where they went and how they came back.

He came down the path, moving easily through the bright morning air, holding his coffee in his right hand, his left tucked into his pocket. I did not know if my father was old or young. Those judgments didn't occur to me. He was just my father. She was just my mother.

When he came up next to me, he put his hand on my head and said, "You're so curious," and then wrapped me in a one-armed hug, my head pressed to his stomach. I could smell his deodorant, at once musky and minty, and the coffee in his cup, and traces of woodsmoke in the fabric of his shirt. Then he released me and looked down into the stump. "Oh, hey," he said. "Is that what you've been looking at?"

"Yeah," I said, a little humiliated.

"Look at them. Little worms or something. They don't stop, huh?"

"No." I was conflicted, because I loved to share things with my father, but I really did feel that this was my discovery—that I was in some way responsible for the fidgeters, and that exposing them to the scrutiny of adults would compromise them, or put them in danger. I also worried that Dad was gently making fun of me, a slight I seemed always to be the last to intuit while it was happening.

"I wonder what they are," he said. "We'll have to look that up." Then he tousled my hair again, and strode off toward the garage, and to his day's chosen work.

—

Nights later, the moon rose so full it threatened to spill over. Dad wanted me to see it. We left Mom on the porch, where she was reading on her phone, and picked our way slowly along the path and up to the road, where the sky was more open. There was one large cloud in the sky, and the moon appeared in a cleft at the top of it so that the cloud seemed to be hung upon the moon, and its edge limned in an ethereal light, silver and feathery.

"Look at that," Dad said, "so big and beautiful. Is that the Hay Moon? Strawberry? No, that's June," he continued, in conversation with himself. "July's the Hay Moon."

"Why?"

"I guess that's when farmers cut hay for their livestock. All the moons are like that—they tell people when it's time to do things. People before. People other than us."

We stood in silence awhile as the moon poured its ghostly light over us, filtered by the cloud's edges. There was only the slightest breeze, but in time the cloud moved on and our surroundings became starkly visible.

Half a million people had died of the virus. The global economy was devastated. Our borders were closed. There were shortages and shipping interruptions for basic supplies. It seemed entirely possible in those days that the entire human experiment had apexed, and was now in its death spiral as nature began clawing its way back to primacy. There was no certainty whatsoever in our lives, and our lives were better than most people's at that time. It was not easy to remember that the world was in turmoil—not there, on a warm summer night, standing in my father's company, the two of us bathed in moonlight.

"If I can speak honestly, Gabey, I'd love nothing more right now than a cigarette. I'm not supposed to say that. I'm supposed to tell you that cigarettes are bad. They are. Terrible. Never start smoking them, not even one. I haven't been a regular smoker in fifteen years, but I still love it. I love thinking about it. I'm thinking about it now. About blowing big, fat smoke rings up at that moon."

"Because that cloud looks like smoke?"

"Maybe. But likely just because it's in my blood. It never leaves. Being strong is hard. You learn that the hard way."

What is the appropriate response at such times? I guess that's the whole problem: both of my parents' reactions—his anxiety, her renewed purposefulness—seemed as reasonable as not. The lack of urgency in our very particular situation lent itself to any number of interpretations. My father might very well have been right about this being a hinge point in human history. We didn't know. No one on Earth did.

I felt sheltered with him standing behind me, protected from any attack from the rear. As I listened to his breathing, there rose a distant pained sound, a far-off keening both proud and lonely. It could have been wind, or music, or something more spectral and mysterious. The voices of the dead.

"Hear that?" Dad asked.

"What is it?"

"Those are wolves." He exhaled slowly, making it sound as though he was blowing smoke rings, and he drew the last word out like he was telling tales around the fire. He wanted to frighten me, but even before he'd finished the word his thinking changed—it was audible—and he didn't want to frighten me. His ten-year-old boy.

"Wolves? Here?"

"Out there. Yeah."

"Will they get us?"

"They're not as close as they sound. We're safe here. But keep them in mind. They're out there."

The moon shimmered, bright and lewd, and the air thrummed with stale warmth, nocturnal mammals, and scavenging insects. Microbes replicated, and the soil beneath our feet wriggled. Life went on.

"We should get to bed," he said. He put his large hand on the crown of my head and steered me back to the cabin, where I mounted my ladder in the dark and went to sleep with the sound of the wolves' cries still echoing in my ears.

Years later, my mother would tell me that after I was well and truly asleep and the moon had swung halfway across the sky, my father rose from bed and went, shirtless, out into the night again to stand in the forest. To hear the wolves, she believed, and to feel the moon on his skin. To feel the world turning under his feet. To measure himself, and his ability to survive, against anything that prowled out there. But clouds had rolled in to blot the moon, the wolves had gone quiet, and he felt only the mosquitoes.

❧

I slept late. When I got up, the cabin was empty. I found my parents at the dock, Mom sitting cross-legged and cradling a mug of coffee in both hands. My father was standing up to his waist in the lake, leaning his elbows on the dock, facing

Mom. His mug was between them, empty. He was shirtless and in his cut-offs, his hair dry.

"There he is," he said when he saw me coming down the path.

"Morning, sleepyhead," Mom said, turning to me.

"Hi," I said. I came abreast of her, and she put her hand on my leg.

"You were tired," she said, looking up at me.

"I guess."

"You're just in time to help me fix this dock," Dad said, slapping his big palm on a rotting grey board.

Often, when there was something I wasn't ready to face, or something I hoped to put off, I would try to lure my parents into storytelling sessions. They enjoyed sharing their memories—it was a weakness I was aware of, and I sometimes tried to use it to my own benefit. This was one of those times.

"Mom," I asked, "why was I born early?"

"Premature," she said. "That's what it's called. You were about five weeks premature."

"But why?" I said, sitting on my knees next to her.

"Not sure, really. You were just ready to come."

"Impatient," Dad said, bending to shift a rock beneath the dock's wooden crib and wedging it more tightly among the other rocks.

"Dad and I were watching *Law & Order*, sitting in bed, and you were like, 'Nope, now you need to go to the hospital.' So Dad drove me, and pretty soon there you were."

"Then I stayed there, right?"

"For about three weeks. They had a room, a department, the special care nursery. Up on the fifth or sixth floor. There was a team of nurses that cared for you. You were in a little clear plastic box."

"Remember the goggles?" Dad said to her.

"I had goggles?"

"It was a blindfold, but it looked like goggles. It Velcroed around your tiny head. It was to protect your eyes from the UV light they shone on you to treat your jaundice."

"I had jaundice?" I did not know what that was, but it sounded serious, possibly even life-threatening, and a jolt ran through me; I recognized it as excitement at the thought that I might have survived something potentially deadly. It made me feel interesting, though at the same time the proximity to oblivion terrified me.

"It's not so unusual in babies," Mom said, deflating me. "Especially preemies like you. They fix it with those lights."

"Oh," I said.

"Remember that nurse, Art? Carey, I think? God, she was just amazing. They were all amazing, but she was something else."

"Carey sounds right," Dad said.

"She was my favourite. I think I'd have gone nuts if it wasn't for her. They kept me in for a few days, Gabey. Then your dad and I were both home, but we would go in to see you three or four times a day, and help feed you."

"Through your nose," Dad said.

"What?!"

"You had a tube," Mom said, laughing, "in your nose and down your throat to your stomach, so the milk would go right in. You didn't know how to eat yet."

"Gross!"

"It was kind of gross," Dad said.

"It's normal," she said, swatting the air between them, pretending to slap him. "Carey was so patient with me. I was so worried I was going to do everything wrong. She was so calm and friendly. Just what I needed."

"She was the same with me," Dad said. "She was great. Sometimes I'd go in there alone, because Mom was home sleeping, and the nurses had to teach me everything. How to hold you, how to change you. Yeah, Carey was great."

"I saw her later," Mom said. "I don't remember why I was at the hospital, an appointment or something, but I was taking an elevator, and she got on. I smiled at her for too long—it was before we had to mask—and then I felt awkward so I looked away. I start to realize then: she doesn't recognize me. Of course she doesn't. Why would she? All the women she's helped, and all the babies. Thousands, probably. And I was so overwhelmed by that—by her ability to do that, her huge capacity for care, for giving and doing and being everything that a new mother needs in the scariest moments of her life, when her baby is only just barely alive..."

There was a catch in my mother's voice, and Dad reached forward and put his wet hand on her bare knee without saying anything.

After a moment she said, "I was embarrassed. I was so overcome, just a total mess. I got off the elevator early. I didn't say anything to her, but somebody had called for the elevator on a different floor, and as soon as the doors opened I raced out. I walked up the stairs the rest of the way, just sobbing, tears, snot, everything. I couldn't stop. It was so weird."

Dad's hand was still on her knee, his fingers moving gently until she put her hand over his. They looked at each other. I didn't know what to say, so I said nothing.

I spent the morning on the road, tossing small rocks at the trunks of trees while my parents attempted to reshape the dock. We had lunch, and then in the stillness of the early afternoon Dad lay down on the bed and dozed, the filmy white curtains lit brightly by the hot sun, their loose weave illuminated, stirring gently in the small breeze coming off the lake. Mom sat crosswise on a chair in the porch, her bare feet up on the chair next to her, a crossword in her lap and a pencil in her mouth. I think now that it must have been a Sunday, that day. There was never any religion in our family, but by custom our Sundays were usually a tick slower than other days of the week. It was such a lovely, somnambulant afternoon—Dad lying down, Mom lounging.

"I'm going outside," I said to whoever might hear me.

"You gonna go do some exploring?" Mom asked.

"I think so," I said.

"Just don't go too far," said Dad, his eyes closed.

"Back by dinner," Mom said, which I thought was a joke, but was not entirely sure.

I first checked on the fidgeters. Their water was low, but they still turned suspended somersaults in what remained. The afternoon was congealing in the heat, and I wanted to lie down. So I found a spot among the ferns: a warm, green, fecund scene on an unspoiled planet from the unimaginably non-human time before the rise of the dinosaurs. I was somehow stranded there, but safe. No predators. No dangers. Just wordless, spineless life covering all land masses, and oceans full of strange creatures, the rough sketches of animals that humans would later know. I lay there on a bed of humus and leaf matter, ignoring the mosquitoes, breathing the loamy aroma, with my eyes lidded, nearly shut, seeing only a curtain of chlorophyll green. I don't know how long. I might have fallen asleep. I felt ants on my scalp, but I didn't budge or panic.

Eventually, I startled and sat up. There were voices coming from the cabin, my parents' voices, raised at one another, but I could not make out their words.

I stood and walked away from the lake and the cabin, with no plan other than to be out of range of my parents' heated exchange. Soon I was walking the road, right up the middle of it.

All of my life I have relished opportunities—late at night, between stoplights—to be in the middle of roads. To thumb my nose at danger, stealing moments in a place hostile to the human body. I would sometimes imagine hands—my parents', or some other guardian's—reaching out to stop me, grabbing at my shoulder or my arm, for my own good. I always slip their grasp in defiance and make my way across the paths of past and potential vehicles—my stomach dancing, heart skipping—to safety, the delicious transgression over but for the savouring.

I don't know if it began that hot afternoon, but as I walked through the deep green tunnel of trees which overhung the dirt and gravel, I felt an electric charge—the possibility of risk, and the allure of courting it. I felt, too, that walking in the middle of the road would give me an extra millisecond of precious time should something slithery, feathered, crawling, clawed, or predatory spring out of the thick ground cover on either side of the road. I kicked stones and twigs, and picked up acorns, filling my pockets with as many intact ones as I could find, coveting their smooth round shapes and perfect tam-o'-shanter caps.

The road at intervals cut across trails which led toward deeper bush, or one of the lake's many irregular inlets. Game trails and walking paths, little used and overgrown. About halfway up toward the highway, the road intersected with a wide trail, presumably used by snowmobiles in the winter and ATVs in the summer, though I never saw any of either.

One trail appealed to me for reasons I can't name. It led off to my left, down toward a huge, ancient, and moss-covered oak tree, and beyond it into a dreamy sort of green light, edged by ferns and rushes. Another old oak was draped in thick vine, its serpentine trunk covered in a rusty bark, its leaves broad and flat. I walked the trail quickly, a moving target for the shapes I imagined rushing in behind me. The air was thick and unmoving, scents of pine and warm earth. It soon grew darker along the path, sheltered by great cedars and little else, the floor soft underfoot. I was a little terrified and very happy. This was the sort of adventure I had hoped to find: the possibility of getting lost, or of making great discoveries, or both.

I walked down into a slight depression where the cedars thinned and gave way to deciduous cover, allowing a mottled, brighter green light to reach me. Moving around the trunk of a thick maple, my eye caught on an unnatural shape—something that clearly belonged in the human world. It was rectangular with round adornment. A car.

I walked slowly around it, worried for a moment that there might be people inside, dead, and in some horrifying state of decay. My heart thumped as I rose on my toes and peeked over the doors, through windows missing or clouded over with age. I only drew closer when I was sure it was empty.

The small sedan sat as though it had been parked there long ago and abandoned, and the forest had matured around it. A sapling grew up through a sizable rust hole in the floor of the back seat, craning its way toward the missing window. There was a thin steering wheel, almost skeletal in appearance, just a metal ring, its fabric cover rotted away. The exterior paint had faded, but might once have been spring green in colour. There was no identifying mark on the hood. The tires had fallen away, torn and twisted ropes of rubber like muscle and tendon lying half-buried in the ground, the car resting on partially submerged, rusted rims. The whole carcass was sunk into the ground, tilted just slightly to the driver's side. The front bumper had fallen and was resting in place, but the rear was still intact, the chrome eaten in spots but hanging on in others. The trunk was closed and either locked or rusted in place, while the hood gaped open, showing teeth and organs I could not identify. Inside, affixed to the steel chassis, was a manufacturer's tag; it said *VAUXHALL*.

I wanted to open a door or grab the steering wheel to see if it could be turned, but I didn't. I didn't dare touch the car at all, thanks to what I'd been told about corroded metal and tetanus. I thought a single prick of my finger meant my blood would be fatally poisoned, so I treated the car with forensic deference.

I surveyed the spot. How had it arrived here? Who had left it? Had they died tragically and suddenly, or had something caused them to forget where their car was? Each scenario I imagined was stranger than the last. This old and abandoned car made it seem possible that the end of the world had already come—that what we were living through was not preamble, but aftermath.

I ran home, back up the trail and out onto the road and all the way back. I ran with a mixture of exhilaration and panic, though I couldn't say why the latter. Even though I fully intended to tell my parents about what I'd found, I ran as though I had a secret. It felt to me that hours had slipped by since I'd stood and left the ferns, though it'd likely been only twenty or thirty minutes, but I figured enough time had passed that my parents had settled their conflict.

I burst through the screen door and said, "I found something."

"Back already," said my father, sitting at the table, looking at his phone.

"Hi, Gabey," Mom said casually from the porch, where she was sitting in the sun with another crossword puzzle.

"I found a car," I said.

"What?" Dad shouted, tensing up. "I hope you stayed the hell away from it," he said as he pushed his chair back and made to stand.

"Oh, neat," said Mom. "Whose?"

"There was nobody in it."

"Where was it?" Dad said.

"On a trail, up the road."

"A trail?"

"It was parked. Like, left there."

"Where would they go?" said Dad.

"No," I said, "there's no people. It's really old."

"Old, like, before the pandemic?" asked Dad.

"Older. It's like a ruin. The wheels are gone."

Mom said, "It's a ruin in the woods? That's cool."

"You didn't touch it, did you?" asked Dad.

"No, just looked."

"Good. Good boy. Probably full of jagged metal and glass, right? I knew a kid who stepped on a rusty nail, went right up through his shoe and all the way through his foot. He could never run after that. It didn't heal right."

"Is that true?"

"No," Mom said, "it isn't. Or not strictly true, I'm willing to bet." She had put down her crossword and come into the cabin. She put her arm over my shoulders and kissed the crown of my head.

Dad continued. "We called him 'Clubfoot Mike' until we graduated high school. Then I think he went off to join the freak show."

"Stop that," said Mom. "Come on, now. Is anybody hot enough to go swimming yet?"

The sky opened that night. As I lay reading in the loft, I heard the first drops fall on the roof just above my head, and in a moment my ears were filled with the choking, gurgling sounds of a torrential downpour. I fell asleep listening to it.

In the morning the rain was lighter. After breakfast I put on my yellow raincoat, pulled up the hood, and ran to the stump to see if the fidgeters were swimming right up at the rim. But there was no water in the trunk, and no worms that I could see.

Dad appeared at the cabin door, coffee cup in hand. The water pump had recently been lurching into action even when no one was using water, which suggested a leak in the pump itself, or the line up from the lake. He and Mom had discussed over breakfast how he would spend the day finding and repairing the leak, while she meant to untangle old fishing lines and organize Papa's tackle box.

"What are you up to today?" he asked me.

"The worms are gone," I said.

"Well, yeah. I drilled a hole so the water wouldn't collect there. Those were mosquitoes. Their larvae."

"They were tree worms, not mosquitoes. They don't have wings."

"Yeah, now," he said, taking a sip. "When they get bigger they'll be mosquitoes. We don't want that. I know you hate mosquitoes, don't you? They grow up in that sort of standing water. It's bad news."

"But they weren't yet. They were just swimming."

"You have to think ahead," he said sternly. "Last thing we need is an extra swarm of mosquitoes. What if they have West Nile? They bite you, you get sick. Do you see a hospital out here? Any doctors?"

"No," I said, my bottom lip stubbornly quivering even as I fought it.

"No. We're on our own. We need to be smart. Think. Always think! Pet mosquitoes would not be smart."

"Okay," I said, turning my head away.

He could see he'd hurt me, I think, because he softened a bit. "Sorry, buddy," he said, "but they had to go. Nothing but bad news. I didn't know you would be upset."

The last part struck me harder than the fact that he'd gotten rid of the larvae. It meant he didn't really know me, wasn't aware of how interested I was in the strange little dancing commas.

In his mind I'm sure this seemed like a valuable lesson: that stoicism and sacrifice were required in order to live in the world, especially the world he imagined I would inherit. He didn't try to express that, though. He just smiled and said, "Come on and give me a hand with the pump."

"I can't," I said, beginning to walk away. "I have something else I'm supposed to do." There was nothing else, but I had to get away. I ran off toward the road where I sat on a rock out of view and sulked.

I would remain sullen for days, replying to his questions in monosyllables.

One dazzling morning, I awoke to find Dad drinking coffee at the table alone, looking at his phone.

"Where's Mom?" I asked.

"Dock," he said. "Fishing."

I went out in the previous day's clothes, which I'd slept in, and my bare feet. Mom was standing on the dock with her rod cast. Next to her was the tackle box, a pair of needle-nose pliers, and a red plastic bucket. It was full of fish.

"Whoa," I said.

"Morning, baby," she said to me. "Sleep well?"

"I guess. You caught all these?"

"I did."

"I didn't know you could fish." I'd never once seen her do it, and when she took up the day-long job of fixing up the rods we'd found in the garage I had assumed it was so that Dad and I could use them.

"Of course I can fish. Your grandad taught me. We did it a lot when I was a girl."

Why hadn't I learned how to do any of these things? What kind of an adult would it make me if I never learned them?

"I love fish," she said, smiling over her shoulder at me. "We'll fry these up tonight. You like fish, don't you?"

"I don't know," I said.

"You'll like 'em the way I make 'em."

"Can I help?"

"Course you can. I could use it."

Mom sent me to the garage for a pair of gloves because she thought the fish's spines would hurt my hands. She continued casting and caught several more smallmouth bass, and taught me how to hold a fish while taking it off the hook. We put each in the bucket without water and let death come to them slowly—she said she didn't have the stomach required to whack them on the dock, which is what her father did. The fish lay massed together, flipping and bucking, their big eyes staring blankly and their mouths gaping. Slowly they stopped, one by one. Mom said she wasn't sure I was ready to help with cleaning, but I said I was, so right there on the bright, hot dock she showed me how to run the long, thin knife up their bellies and scoop out the guts.

The dock's wooden planks glistened with blood and scales and viscera, and the thighs of Mom's shorts became dark with the same, from her wiping her hands there. There was a smear of blood on her cheek below her right eye where she'd rubbed the back of her hand across her face. The smell became overpowering.

When she was done, she took the gutless fish and put them all into plastic bags and then into the fridge. She said all we needed was butter and lemon, but maybe I should go up the road to pick the wild chives that grew there. Then she went back down to the dock, and using the same red plastic bucket the fish had died in, she took water from the lake and splashed it across the planks to wash off the mess, the blood and scales and guts all sluicing down into the dark water below.

After lunch I did as she'd told me to do, walking up the dusty clearing to the two places where I knew there to be clumps of wild chives. I didn't like onions, but I liked these fresh chives very much. I would cut the shoots down near ground level with a pair of kitchen scissors and put the bundles into a plastic bag—all except for the longest, or greenest, or fattest one from each bunch. Those I would pop into my mouth and chew, tasting the sharp tang.

By the time Mom presented us with dinner plates of fried fish with scalloped potatoes, Dad and I had wordlessly reached a kind of détente, an easing of tensions. He smiled at me in a way that asked if I was still angry about the mosquitoes, and I smiled back because I was hungry and the fish smelled hot and delicious. I didn't feel any anger—but I did not exactly feel forgiveness, either.

After Dad washed the dishes and I swept the floor, we sat on the porch. The sun's last blaze lit up the surface of the bay, and insects hurled themselves against the screening.

One afternoon, a man approached the cabin. He came up the road on foot and called hesitantly from the edge of our property.

"Hello," he shouted.

Mom and I were in the garage building a birdhouse, and Dad was on the lakeshore painting the upturned canoe a fresher blue. When she heard the man, Mom started as though she'd heard a shot. She stepped in front of me, shielding me with her arm as she pulled her shirt up over her nose and mouth in lieu of a mask.

"Hello," she said. She walked out to the mouth of the garage and said quietly to me, "Gabe, stay where you are, okay?"

"Hi. I'm Daniel," said the man, smiling somewhat nervously. "Dan Evans."

He wore a T-shirt and shorts, brown leather sandals on his feet, and he had dark curly hair spilling out from beneath a tan cotton bucket hat. He was older than my parents, but not very old. He held his right hand out in front of him. I could not tell if that was meant to reassure us or to keep us from getting too close to him. Either way it was unnecessary; we were thirty or forty feet away from one another.

"I just bought the land back toward the highway," he said. "Just wanted to take a look around, say hi."

"Hi," said Mom, and a beat followed when I think the man expected her to offer more detail, but her silence was meant to tell him that he didn't need to know more. She didn't offer our names, our reason for being there.

Dad came up the hill in a slow jog, turning the corner of the cabin with his chest puffed a bit. In normal times I wouldn't have been scared, but my parents' reactions told me that alarm was the right response. I took a step back toward the rear of the garage, looked around for anything I might use as a weapon, but could only see a broom.

"Hello," said Dad in a kind of accusatory tone.

"Hi," the man said again. "I was just saying hi. I'm Dan. Just bought the land—"

"Back up the road," said Dad. "Right. Good."

"Yes," said the man.

"Okay," said Dad. "Is there anything wrong?"

"No, nothing wrong at all."

"Well, good. Okay, then. Nice to see you. Have a good day."

"Okay," said the man. "Just wanted to assure you that I'm not going to be doing anything drastic up there. Not knocking down all the trees or anything. Probably won't build on it for a few years."

"That's good news," said Dad.

"Just have our little trailer there for now. Getting the lay of the land."

"Okay. Thanks, Dave."

"Dan. Well," said the man, "okay. I suppose I'll see you. Have a good one."

"Yup," said Dad, clearly impatient.

Daniel Evans took several steps backwards, still looking at us—unsure, it seemed to me, whether or not the conversation was truly over. Eventually he gave a weak half wave, turned, and walked away.

"Shit," said Dad. "Shit, shit, shit."

"It's okay, Artie. It is. No big deal."

"Very big deal," he said.

—

We kept busy with our little jobs until the late afternoon. When the sun seemed at its hottest, we quit. We did not swim that day. Instead we sat in the blistering heat of the windless porch, watching the canoe's paint dry and silently assessing the damage from our meeting with Daniel. Why we should feel injured by his presence, I wasn't sure. Maybe he reminded us that we were not wholly isolated from the wider world and its continued upheaval.

"Whole point in coming here was that we wouldn't have neighbours," said Dad. "But we got 'em anyway."

"Wonder what he paid," Mom said.

"Big enough lot," Dad said, then sipped from his beer. "Don't know how many acres, but it's big."

"No waterfront, though," said Mom.

"Little bit of the river goes through it," said Dad. "Don't know if you could get a boat in there."

"Hope he doesn't build anything too big. This'll be the Muskokas soon."

"Yup. Assuming the world is ever right again. People coming up from the GTA. Jet Skis, golf courses. They keep pushing out of the city, like a plague."

"Wouldn't hurt the value of this place, though."

"No, it would not. Could probably get some fool from Toronto to give us a million for this. They're all trying to get away from it. If things get worse they'll be up here building bunkers, siphoning all the water."

"Art."

"Maybe we should jump on this, take advantage of their desperation. Then we could get something more remote. Go further north."

Then they were both quiet. I didn't want to leave Papa's cabin, and I didn't want to think about someone else owning it, but my parents were speaking in the manner they reserved for blue-sky speculation, not real action. This was an idle brainstorm, not a plan, so I wasn't truly worried. Here was more proof, though, that the real business of the world continued—that we were not quite as alone as I had believed, or most fervently hoped.

That night I lay unsleeping, staring at the shadows playing on the ceiling above my head. Through the noise of the trees' swaying and the insects' chirping, I realized I could hear the sound of cars passing by on the highway. That realization sent a jolt through me.

When I finally fell asleep, I dreamed of swimming—of the feeling of the water, and the wavy, tremulous light beneath the surface, where there was a more permanent silence.

The summer grew hotter, stretched out. It was green and close and shimmering. At night the air was thick and slow. The lake grew warmer and warmer, and in time it felt like bathwater; we swam anyway, though it was not as refreshing. We swam in blazing sun and torrential downpours. We only got out of the water if we heard thunder.

Only when we crawled into August did I catch a glimpse of how strangely time was advancing. It came when, for the first time in ages, I thought of Max.

He was my closest friend. Before the virus we'd usually spent our recesses together, throwing a ball against the wall, or floating stick boats down the wide gully that would form through the middle of our school's field after heavy rain or as the snow melted. Max had been in my class since kindergarten, and we also saw each other twice a year outside of school, for his birthday party in September and mine in April.

For his last birthday before the pandemic, we'd gone to the Havoc Palace Laser Tag Arena, a unit in a big, square building in an industrial park at the south end of Peterborough, set between a used tire store and a do-it-yourself pottery studio. There were about a dozen boys at that party—the largest of any of our gatherings up to that point, which reflected less Max's growing popularity, and more the frenzy ten-year-old boys then had for pointing fake guns at one another.

Mom had been in the process of planning my own birthday party when things halted. She'd asked me if I'd rather she rent the party room at the local movie theatre or book a couple of hours at the Havoc Palace. I said laser tag. She prepared nine invitations that I took to school and gave to my classmates, and each of those nine boys stuffed the invitation into his backpack and brought it home. Mom and I were anxiously awaiting RSVPs when the government announced that all schools would be shut down for a couple of weeks to flatten the curve. When, as the end of those two weeks neared, they said that schools would remain closed indefinitely, Mom contacted each boy's parents and said that she would reschedule. The months passed, and though Mom never actually said so, I came to understand that I just wouldn't be having a tenth birthday party. But I was okay with it—nobody else was having a tenth birthday party either.

Of the nine boys invited, Max was the only one I'd have said I'd be sorry not to see for months on end. But the truth was, I thought of him very little during all that time in lockdown. I suppose Max and I didn't have any abiding passions in common—we were just very familiar with one another. My parents weren't close with his parents either. I don't think they saw each other at all, except to drop us off at our respective parties, whether at our houses, the Havoc Palace, the movie theatre, or once, for my eighth birthday, the small local zoo.

But as the lockdown wore on, all of it—Max, school, laser tag, going to the movies—seemed so distant that it might as well not have been a part of my life at all. I didn't treasure or long for those things any more than I did a haircut, or a visit to the doctor. I accepted the new borders of my world. When we moved to Papa's cabin, I was excited and happy. I would say that I had all that I required, even though there wasn't another kid around to play with. It was made very clear to me that playing with other kids wasn't an option, but I was told I could play all day with my friends when a vaccine was developed and everything went back to normal. It made no sense to me to mourn this loss. I came to see that I had myself, and that was enough. In the absence of abundance, I learned to make do.

And I did. In spite of the awful state of the world, I had the best summer of my life. I was a ten-year-old boy, and I had my parents' attention. I had trees and a lake, fishing rods, rocks, campfires. I had a stack of Hardy Boys books, and clear nights of blanketing starry skies. Very few things seemed capable of finding me there, let alone harming me—other than the wolves, that is, whose nearness sent a jaggedness through me every night when it grew dark.

One evening, after dinner, we went for a walk. It had rained most of the day, shutting us inside, but about dinnertime the sun came out and made a show of drying out all the full, lush dampness. Mom suggested we hike up the road to the highway and back, and when we finally set out it was approaching dusk. Leaves dripped little globes of light in the golden late-day sun. Puddles lay in the road's dust and gravel, and the air had a new, sweet coolness to it. Cattails bobbed gently by the side of the road, growing taller than I was out of the low wet places. Where it was drier there grew tall grass gone to seed, which I pulled between my fingers as we passed to make bushes or trees, just as Max and I would do along the fence in the schoolyard. The forest exhaled its rich, wet breath onto us.

We'd brought no flashlight. I don't know why—it was clear to me that it would be dark by the time we were returning. The sun dropped behind us as we neared the highway, and the darkness off in the trees on either side of the road became thick and menacing. We'd gone as far as the signpost that supported the red *FIRE ROAD 26* sign, touching its galvanized surface as a way to signal the end of our route, my deepest foray into the wider world since we'd arrived. Then we turned back again. The sun was just a glow between the trees, and an inky violet was overtaking the sky, from the east up toward the zenith. Fireflies began to appear, winking on and off on all sides of us.

We rounded a bend, and in the dark space between the trees there was a spot of greater dark and sudden movement. Something animal, hunched and large. It was too big to be canine, and it galumphed rather than trotting or bounding. On our approach, the dark shape—a void of almost perfect darkness in the already dusky air—scrabbled and collected itself into a run. It moved along the road further around the bend, then appeared to continue into the brush and dense forest.

"Oh god," said Mom. "What was that?"

"I'm pretty sure that was a bear," said Dad.

We stood close together for a long time, not moving or speaking. I heard my parents' breathing and my own heart thudding, but nothing else. The back of my neck began to crawl. I felt shivers deep inside my chest that I was certain would spill out as gasps and chattering teeth if I opened my mouth, so I kept it shut.

"We don't have anything, do we?" asked Mom in a voice above a whisper, but below a normal volume. I could hear the strain at the edges of it, and I knew she was trying to sound calm despite the fear in her.

"Anything?"

"Like, I don't know. Like bear spray? Or a knife, or something?"

"No," said Dad, patting his pockets.

"We should have brought a light to shine in its eyes," she said.

"I think it's gone. It went into the trees. They want to get away from you even more than you want to get away from them." He tried to sound reassuring, but did not sound reassured himself.

"Sure, but the sound just kind of stopped," Mom said. We were maybe forty metres from the spot where we'd last seen the shape, but we were not moving toward it. There was no other way back to the cabin. "Are you sure it was a bear? It might have just looked bigger than it was. Could have been a coyote. Racoon."

"Or a wolf," I said.

"No, it was a fucking bear," Dad said, speaking to a certainty I'm not wholly sure he possessed. He might have been trying to imagine the worst-case scenario. That was something he was prone to doing.

"How long do we wait?" I finally said, my voice small and weak and jostled by the trembling in my chest.

"We can probably go now," Dad said. "But we should make noise so we don't sneak up on it again. You're supposed to make noise. Warn it that you're coming."

"Hey," Mom shouted. "Hey, bear!" She clapped her hands and whistled. "Gah!"

"Go on, bear," Dad yelled, also clapping. "Get!"

I joined them, screeching, "Get away! Get away! Go on, bear, get away!"

Nothing moved as we crept down the road, yelling and clapping. When we reached the approximate spot where the shadow had disappeared, we called louder, then turned to walk backwards as fast as we could, still making our noise, trying to protect ourselves from an ambush.

"I think we're good now," Dad said.

We turned and jogged all the way back to the darkened cabin, where Mom closed and locked the door as though the bear had been right on our heels the whole time. Then my parents began to laugh, in between big breaths. They became lighter, and the fear seemed to rise up off of them. Soon they were in the screened porch with cold beers—Dad with his small glass of whisky too—laughing and telling stories of past encounters with bears and other wildlife.

They sent me to bed, but I couldn't sleep for the violent beating that continued in my chest. It was like a heavy living thing outside of me. Something in pursuit.

———

When I was seven, Mom and Dad took me to Florida for March break. It was not a normal thing for us to do as a family. I don't think we'd ever gone away in the spring before. But Mom and Dad, for reasons I didn't know then, were flush, or at least willing to take on a little short-term debt, in order to take me to Disney World.

We drove all night and through most of the next day to get there. I slept through blowing snow in Pennsylvania and West Virginia, and when I woke up in South Carolina the sun was beating down on my head. I said, "I have to pee." We stopped at a McDonald's and watched CNN on overhead TVs while we ate flapjacks and my parents sipped from cups of coffee as tall as flowerpots.

We stayed in a hotel in Orlando. I watched a lot of TV and spent three long days at Disney World, but I was too scared to get on any rides, and the heat made me feel sick to my stomach. When a park employee dressed as Goofy approached me, I tried to hide behind my parents and would not respond when he offered his big, gloved hand. I complained just about the whole time, but at the end of our third day, after dark and shortly before the park closed for the night, the fireworks exploded over our heads and the colour lit up my parents' faces, and I was thrilled by all of it.

We drove back north, stopping at a Best Western in Virginia for the night. It was in a small town bisected by the interstate and it looked to be made up entirely of motels and family restaurants. We brought takeout burgers into our room and sat on the ends of the beds watching TV. There was a news report of a school shooting, and my father sat mesmerized.

Mom said, "Artie, change it." He seemed not to hear her, so she went searching for the remote control and when she found it she aimed it at the screen and it went suddenly black. "Is there anything else to watch?" she asked sharply.

"I think there's a big college basketball game on," he said, as though he'd been awoken from a dream. I'd seen the one he meant on the TV in the lobby when we checked in and the clerk seemed too distracted by it to speak to Mom in full sentences. We watched the game and then turned out the lights, but after a while Dad turned the lights back on. He and Mom spoke in whispers, and then he put on his pants and shoes and left the room.

"Where's Dad going?" I asked Mom.

"He might have left something in the car, maybe," she said, looking at the door, and with a small bit of worry in her voice.

I got up, went to the window, and pushed aside the heavy blackout curtain. I watched him walk across the parking lot to its edge and stand beneath a light standard, his back to the building, his fingers laced together up on top of his head. He was staring into the scrubby brush at nothing, or so it appeared. Just into the darkness there, the moisture, the decay, the neon thread of violence that snaked its way through everything in America. It was a cold night, and I could see his breath rising in slow clouds up toward the orangey light. He was my father, but he looked like a stranger. He put his hands on his hips and turned as if to come back inside, but stopped and faced the bushes again.

"Why isn't he coming inside?"

"He just needs some air, probably," Mom answered.

I went back to my big bed and slid inside the starchy sheets and tried to stay awake until he returned, but I dozed off. I awoke sometime later to the sound of the door opening. He took off his shoes and pants and sat on the edge of their bed and looked at me. I could smell the night on him—the cold air, the exhaust from the highway rigs, the French fries he'd eaten, his stale breath.

"Is everything okay, Dad?" I asked.

"Everything's fine," he said. "Get some sleep." He smiled a tired smile.

I rolled over and closed my eyes, trying to take him at his word.

One dark, starless night, a few days after we saw the shadow of a bear, I found myself lying awake in bed. I knew Mom was asleep because I could hear her breathing slowly and loudly, but Dad was awake too. He was sitting up in bed, I thought, thinking, or stewing. I heard him stirring, moving, sometimes muttering to himself.

From outside the windows, in the leafy, sighing darkness, there came a strange, trilling bird call, a bar of music that rose at its end so that it sounded like a question.

"What's that?"

"I think that's a whippoorwill," Dad whispered. "They're named after their sound. Hear it?"

"Like it's saying its own name."

"Right."

The bird continued to call. It sounded tropical and exotic. It made me think of the dense vegetation that rings Florida parking lots and the strange animals found in there. I said to Dad, "I liked Florida," though I'd never had a good word to say about my memories of the place. Perhaps I was trying to find some common thing we could both smile about, a scene from the pre-pandemic world, something my parents had perhaps enjoyed, and something to look forward to. "Maybe we could go back there."

"Florida," he said. "That's the hot spot right now."

"Is it bad?"

"It's all bad," he said. "We won't be going to the States anymore, that I can tell you. It's awful. They're done. The whole country is done."

◆

Dad and I canoed out to the cliff with two musty sleeping bags and a small canvas tent he'd found in the garage. We had two cans of Quebec-style baked beans in maple syrup, three bruised bananas, a bag of all-dressed potato chips, a one-litre bottle of water, and a five-hundred-millilitre bottle of iced tea. Dad had a Mason jar of rye, a Swiss Army knife, and one pack of waterproof matches, their tips daubed with shiny green wax and their box depicting a Newfie in a sou'wester rowing a dinghy.

He'd mused aloud about us coming out here one afternoon when we were swimming, and days later there we were, doing it. Our own little adventure, just the two of us. I think it was his way of patching up any damage he'd done by drilling that hole in what I'd thought of as my tree stump.

When we landed Dad pulled the canoe onto the rock and turned it over so that it resembled a beached, supine aquatic mammal. Though it was out of the water, he tied the yellow nylon rope from its bow around a stout cedar, double-knotting it. "Wind," he said as I watched him do this. "You never know."

I helped him set up the tent by handing him the poles from the bag as he asked for them. He erected it on a small flattish depression of dry, spongy lichen on the backside of the rock, away from the water. From that spot I couldn't see any water, and already this was a departure from how I'd imagined this adventure—in my mind's eye we'd sleep right up on the very highest point of the rock, overlooking the lake, and the moon and the stars would be reflected in the gently rippling water. I tried to shoulder past this disappointment.

He tried and failed to drive the thin metal tent stakes into the ground, so he sent me off to look around for stones— "The size of my fist or bigger." It took me several sorties, but I made a pile of a dozen or so. He tied the guy wires around the stones and placed them around the tent like idols to ward off bad exhalations. Then he unzipped the tent's door and unrolled our sleeping bags inside.

We swam after that, in the clothes we wore. We'd brought no towels, so we sat on the sunniest open spot in the early evening sun until we dried, and I felt the skin of my face tighten and redden.

Dad sat cross-legged on the high point, looking toward the western horizon, across a great distance and many years. He could occasionally look boyish, and he did in that moment, with his fine features and the sun on his face.

He sent me to look for kindling. "Get some birchbark, if you can find it," he said. While I did, he scavenged driftwood and deadfall, placing long sticks against a boulder and then driving his shoe's heel into the middle of them. Their dry cracking sounds were like gunshots as they broadcast down the lake and ricocheted off the rocks opposite us.

I ventured to the edge of thicker forest cover, not far away. There were two or three birches there, so I tore off curled strips of their bark, which was so easy that it was addictive. I stuffed the little rolls in my pockets and then filled my hands with sticks and twigs and walked back toward my father.

"You want to go smallest to biggest," he said, kneeling on the rock above a small indentation where he'd placed the birchbark strips in a jumble. "Your easiest fuel—paper, or bark in this case—and then the smallest, easiest-to-catch twigs."

He narrated as he did all this, building a small pyramid overtop the bark.

"Bigger twigs on top of those," he said, enclosing the first pyramid inside a slightly larger one. "Eventually your big logs go around the outside. Smallest to biggest. Then you just have to hold a match to the paper, and boom."

It took him several tries to strike the match, which he then held to the edge of one of the curls of birchbark. It flared immediately, and in the blink of an eye all the birchbark was consumed. Dad knelt, his face close, eyes fixed.

"Yeah," he said, "that's it. She'll go."

He blew into the base of the flame a few times and then sat back on his haunches. The fire leapt up tall and hungry before settling down, Dad's pyramids collapsing gently to one side, the flames growing hotter and steadier. He used the can opener on his pocket knife to crack open both cans of beans, which he placed at the edge of the fire, turning them every few minutes using two sticks like a pair of primitive pliers. We passed the warm, sweet iced tea back and forth. He stirred the beans with a barkless stick he'd found, and when they were warm and steaming he took the cans away from the flames, placed one just in front of me, and one in front of himself. He handed me a spoon.

"Careful," he said. "It'll need to cool."

I didn't wait, of course. I tried to pick up the can with my left hand, but quickly let go. "Ooh," I said, and blew on my palm while Dad chuckled. Then I put my spoon in and scooped it full of the warm beans and the sweet maple syrup, and when I put it in my mouth it scalded my palate and tongue. I chewed with my mouth open, trying to cool it down.

Dad chuckled some more. "Sure," he said through his mouthful of beans. "I mean, why would you listen to your old dad? Why benefit from my years of wisdom? Better to do it your own way, right?"

The burn lessened the flavour of the rest of the beans, but they filled me up. When I was done, I asked what we would do with the cans. "Will we just burn them?"

"No, they won't burn. We'll take them home. But we can't have them lying around here tonight. Great bear bait. No, thanks."

He produced a mesh bag, holding it up by its corners for me to see. When it was clear I wasn't sure what he meant

to do, he stood and indicated with his head that I should
follow him.

"Bring the cans," he said.

He walked down to the water's edge and crouched,
then took the cans and dunked them into the lake, where
he swished them about and dumped them out. Then he
bent the lids, still attached, into the cylinders, and he put
both cans in the mesh bag and cinched its top. He moved
a rock just beneath the water's surface in the shallows near
his feet, then he pushed the bag of cans in, filling them,
and placed the rock on top of one edge of the black mesh,
weighing it down.

"There," he said. "They won't smell that. We just have to
remember to bring that with us when we leave tomorrow."

It seemed like a good solution to me.

The dusk was growing thick with pollen and birdsong,
the western sky streaked in peach and lavender while over
us a patch of clear sky shone with the first few stars.

"Might be good stargazing tonight," he said.

I sat that way, hugging my legs and looking up at the
stars, until my neck began to ache, and then I lay down like
my father. We didn't speak. There were few sounds beyond
the birds, and the hiss and crackle of the fire. The sun disappeared and the sky grew darker, the stars brighter.

"Do you think there's aliens?" I said.

"Probably. If you think about it, how could there not be?
How could it be just us? They already know; they just won't
tell us. I think the billionaires are getting secrets from the
aliens, and they know enough to be leaving this planet."

"Really?"

"Oh, I don't know. Probably. And the rest of us are
screwed."

I didn't know what to say to that, so I said nothing. I kept hoping my father would offer something more optimistic to allay my fears, but he was silent for a long time. Bullfrogs began their chorus in the wetlands nearby.

"I mean," he finally said, "I guess it makes sense for them. If you're rich enough you can just go somewhere else to find new resources to exploit. But that makes what the rest of us down here do that much more important."

This was, at least, a partially hopeful comment. "Are there planets like ours?"

"There has to be," he said. "Look at everything up there."

The Milky Way had emerged, like the image on a print soaking in developer, arcing over our heads from one horizon to the other.

"Will people go?"

"We have a lot of shit to figure out first," he said. "We have to survive this thing, first of all."

"Do you think we will?"

"Well," he said, turning his head toward me, "I intend to."

"Here?"

"Better than in the city. Too many people there. It's just simple math. There's nobody here to give it to us."

"Mom thinks we'll be okay there."

"Mom's hoping that's true. She doesn't know. Nobody knows."

"Nobody?"

"Nope."

I had more questions than I could process, so none came out. Instead I stared up, realizing that if I fixed my eyes on a seemingly blank patch of sky, more stars would appear, first in my peripheral vision, and then exactly where I was looking. The notion of infinity came tantalizingly close to my grasp before it slipped off, leaving me with even more questions. The totality of things seemed crushingly incomprehensible.

Before long, I realized that Dad had fallen asleep. The fire was all but gone. Mosquitoes attempted to get at my brain through my ears and nostrils. "Dad?"

"Mm."

"Bedtime, I guess?"

He roused himself and brought the empty iced tea bottle down to the lake, filling it with water that he poured on the fire, making it hiss loudly and emit a thick, warm steam. He did that twice more until no glowing coals remained, and he stirred the ashes with a stick to be sure. We took off our shoes and left them outside the door, and we zipped ourselves inside the tent, inside our sleeping bags. The ground at the spot he'd chosen was springy and almost comfortable. I fell quickly asleep with the night so quiet and close—just the bullfrogs and the sound of my own circulation thrumming in my ears, and no wolves—and I believe he did, too.

━

I woke first, moist and hot. I unzipped my bag and crawled out the door, put on my shoes, and peed on a small tree. Then I walked up to the rock's apex, where I sat cross-legged and watched the sun rise over the marshy end of the lake where red-winged blackbirds were calling, landing and taking off from cattails and tall grasses that waved and bobbed in a gentle wind.

"Gabe?" Dad's voice was a little grumbly and quiet. He'd just woken up. I knew he thought I was still in the tent, but everything was so still and hushed that I could hear him as though he was right next to my ear.

"Here, Dad."

"Oh, good," he said. "We made it through the night. Survival is an accomplishment."

"Just watching the sun come up."

"The early bird. You okay?"

"Yup. I'm good."

"Okay. I'll join you out there in a minute."

But then I believe he fell back asleep, because I didn't hear from him again nor see him until the sun was higher and very hot and I had used sticks to build a bridge across a narrow, deep fissure in the rock, which I then paved with tiny stones. I watched an ant make its speedy, jerky way across it, and I thought I had solved a problem for him and his colony. I had bridged this crevasse which had vexed them and their ancestors for millennia.

The sharp sound of the tent door's zipper announced Dad's rising. He stood and stretched and winced into the sun. Then he located me.

"Hey, there you are. Have you eaten?"

"No."

"Go down to the boat; the bananas are there."

He'd left them beneath the upturned canoe, and somehow, miraculously, they'd made it through the night. We ate one each and split the third, shared the bottle of warm water, and then broke camp, stuffing our sleeping bags into their sacks and wrestling the tent into its bag. I straddled it and pushed the zipper's teeth together while Dad zipped it an inch at a time.

"Always the worst job," he said.

The wind was kicking up as we pushed off, and the paddle home was hard and slow. The headwind eased as we slipped into the bay, and soon we saw Mom waiting on the dock, her feet in the water, a can of Diet Coke in her hand.

"There they are," she said as we neared, "the brave adventurers."

"Hi, Mom."

"How was it?"

"Good," I said. "Fun."

"No bear attacks? No monsters?"

"Just mister here," said Dad, "and his snoring."

"And you didn't burn the forest down?"

"All blazes safely extinguished," he said, holding his paddle so Mom could grab it and pull us into the dock. When we were safely out of the canoe, our things piled on the dock, Dad said to her, "And what did you do last night?"

"Cowered, of course. Without my men here to protect me? I hid beneath a blanket and shivered out of pure fright until the birds woke up and the sun rose. Thank god you're home."

"Mom."

"Sat on the screened porch, drank a beer, did a crossword, slept like a baby. Same as I do when you're here. Was I supposed to throw a party?"

◆

Of course there was a gun.

The cabin had been Papa's hunting and fishing lodge. There were fishing poles, and there was a gun. Dad found it when he was cleaning and organizing the garage, only days after we'd moved up from the city. It hadn't been locked away, though the clasp on the green metal case was stiff with rust.

It was a rifle. I don't know what kind. I had a shiny, wet-looking barrel and a smooth, dark wooden stock. It smelled of metal, oil, and age. When Dad placed the dull-green case on the garage's long workbench one afternoon to show me—unhooking the latch and prying it up, slowly raising the lid to dramatically reveal its terrifying contents—I think he believed he was giving me some understanding both of the direness of our circumstances and the great responsibility now invested in us, in me. That in removing the rifle from its case and holding it to his shoulder and softly whispering, "Boom!" while mimicking a slow-motion recoil, he was transmitting a lesson to me about self-reliance and doing what's necessary—the messy business of survival.

"What do you think?" he said.

"Is it real?" This was an understandable question, I felt, as I'd never seen anything like it before, only screen depictions and police officers' holstered sidearms.

"Is it real? Of course it's real." He ran his hand along its flank as though petting an animal, and stared at it appraisingly. He was a livestock judge at a county fair.

"Was it Papa's?"

"It was. He'd use it in the fall. For deer."

"To kill them."

I had never watched an animal die. Fish, and insects, I suppose, but only those. And the dove that I'd found dying in our yard in Peterborough. But I'd never seen a dead mammal or watched one die.

"For food," he said. "It's natural, a normal part of life. You watch, when the cold weather comes up here you'll hear guns. People getting ready for winter." He glanced at me to size up the impact of his words, but once he had my eye he returned his gaze to the oiled muzzle. "We'll learn how to use it together."

"Really?"

I was certain he was not serious, and I did not want him to be. The thought terrified me. But still I wanted to please my father, to be a young man he could feel pride in, and in whom he might see some of himself. My best efforts at earning his love were acts of imitation.

"Soon," he said. "Soon. For now just remember that Mom doesn't know, and it's better if I tell her."

"Okay."

"I'm serious, buddy. Got it?"

"Yes."

He turned away from me then, setting the rifle back in its clumsy case and closing it as you would a vampire's coffin, carefully but firmly, hoping it wouldn't stir. His manner suggested we were done, or that he was done with me, and I knew that I could walk out of the garage without a word and not be admonished for rudeness. My father could be like that—like a searchlight: when his gaze and notice were upon you, you were bathed in it and he was aware of everything you did, but once it swung away, to another object or person, he'd forget you altogether. So I wandered out the big open doors and into the sludgy afternoon heat.

Everything sang and ached—the crickets, the clouds, the trees. The large, showy sky looked to me like yearning. I felt it on a distinctly wordless level, though I didn't know what it was I yearned for.

◆

Dad began chopping wood in early August. The axe had been suspended on pegs above Papa's workbench, and for a block Dad dug out from beneath the cabin a thick, broad stump which had been sanded and finished with a yellow-tinted varnish—Papa had likely meant to turn it into a table or a stool. Dad placed it on a level spot of ground between the cabin and the garage. Then he took the axe down from its perch, swung it into the block, and left it there at a crude angle, the thinnest edge of it bitten into the middle of the block, bisecting its concentric rings, while he began to sift through the logs remaining in Papa's stack against the back of the garage. I could see that most of them had gone to rot, soft and papery with holes in the middles, or chewed up by carpenter ants, the bark falling away as Dad picked up each piece. But some remained solid, and these he began to pile next to the block. Then he started in on splitting.

He would bend to pick up a log from the stack, his hands gloved in a tattered pair of Papa's leather work gloves, and place the log carefully on its flattest end in the middle of the varnished block. Then he would look at his feet, shuffling them slightly to ensure they were the proper distance from his target. He would pick up the axe, which had been stuck into the dirt near his feet, gripping its handle tightly, flexing his fingers, wringing the blond wooden handle. Raising the head, he would hold it straight out, a direct line between his shoulders and the glinting metal wedge, and hover it just above the waiting log. Measuring. Then he would bring the axe in a wide slow arc behind himself and over his head before swinging it violently down and through the wood, his knees bent and his face puffed out in a sudden exhalation, the axe head cleaving the block and the two halves toppling to either side to fall to the earth with a soft, pleasing thud. After each blow he would sink the axe into the soft earth with a quick chop and use his hands either to pick up the two new logs and pitch them back toward the garage or, if they were still too large for the wood stove, balance one of the halves again on his block and split it once more. He worked that way all afternoon until he'd split all the logs worth splitting, and hauled the bad wood up to our firepit, dumping it all in a haphazard pile. The good logs he carefully stacked against the back of the garage, as Papa had. Then my father stood back and admired his work.

Dripping with sweat on what had become a cloudy and terrifically humid afternoon, Dad said, "Jesus. Time for a swim." So we all got in the canoe and paddled toward the cliff.

"Hard to believe how fast this will change," Dad said. "Summer's nearly over."

"It's still summer," said Mom happily, reassuringly.

"The change will come quick."

My father's fixation on the change of seasons caused a rattling in my heart. I wanted summer to continue forever—I wanted to be submerged in it. That was why, that afternoon, I finally climbed much higher up the warm rock. Without saying a word I scrabbled halfway up the slope and stood looking down at the unmoving water. For seconds that seemed interminable I thought about the pain of hitting the water wrong, the consequences of not jumping far enough and grazing the rock on the way down. I thought of the feeling of water up my nose. I thought of hitting the bottom, or brushing up against something slick and dark when I went under. But then I thought of summer ending, and I thought of the confusion and anger I felt when Dad talked about summer's end, and winter's approach, and never seeing Max again, or going to the movies, or playing laser tag.

And so I jumped.

The fall sent an electric sensation up through my stomach and heart, and the rush of air in my face and ears was unlike anything I'd known before. I couldn't hear my parents, though I knew that they were likely calling my name. My arms spun and my legs cycled. I thought about what I would do if I found myself upside down, but that didn't happen. As I neared the water I stiffened and pointed my feet and clamped my arms to my side. Then I hit the surface, and was aware of an instant change in temperature, and of the water opening to accept me. My nose stung as though it had been scoured with a wire brush. My ears popped, and there was a terrible squeal inside my head. When I felt my downward momentum stop I began kicking hard and clawing for the surface. I had never been so deep underwater before, and my lungs felt as though they might collapse into themselves. I wanted very badly to reach the surface again, though I was also glad to be in there amid the violent bubbling and the insulated, amniotic sound, the water pressing against me. I opened my eyes very quickly to see a soft gradation of light, from white-grey above me to brown murk in front of me, and blackness below.

I broke through and shut my eyes again, pushing my chin toward the sky. Ordinary sound returned—first to my right ear, and then to my left—and I heard Mom shouting, "Wow, Gabey!" with a mix of happiness and concern. It was the same tone she inadvertently used whenever I showed some small bit of independence or capability.

"Good job, Gabe," shouted Dad from atop the rock, and then he too leapt. He brought his knees to his chest, hugging them all the way down until he hit with a thunderous concussion, the water pushing away and then healing itself, pouring green and white from all sides to meet at the very spot where he'd landed, then clapping against itself and mushrooming up into the air. He popped up several metres away and said, "Woo!" and then, "soon you'll be doing those off the very top!"

When we sat down to dinner that night, Dad was unusually buoyant and talkative. He said that it would be easy to insulate the cabin, and that the first and easiest thing we could do would be to caulk around all the windows and doors. He said that Mom should pick up some caulking the next time she went into town for groceries. "We'll put the CERB cheque to good use. Other thing is we don't have enough wood. What's there won't last until Christmas."

"We're going to be here for Christmas?" I asked.

"We don't know yet, hon," said Mom.

"Well, you know, I think we should be thinking in those terms," said Dad. "In terms of, okay, what do we need to do to get through the winter?"

"Is this road even plowed in winter?" Mom asked. "We've only been up here when there's, like, no snow."

"Don't know that," said Dad. This seemed to stump him. He sat chewing his lower lip for a moment. "Yeah, I don't know."

"So we're up here and we get thirty centimetres" she continued. "Do we, what? We shovel all the way out? Put a plow on the Honda?"

"No, in that case we probably hunker down for a few days."

"A few days…until April? What do we eat until April?"

"There are," he said, and paused. "There are a few things we'd need to think through."

"Does Dad mean we're going to stay until next year?" I asked.

"Gabey," she said, her tone softening for my benefit, "I think what your dad means is just that it's good to be prepared for a few different possibilities."

"What your dad means," Dad cut in, "is that the safest thing to do is continue to lay low here, and that his biggest problem seems to be talking any sense into your mother." He'd leaned forward with one elbow on the table, and was looking directly at Mom. "This is it. This is where the rubber meets the road."

"Oh, my god. When did we lose you? When did all this infect your brain?"

They were both silent then, but a long, hard look passed between them. I dragged my fork through my spaghetti, cutting a valley, the tine marks making the plate look like little furrowed fields of red earth.

"We're trying to figure out what makes the most sense for us," Mom finally said.

"Anyway," Dad said, "we'll need a load of wood."

"Could you just cut down some trees?" I asked.

"We could. But you can't burn a tree as soon as it's cut. You have to wait and let it dry out."

"How long?"

"I think a year, about. At least. That's what they call seasoning. You need the wood to dry out so it burns well."

"A year?"

"I think so. I'd need to check that."

"Couldn't you look it up on your phone?" I said.

"Well," he said, "we could, but no. Not right now."

"We're taking a little break from our phones," Mom said, a small crack in her voice. "Unless we absolutely need to use them."

She shifted uneasily. Dad nodded.

"They just bring us bad news," he said.

Mom excused herself to the bathroom and was quiet in there for a long while, as Dad and I sat silently at the table.

I stared into my remaining spaghetti, and he slumped back in his chair and stared out the window. Eventually Mom returned seeming composed, having brushed her hair and splashed water on her face.

"Everybody full?" she asked.

"Stuffed," Dad said.

After cleaning up we went up to the firepit. My father built a small pile of wood he'd deemed unfit for the stove, then squirted a small amount of lighter fluid from a little plastic bottle onto the kindling and logs. He pointed a barbecue lighter into a recess and clicked its trigger, and the flames leapt blue and white into the heavy twilight air. It was a warm evening, so we positioned our folding camp chairs well back from the blaze.

Over the crackling and popping we heard a distant howling, a chorus that seemed to mock my parents' earlier disunity.

"Those are wolves," I said to my mother, proud of myself for identifying the animals, and confident I'd provided her a service by passing along this vital piece of information.

"Wolves or coyotes," she said, nodding.

"I think wolves," I said.

"Those are wolves," Dad said, backing me up. He projected certainty, but the look my mother slid toward him suggested that she knew as well as he did that he had no idea what he was talking about.

The half moon rose orange and wet-looking over the trees to my right. I stared at it, shielding my eyes from the fire with my hand, and tried to imagine the rest of its perfect circle. A rock floating in space. I wondered, not for the last time, how large the universe was.

"Wolves," Dad repeated. "They're something, aren't they?"

For days after, my parents shared few words. I assumed their animosity was the result of the wolf-versus-coyote dispute, and I failed to plot it on a chart of greater disagreements. The weather turned grey and threatened rain, and the nights were noticeably cooler, as though confirming Dad's concerns: summer was going to end, whether we were ready or not. This confirmation, which we all felt, seemed to animate him. He found a phone number for a firewood seller and placed an order for two bush cords, which would be delivered in a few weeks' time. He asked Mom again to pick up tubes of caulking when next she was in town. "You can get them in a contractor's pack," he said. "I think it's twelve. That'll do us."

Mom grew more and more steely, like someone with a secret threatening to spill out if they opened their mouth. When she kissed me on the top of my head I knew she was staring out beyond me, and when she said goodnight it sounded not like a word of comfort, but like a question.

⬗

The next time I saw the rifle it was in my father's hands.

The morning was uneasy, with a wet breeze from the north. I'd woken early with nothing particular in mind but a desire to stand beneath the trees as they flashed their leaf bottoms in the roiled air. I'd crept outside to keep from waking Mom and Dad, and once in the open I tiptoed up the path toward the garage, and beyond that toward the road.

There was a flash of movement. My first, terrifying thought, which froze my blood and made me seize up, was that it was a person—perhaps the same man who'd come up the road all the way back in July. The implication eluded me then, but I see it now: I had become more afraid of people than of wolves or bears.

But as my eyes widened in fear, I saw it. A solitary deer, maybe fifty metres up the road, bending to nibble on some leaves. It straightened itself up slowly, regally, impossibly lithe, the early light giving its coat's sheen a soft, almost hazy quality. The deer flicked its white tail and stepped backwards on hooves gently jabbing at the ground. It turned toward me, and even at that distance I could see the large brown orb of its eye, but either it did not see me, standing as I was in the cover of deep shadow, or it did see me and determined that I posed no threat. It took another series of steps down the road and then bent again to eat, so that what I saw most was its rump and white tail.

Then there was only the slightest movement beside me, registering not as a sound but as a blot against the mottled light on my left, a change in the way that sound moved around me. I slid my eyes in that direction and then slowly turned my head just a few degrees.

There, nodding at me, was Dad. In his hands, pointed at the ground, was the gun.

Don't, I mouthed.

But he was not looking at me. He was focused on the deer. He raised the gun to his shoulder, the barrel parallel to the ground, the dark wooden stock wedged into the soft indent of his shoulder. All his muscles clenched, shoulders hunched.

I knew that I could yell and that the deer would likely bolt if I did so, running to safety before Dad could get a shot off. But I also knew that if I did that, my father would be angry with me. I felt helpless. I closed my eyes as tight as I could and shook back and forth whispering, "No, no, no."

The sound of the shot split the morning in two jagged halves. I grabbed at my left ear, which I was certain had begun to bleed, so intense was the sudden ringing.

With my eyes now wide open, I watched as the deer recoiled and then staggered a bit, as though uncertain where the ground had gone. It began spinning in a tight circle in an effort to evade the pain as blood started spurting from a bright-red wound on its left flank.

I looked at my father and screamed. No words, just anguish.

The gun was still at his shoulder, but Dad had relaxed his body, and his face was slack and uncomprehending.

The poor deer straightened as best it could, like a partially crushed aluminum can left standing on a table. Then it broke into hobbled motion, dashing woozily down the road. My father, apparently stunned, could not manage to fire a second time, and in a moment the animal had leapt off the road, dragging itself behind its overworking front legs, and crashed unsteadily into the bush where we could no longer see it.

We both stood looking down the road, not speaking. I was sobbing, but I did not want him to hear me, though tears fell down my face. We both heard the cabin door open and then shut, and my mother's sprinting footsteps coming up the path toward us. She appeared, red and puffy with sleep, hair matted, hugging closed one of my father's flannel shirts. Her feet were only half in her running shoes, and her legs were bare. I thought she must be cold in the morning air.

"What the hell happened?" she said. "What's going on?"

We were both facing her now, the gun down by my father's right leg.

Mom looked us both over, her mouth open, and she said, "Jesus, Artie, what the fuck have you done?"

She kept one hand on her breast clutching the shirt fabric, and as she fixed her eyes on Dad's she held the other arm out in a gesture I knew meant that she would hold me. I ran to her and pressed my face into her side, and she closed her arm around me, rubbing my back.

"What were you thinking?" she said to Dad, hissing, almost a whisper.

"There was a deer." I sobbed. "I think Dad shot it."

"Venison for winter," he said. "I was only trying..."

He stopped before finishing the sentence. A minute passed in heated silence.

"Where is it?" she asked, accusingly.

"It bolted," Dad said. "I couldn't get another shot off."

"It was hurt," I said. "He got it a little bit, but he didn't kill it."

"Come inside," she said to me, rubbing my back one last time before turning me toward the cabin.

We shuffled inside together, and Mom kicked off her shoes, scooped me into her arms, and folded us both inside the bed covers, where it seemed she meant to keep me safe inside the cocoon of her body and old flannel sheets.

Something in Mom's life had instilled this habit: she always met bad news, harrowing events, arguments, or unpleasant unexpected developments by going to bed. And it was a habit she'd passed on to me. Even now, whenever I am beset, I climb beneath a duvet and fall into a deep, hot sleep, and just before I drift off, my whole body huddles in a ball.

The door did not open again after us. I figured Dad was hiding out in the garage, or had gone down the road in a vain search for the deer. Maybe he knew that it would have done no good to follow us into the house and try to talk through his line of thinking. My parents were, by then, simply too far apart.

Mom said nothing, and I breathed the hot, stuffy air of the bed and her body, and in time I fell asleep.

PART 2: DIAPAUSE

WHEN I WAS TWENTY-TWO, I lived in a world overly dense with meaning. Codes and signals zipped around me; every object was an information gun directing streams of data toward me, through me, off me. I was an antenna, buzzing. Weather contained messages. Entire complex histories were suggested by qualities of light, strangers' wardrobes, songs overheard. The order of news presented to me in my feed was not just concocted algorithmically, but also belied sinister intent on behalf of faceless entities operating in the shadow realm where finances and futures were decided.

Beyond my doorstep the world spun on—or spun further out. Democratic assemblies from the UK to Denmark, Australia to America had slid into constant states of deadlock, with populist obstructionists at last open about their sole objective: to fuck everything up.

Megastorms had emerged, with Hurricane Zelda having two years previously steamrolled its way inland as far as Chicago, spawning two hundred tornadoes along its path. The northern wildfire season stretched further and further with each passing year, beginning earlier and ending later. Super-megafires routinely burned for six or eight months, devouring hundreds of thousands of acres, choking a continent, messing up transportation, but also turning the whole atmosphere a ghostly orange and making for some really great photos. Every year we missed another set of emissions targets; every year they were torn up and redrawn as the most obstinate petrostates continued to be sand in the gears of decarbonization.

The Mass Glitch had knocked out most of the world's internet-connected devices for eleven and a half minutes the previous February. No official explanation had yet been offered, though every platform was alight with theories, the most popular involving a coronal mass ejection that the world's space forces had failed to forecast, though scientists insisted no such storm had occurred. Ransomware attacks were regular and often disastrous; many of us carried a small non-connected chip around—tucked in a pocket or a wallet, or worn on a chain around the neck—where verified personal data was backed up.

I was in Ottawa, where I had gone to begin university, drop out, make deliveries (food, liquor, weed, opioids, and mysterious packages, their contents happily unknown to me) through a wildcat app, wreck my car, lose my apartment, and cover the shame of the above with alcohol and pills. I did not call home once—even when I was at my most desperate, mired in the overlapping messes I had made for myself—because I didn't want to dilute my own sense of disappointment. I didn't want my mother, who was still at home in Peterborough, to tell me things would be okay. She was busy buying second-hand gingham dresses, growing tomatoes, and hosting a book club, and she didn't need my shame, my failure. She'd had enough of that.

There is an unmistakable pause, an extra hitch in the breath or a tilt of the head, that every parent possesses, whether they are aware of it or not—one that speaks honestly and nakedly to a sudden and unforeseen sense of disappointment. With my mother it was a held word, a beat that extended a fraction of a second too long. Once she caught herself she would endeavour to glide right over the feeling, and in all honesty she was pretty good at it, but that extra half measure of silence, though unreadable to others, was conspicuous to me. I've always known it, and I couldn't bear to hear it. So I didn't call. We would text, and I would send her little video messages around her birthday or Christmas—but I never let her hear my voice so that I would never have to hear hers.

In a normally functioning adult, this sense of duty to their mother might keep them from committing unsavoury acts, or putting themselves at risk of censure or incarceration. In me it only heightened my anxiety, made me doubly afraid: I'd get caught and face whatever punishment was coming my way, *and* I'd disappoint my mother, who remained the greatest person I'd ever known. Between those two fears I could lose whole weeks of sleep. And yet, for all my gnashing and fretting, I couldn't seem to pull myself out of my crimes of convenience, nor extricate myself from the low-level addictions that I found easier to nurse than discard. Through a series of bad decisions on the heels of minor crises, my only talent seemed to be an ability to stay one step removed from trouble, though I expected it to appear around every corner. Whatever benign presence in the universe that kept me from real consequence continued its watch, and I skated through. Slippery as an eel, accidentally diabolical, or at least as diabolical as a petty thief and occasional addict can get.

By way of illustrating: I had managed to replace my car with one so ridiculously affordable that it was almost certainly stolen. This allowed me to deliver food again, spending my nights tapping nervously on the steering wheel and waiting for my phone to make the little dinging sound I had come to associate with the rapidly successive feelings of hope (for money), resentment (too little money), and resignation (How else am I going to make money?).

It was in the midst of all this that I first encountered Rhonda.

◆

I was at a meatless steakhouse—bright, modern, and bobbing on a sea of suburban asphalt—to pick up a boxed vegan surf and turf for a customer dangling a brazen tip. Rhonda was kibitzing with the host at the fake bamboo podium immediately inside the double doors. She smiled sideways at me, and I made a resolution. After the delivery (where I learned that the customer and I had different definitions of *big*) I sped back to the restaurant and asked the same host to seat me in her section. He refused, which was the right thing to do, but she overheard all this and told me to sit at the bar for forty-five minutes until the end of her shift.

I turned off all incoming orders on the app, sat in a high swivelling chair, put my elbows on the bar, ordered a non-beer, and paid with the phone. I nursed the drink slowly, with an eye on my uncertain financial situation, not completely sure how much money dwelled in the account of someone named Griffin who, until quite recently, had owned said phone.

I watched sports highlights on the bank of screens over the bartender's head until finally, blessedly, Rhonda sat down on the stool next to me, draping her long corduroy thrift-store coat and big bag across her knees.

I registered the nearly invisible markers that told me she was from my precise cohort. As the first generation to come of age with legal marijuana, we'd been forced to get creative in order to maintain an illicit edge to getting high. Some people went hard into other substances, still decidedly illegal, while others—and Rhonda was a prime example of this—had fashioned themselves into warlocks or witches and invested in the idea of potions, concoctions, unholy combinations. Exotic superstrains, rank and gummy tinctures, powdered mushrooms mixed into tar-like compounds and scented with essential oils.

Rhonda had a small satchel sewn of scraps of fabric—denim, paisley, fleece—tied with a length of rough leather binding, and worn around the neck at the end of a long strand of tie-dyed silk of aquas, washy blues, a vein of creamy yellow. Her hair was just the right degree of wild, its waves and curls now loosed from the bun she'd worn while working, and what little makeup she wore was inexpertly applied. Wan pink lipstick, a little liner beneath the eyes, some concealer failing to conceal a red spot at the end of her nose. There was a tiny scar on the roundest outer rim of her left nostril, where she'd once worn a nose ring. The dress she'd changed into was sack-shaped, though pulled in at her waist, and from beneath peeked a dark grey bra strap, frilled and curlicued with cheap machine-made lace. Her dark brown knit tights bunched below her knees as though someone else had worn them in. There was pilling. On her left wrist, just before the veins branched and ran into her palm, there was a mark: a tiny tattoo, a crude, hatchet-mark depiction of a beaked mermaid, the ink starting to spread murkily, and below it, centimetres shy of the meat of her palm, four Japanese characters.

These things, so subtle on their surface, spoke loudly to me. I could have told you what music she'd listened to, the song that was playing during her first kiss ("Ancient Gestures," by Doppler and the Redshift). We were almost precisely the same age, which meant there'd be some short-hand to our communication.

She said, "I'm Rhonda."

"Gabe," I replied, smiling idiotically, pointing a thumb at myself.

"So what's your plan here?"

In the time I'd been sitting there I'd thought many things, most of them clustered along a strong through-line of escape, and of a kind of conspiratorial chemistry that would carry us together to some new hiding place. But I had not thought of a *plan*.

"No plan, I'm afraid."

The statement was true beyond the immediate moment—it described, more broadly, my general situation. I could sense no direction in my life except the standard one, away from childhood and toward darkness. The stolen phone in my pocket was a janky old Motorola with no more storage space. I wasn't going to be able to pay the rent on my 160-square-foot apartment, which was due in a few days' time. I had two pairs of pants and five shirts and one pair of boots. I'd left my coat somewhere I couldn't remember and cold weather was coming, Arctic systems loading up and preparing to descend on southern Canada. My car, which was my sole means of securing a halfway legitimate income—meagre, unpredictable, insecure—needed work, had no winter tires, and was seldom fully charged. It should go without saying that it was uninsured. My head throbbed.

And yet despite all that, in my mind's eye what Rhonda saw when taking me in was devastatingly alluring: the way my pants hung off my hip bones, advertising genuine and unambiguous danger, my having been totally transformed, I perceived, from the malodorous and desperate teenager I'd only recently been. In retrospect I wonder if what she saw was as simple as a free ride home. She couldn't have anticipated the baggage, though maybe she should have.

"You've been sitting here nearly an hour and you haven't come up with a plan? Pretty weak, Gabe."

"Admittedly."

"So?"

"How about we go for a drive?"

Miraculously, improbably, the car was mostly charged then, though only because that very afternoon I'd come into a credit card. I had about two days to use it, so I plugged in the first chance I had. I also bought some food and put some funds—not enough—aside for rent. I thought I'd live a little lavishly, thinking abstractly that I'd earned it, before going back to my lean lifestyle. Simple, I called that life, willing myself toward optimism. Precarious, really. Eventually, hopefully, another set of digits would come my way. I had an old roommate who was good for that, but he and I had recently fallen out for reasons that were hazy and much disputed. I'd need to find another source.

"What the hell," she said. "That'll do."

She leaned into her bag—the large vintage cracked-leather tote on her lap, not the small pouch hanging from her neck—and pulled out her phone. Maybe I should have been wary of her baggage, too, but I was busy receiving her. There was such energy, such life, jumping and strafing the air between us. She tapped out a message, likely a heads-up to a friend that she was about to climb into a car with a strange man, and to check in later, and if there was no response to get help. I understood that. It made sense.

Then she looked up at me, erratic strands of her brown hair falling in front of her dark blue eyes—almost navy, a shade I'd never seen—and said, "Let's go."

We drove under a flat, starless sky into a stiff wind that rattled the car at stoplights and blew grit against the windshield.

"This is a bit random and probably stupid," she said, "meeting you like this, and now I'm in your car."

"It's one hundred percent random."

"Right. But I need a bit of random. Everything is kind of terrible. Oh, I know, how about I jump into a stranger's car? Great idea. Really sharp. You're okay, though, right? I can trust you?" She had turned sideways in her seat to interrogate me, leaning back against the passenger door.

"Oh, like, absolutely," I said, "but, I mean, what would I say if you couldn't?"

"I know," she said, "but I'm getting a good feeling. I just needed something, anyway, a jolt, something different. I get like that. Like I'm stuck and I have to force my way out or I'll get glued down."

"I know that feeling," I said, believing that I was receiving all of her signals, the overt and the concealed alike.

"What do you do to get out of it?"

"Driving is good. Sometimes I'll walk a long ways. Meet somebody new."

"Like me."

"Mm. Talking to someone I've never met tells me that there are still new things in the world. Terrifying but unthreatening. New people, new places, new things to experience."

"Terrifying but unthreatening," she said. "That's good. Hey, let's have a new experience together."

My radar lit up with intense magentas and lurid oranges. She was unambiguously offering what I sought: connection. All kinds of connection.

⌐◄

I didn't know where we might go, because without an address tapped into the navsys I didn't know Ottawa well. Just the area around the university, my apartment, and the neighbourhoods where I'd made deliveries. None of it was second nature yet. She was a native, though, so she directed me, telling me which direction to go at each light and stop sign. But as we moved out toward the city's eastern extremes, she found herself a bit lost too.

"It's so weird out here," she said.

"It just keeps going," I said.

"I don't recognize any of this."

"Did you grow up out here?"

"No, I was an Alta Vista kid. Only came out to the east end when there was a party. There were some ragers in the bush not far from here, but it doesn't look like it's bush anymore. Just more houses."

"Everything changes," I said.

"Everything and nothing."

"Is this okay?" I said. "Is there somewhere you want to go?"

"No, just keep going. Go left, turn right, whatever. I just want to be moving right now."

We were on a wide boulevard, a big, sweeping curve lined with trees and lit up by tall sodium lights atop concrete stanchions. There was a broad expanse of grass down the median, and grassy embankments on either side that disappeared into darkened tree cover. Not a building in sight on that alien plain. No houses, no stores, not a charging station. Just lights and empty roadway.

"You know," she said absently, "I try to stay away from seeing people from work. Not that you're from work, but you kind of are. I did it once. Marcel. He was a cook there. He was my last boyfriend, actually. Told me out of the blue he was moving to Vancouver. We'd been together, I think, like, eight months. Didn't ask me to go. Just went. I was like, the fuck? That was about six months ago."

"That's awful."

"I didn't love him, and I don't miss him. I just wanted to love him and miss him."

"That's sad."

"It's *fucking* sad." She turned on the satellite radio and found a station she liked. Slow guitars and a man singing a song I didn't know about someone dancing across water.

"I love songs on the radio," she said. "Do you know this one? It's what's-his-name."

"No."

"Oh, you know. Canadian. Come on."

"Sorry."

"Doesn't matter. What's the one song," she asked me, "that you'd listen to for the rest of your life?"

"Oh, easy, 'Amazing Grace,'" I said, "but it has to be Aretha Franklin singing it."

"Oh, wow," she said. "Why?"

"It was printed on a tea towel that we had. At our cabin. It was my grandfather's, but then he died and left us the cabin. So we went there during the first lockdown, and this 'Amazing Grace' tea towel was there, hung on the wall. It was ugly. Ha! I never thought about that, but it was likely cheap. It had a bagpiper printed on it, the kilt and big hat, and the words, with musical notes. I don't think it was the actual notation, just, you know, notes suggesting, like, *music*."

"Did you sing it?"

"I didn't know the tune. I wasn't even really sure it was a real song, if that makes sense. I thought it was a poem or something. So I knew the words," and I recited the first verse, the wretch being saved, etc., "but I didn't know the music. Then I asked my mom, and she sang it for me, but she isn't very good with tone. Bad singer. Sorry, Mom."

"That's so cold," Rhonda laughed.

"It's true. So I had some idea how it went, but not really. It became this mysterious thing to me. Then one day I heard it. I clicked on it somewhere just because of the title. Aretha Franklin. It killed me. She's just standing in a church, at a podium, and people are clapping and yelling. The choir. It kills me."

"Where was the cabin?" she asked.

I told her all about it, in broad strokes. About my parents, and the mosquitoes in the tree, the canoe, swimming. All of it.

We were driving then far out into the city's eastern extremes, where housing developments had sprouted like mushrooms, spaced between farm fields and dark forest, one of the early pilot super-forest sequestration zones, I think. It was very late at night. A bullet train needled through the darkness next to the road we were on. I felt weightless.

She grew very quiet. "I feel like I bored you there," I said. "That was long. Sorry."

"No, it was nice." She spoke softly, but there was a catch in her voice.

"What is it? I bummed you out."

"No, no. My mom died that first summer. She was fine one morning, and then she felt dizzy and had a fever. Started coughing. She was in hospital that night. Four days later she crashed, never came out of it. We couldn't visit her at all. That was the worst part. Saying goodbye by video call."

"Shit, I'm sorry."

"It's okay. Thank you. I'm okay. I've had half my life to deal with it. I miss her, but I'm okay." She was not crying. Her pain was old and lived in.

"Your dad?"

"Oh, it fucked him up pretty bad. We used to be close when I was little. Not so much since."

"That's awful."

"Did you lose anyone?"

I thought about that for a long minute, and then I said, "Sort of."

She sensed the futility of asking me to elaborate, let the words settle instead.

In that silence, I think we both understood the same thing simultaneously: that I was offering a promise to tell the rest of the story in time, and that she would still be around to hear it.

"And what about you?" I finally said. "What song?"

"I could never listen to just one song over and over again," she said.

I said, "Usually when people ask a question like that they have an answer of their own."

"Nope. How about this, though: if you can find somewhere to pull off the road, you can kiss me."

"That works," I said.

I pulled into the first dirt laneway I saw, an ungated farm road shielded on one side by a row of neatly spaced poplars, a dark cropless field on the other. Beyond were strings of street lights on roads built in anticipation of houses, but as yet without. Empty roads, lit for no one, in loops and crescents, vascular patterns of thoroughfares with curbs bracketing empty dirt lots. I swept my eyes over them as I put the car in park and killed the engine with the push of a button. We sat in silence a moment, and my eyes attuned to the dark. I saw more stars than I'd seen in a long time, and the fast-moving trains of linksats gridding the exosphere in straight, parallel courses.

When I turned toward Rhonda, she was leaning toward me. I leaned toward her, and our heat met and converged like tropical depressions merging to produce a super-cyclone. Our lips melded as our eyes closed, and then I pulled away for a second just to look at her with her eyes closed and her mouth open, and then I leaned into her again and I bumped my lip against her teeth, tasted the smallest hint of blood.

Her breath was stale, and I knew I must have been a little gamey, living as I did, but neither one of us seemed to care, so we continued to kiss and began to twist our bodies as though looking for the correct fit. Elbows and shoulders, the dip inside her clavicle. She mounted me and I fumbled with my belt and zipper and she had no underwear beneath her dress and she slid down over me. I said something overly earnest while pressing my palm into the dimples at the base of her back, and then she shuddered and twitched and said, "Oh, god," though I believe, looking back, that it was too easy, too perfect, and so she must have been faking. Either way, half a moment later I shook and shuddered and then felt every muscle go slack.

She kissed me on the forehead and said, "How was that, Gabriel?"

"That was," I said as she dismounted and slumped sideways, looking at me in the dimness. "Wow. That was wow."

I could only see the glint of her eyes and the dark form of her body. "Gabriel or Gabe?"

"Gabe, usually, but you can call me anything you want."

I leaned over and put my head against her, pressed my ear to her chest and smelled her powdery burnt-coffee scent. I told her she was beautiful and I meant it. I tasted her hair and heard her skin. But what I really wanted was for her to take the wheel and drive on into the darkness, through the night, while I sat safe and warm in the seat next to her, in the glow from the dash and the murmur of indecipherable voices from the speakers. We could talk or not talk. She could talk and I could listen. It wouldn't matter in the least where we were heading, because wherever we reached in the long minutes before dawn would feel like home for her presence. At that moment in my life I was seeking moorage, and I believed Rhonda might provide it.

It should have been clear to me that everything that would come to bear on us—on her, on me, and on our love—was already present that night.

"Well, Gabe," she said, her fingers in my hair, "it looks like I'm your problem now."

I sat up, rolled my shoulders back, and pressed the button to lower my window an inch to let in a jet of cool night air. It was early November, the leaves nearly all gone, no traces remaining of summer's vulgar lushness and fragrance, with all their memories of my mother, perfumed, bare calves, running through tall grass, pine needles, fish scales.

"I'm exhausted," Rhonda said. "Take me to your place so we can sleep for eighteen hours."

"Oh, hell, yes, let's do that."

After some exploratory circles and a stab at manual reorientation, I gave up and turned on the navsys. It pointed to a major artery that sent us back toward the city, and the lights soon rose around us and closed in on us. Ever since my family's flight out of Peterborough and up to my grandfather's cabin, I'd wondered about the end of cities—how their interlaced networks of being and doing seemed so precarious, their complexity their potential undoing. How the difficulty of navigating, with hundreds of thousands of one's fellow citizens, a path to safety could become the very thing that threatens a person's safety. As we drove into the heart of Ottawa, I remembered how I'd come to assume, very early in our time at the cabin, that there would soon be no cities left. It is a feeling that has stayed with me, so that whenever I am in a city I see its existence as temporary, ultimately doomed.

"Did you hear 'Amazing Grace' back there?" she asked me.

"Back there?"

"When I rode you like a wild stallion. Were there angels? Trumpets?" Her voice quivered a bit, betraying both sincerity and a guardedness that suggested she assumed I wouldn't take her seriously. She added a quick laugh to hedge her bets. To avoid the humiliation of vulnerability.

"The earth moved," I said, trying to do much the same thing. I regretted it immediately, even before I saw her eyes shift focus, her lower lip bend inward ever so slightly. "It was beautiful. Truly."

"I don't kiss, usually. During sex. Makes me feel too, I don't know. Open. You know. But I kissed you. I hope you appreciate that."

"I do. Honestly."

"Don't fucking make me regret it."

We drove alongside the university campus's central cluster of buildings spanning nineteenth-century stone, twentieth-century concrete brutalism, and twenty-first-century timber-frame plyscraper, and to the brick low-rise where I lived. I pulled into my insufficiently lit parking space, marked by its perpetually inoperative charging port.

"Home," I said, using a word that suddenly thrilled me.

I wanted to ensconce myself with Rhonda, and the manner in which she leaned into me suggested she wanted the same. To share warm lamplit rooms on dark, inclement nights, to curl, cover, bank. She disrobed freely in the middle of my room, down to her thin black camisole and ill-fitting underwear, and only when she buried herself beneath my comforter and offered her prone back to me, a comma of warmth and contentment, did I strip down to my shorts, kill the light, and climb in next to her.

We slept from then—it was around one a.m.—until the early afternoon, and when I woke up I took great encouragement from the fact that she was still there, that she had not evaporated or disappeared.

"I'm so glad you're still here," I said when she opened her eyes a few minutes later. Her caramel hair was a riot of tangles, and her eyes were puffy, her cheeks red from the heat of the down bedcover.

"I am," she said. "I'm here."

"There was always a chance that I'd just dreamed you."

"You did, but I'm here and I'm staying."

Barely a half day into whatever we were to become, I was securely in her thrall, enmeshed in that hair, held by her narrow shoulders, her neo-hippie beliefs, her draped neck-laces, her bangles and feather earrings. I would run with her across the burning face of the world.

I should probably have recognized in the events of the previous evening the combination of impulsivity, danger-seeking, and manipulation that would eventually undo us, but I didn't. I loved her. I believe that even now.

I rose and made us coffee as cold late-autumn sunlight filled my small kitchen space, three steps from my bed. Her voice muffled beneath the duvet, she told me she was nearly out of options, choices, and favours in Ottawa. "I've been thinking about maybe going somewhere new," she said

My heart sank at this, because I didn't know where or what she had in mind, or if I'd be included. "Where would you go?"

"No idea. New York?"

"The visa situation makes that tricky," I said, perhaps too quickly.

"True. Montreal? How's your French?"

"Non-existent. *Je ne parle pas* French."

I began to suspect here that she was the type to make elaborate plans with no intention of following through with them, but I wanted to meet her energy, to attempt to cast myself into a bit of chaos with the reckless enthusiasm only people our age could access. I pictured myself capable of burning bridges and living with the results. All but my one most important attachment.

"Yeah, mine's not so good, either." She rose, reached down to the floor and from a pile there pulled out her black camisole, which she slipped on over her head and pulled down around her hips. She stood and walked toward me, catching me turning after taking a carton of soy milk from the fridge, and planted a sour, dry, but very welcome kiss on my lips. "We'd learn, though," she said.

Unsure of what to say next, I plucked my phone—the phone then in my possession—off the countertop and thumbed the weather icon. Out sprang an animated depiction of a glossy yellow sun, lines radiating in three directions, its lower left quadrant obscured by a quivering grey cloud.

I have long been obsessed with weather apps. I am constantly checking and rechecking, hoping in my darkest chambers for something severe. Torrential rain, lightning, high winds, tornadoes, whiteouts. A subject change provided by calamity. Any specific wishes I have regarding my eventual end always include large-scale events. Jurisdiction-levelling floods, grid failure caused by lightning strikes. Every death scenario I conjure involves extreme weather—that or, of course, a rogue pathogen leaping a taxonomic divide, or thawing from a remnant of permafrost—and an irrepressible part of me has come to root for these forces. I want my end to come via something hubristic on a civilizational level.

"Supposed to be nice this afternoon," I said to her. "Cool, but sunny."

"Okay," she said. "What is that? Is that a deflection?"

"I was just checking. It could affect our day."

"Gabe, we should address this—it's not a healthy habit. I'm genuinely making plans here. It might not have occurred to you that I was being serious, but I am. I'm looking for a way out of here. I don't know what last night meant for you, like if you just saw me and wanted to fuck me, but I had the sense that it wasn't that, and I can tell you that it wasn't that for me. If I wanted to sleep with just anybody it would've been easier to say yes to whatever idiot in the kitchen was being the most obvious about his wish to plow me last night. Because they've all tried. And at least I know all of them. I *know* how sketchy they are. I've never seen you before in my life, don't know anything about you. But I got into your car and let you drive me wherever the fuck we went because there was something in your light that told me, *Go with him. He's important to the next part of your life.*"

"You took my breath away," I said.

She stopped cold, her mouth slightly open.

"You were the only person in that room," I continued. "I knew I had to be near you. It wouldn't have mattered if you didn't sleep with me, last night, forever. I got caught up in you the second I saw you. I knew right away I'd follow you wherever you wanted to go."

She was silent a moment, and then said, "Yeah," swirling pale-grey soy into her mug. "I know. I've seen that look before."

Trouble.

I drove her to work that afternoon, spent the last part of the day doing deliveries, then picked her up after her shift. She had a box of leftovers that we shared for dinner at my place—fake sirloin and a pile of steamed broccoli, the end of a sourdough boule. I had a bottle of bad red that we opened and drained, then we had sex with the lights on as a means of demonstrating our trust in one another, our commitment to transparency. We were at sea, at the end of all tradition, trying to find ways to relate to one another's actual presence, post-industry, post-art, post-meaning. We sifted through the wreckage of human endeavour to determine our roles, how we could be of value to one another now, though all value seemed to have been bled from the world. Biology prevailed, so we bent to it, looking each other in the eyes.

She showered while I washed the dishes.

"What are you doing tomorrow?" she asked, standing in the bathroom doorway wrapped in my only towel.

"Oh, very busy," I said.

"Oh, yeah?"

"Sure. I have a thing, followed by another thing. Things all day."

"I have the day off. Okay if I move in?"

"Here?"

"We don't really have to pretend it's a big deal, do we? I want it; you want it. Tell me I'm wrong. Am I wrong?"

"No, you're not wrong."

She was slouched against the door frame, hair dripping. One strand fell down her shoulder, curled loosely, its end pointing at her left breast. She began coiling it around her index finger, held it in front of her face, studying its end. When she looked back at me, I noticed for the first time a very slight asymmetry in her face, her right eye the tiniest bit lower than her left. It was devastatingly beautiful.

"Okay, I own about seven things. Drive me to my dad's so I can pick them up?"

"Okay."

"Okay!"

We climbed beneath the covers, wrapped ourselves around one another, streamed *To Catch a Thief.* When Cary Grant as John Robie left the beach and swam through the turquoise Mediterranean to the raft, I said, "Doesn't that look amazing? I can't wait to go swimming with you."

"Oh, god, I don't swim," Rhonda said, and we fell asleep before the costume party reveal.

◆

Rhonda's widowed father was a man named Tom Glaske. He still lived in the house she'd grown up in, on a winding street of California bungalows built in the 1960s in an enclave near Ottawa's old south end. Asphalt without markings edged curbless onto wide, flat lawns dotted with stone landscaping features and flower beds now dormant, shrubs wrapped in burlap, a few eager Christmas displays though we were just two weeks removed from Halloween. Half the lawns were raked of the leavings of mature maple, birch, oak, and the other half would be seen to that weekend. Everything was tidy and well kept. Money lived there, safe but ample, and time passed slowly. Deeds were held by long-time government careerists who'd invested wisely to supplement their pensions. The neighbourhood had clearly aged with its last generation of buyers—the kids had almost all moved out, and the coming wave of young families had yet to gain a foothold, might not even get a chance if interest rates continued their herky-jerky upward trend. There were no basketball hoops over garages, no swing sets, no street-hockey nets. The cars that sat unrusting, snow tires installed, prepared and patient, were late-model coupes and luxury SUVs, not child-friendly vehicles.

This was all so normal in ways that haunted me after the cabin summer, and still does, because my father had convinced me that it was all so fragile. But here it was.

A featureless afternoon was bleeding into an early dusk, and lights were popping on in several windows. Leafs and Jets soon to start on half the TVs, the pre-game experts already jabbering, their faces several feet high on big screens mounted over electric fireplaces. The idea of pulling up a recliner in front of the game and dipping into a case of macrobrew lager was not without appeal, but I sensed that affirming my allegiance to Rhonda meant resisting any such offer.

"Nice house," I said as we pulled into the drive behind Tom's Subaru.

"I can't stand being here," she said, "but I guess it's an okay house."

"What does your dad do?"

"He's a systems analyst at Canada Revenue," she said, a string of words I will never in my life be able to decipher. "Rides his bike to work and back, goes cycling in the Gatineaus on the weekend. Gave up natural meat after his first bypass. Votes NDP because the Greens *aren't viable yet.* Yet! Composts, recycles, believes in solar but is *still* waiting for the cost of a roof array to come down. Dreams of retiring to an off-grid house with geothermal and growing his own potatoes and garlic and recycling his water. Misses my mother— keeps her photo on his bedside and still wears his ring. Will never date again. Ever. What else?"

"That is a very complete portrait."

"Pretends to like every boyfriend I bring home, but actually hates them all because I'm all he has left and nobody's good enough for me. Likes bad movies and Radiohead and Pearl Jam. A *lot.* Speaks in *Simpsons* quotes. Distrusts the press, but only a little. Oh, and he wears shorts."

"Okay."

"All year."

"Oh, wow."

"Like, I guarantee he'll be wearing them when we go in there."

"It's two degrees out."

"It's his thing, his rebellion. His way of asserting, I don't know, control. Being contrary."

"I get it."

"Just don't mention it. Please. Promise me. Because it fuels him, gives him some kind of power over you. Just pretend you don't see it, okay?"

"Got it."

"I'm serious. This has to be a real promise."

"Promise."

We walked in the front door into a wide, tiled foyer. Rhonda called, "Hi, Dad," in a flat, unimpressed voice. He answered from somewhere ahead of us. We removed our shoes and went down a hallway into the kitchen in the back of the house, where he was unloading the dishwasher.

"Ron," he said, "you've returned from the dead. Wasn't sure I'd see you again."

"I texted you. You knew I was alive."

"Hi," he said, looking at me.

"Dad, this is Gabriel." I held out my hand, and he stepped forward and shook it.

"Nice to meet you, Gabriel."

"Likewise, Mr. Glaske."

"Great," he said. "So to what do I owe this pleasure, Ron? Popping in like this?" His tone was hard to miss.

"I came to pick up some stuff," she said.

"Okay, well you know where everything is. You live here, after all. At least, I think you do. You did."

"I'll probably keep staying with Gabe for a while," she said, which was a way of phrasing our arrangement that wouldn't have occurred to me.

Even while caustic, she was smaller in his presence, meeker, likely the residue of her childhood, the complexities of the father-daughter relationship. We all show different faces.

"Have you two eaten?" he asked. "I can put some black bean burgers on the grill."

"We're okay," she said, though my stomach growled at the mention of food.

"You sure? As long as you're here. They're in the freezer. Won't take long to cook. Have a burger, a beer. What do you say, Gabriel? You hungry?"

"I mean, I suppose a little," I said. It was the wrong thing to say, but my body had spoken over my mind. I hadn't eaten since the boxed leftovers and red wine. I was running on fumes.

"Great! Ron, you're staying. Gabriel is our guest." The latter clearly meant to reassert Rhonda's permanent residence in the house—that I was just a detour, a dalliance.

My feeling wasn't that Tom Glaske wanted to continue living with his daughter. She was in her twenties, after all, and had likely always been a handful. Theirs was obviously a strained relationship. But he didn't seem to want her departure to be so sudden and ad hoc either. Maybe he wanted ceremony, a sense that she was moving on to something good, something through which she could progress into a responsible adulthood. Not a fling with an emotionally damaged part-time food delivery driver with a taste for prescription pills and a stolen phone in his pocket. Not that he knew all those particulars about me, but I think Tom picked up more frequencies than he was letting on.

He was somewhere in his mid-fifties, and he appeared to be kind of adrift, at a point in his life for which he hadn't thought to prepare. He limped around on a bad right leg— "Doored by a guy in an old Tesla," he explained to me—and his jean shorts, factory-hemmed above the knee, revealed shins carved and dented by a thousand other bike-related mishaps. Grey wool socks, a black long-sleeved tee with the name of a French bicycle manufacturer printed down the arms, and an orange fleece vest zipped to the chin. This was his winter ensemble, his concession to the cold. His brown hair was short, thinning a bit, and spiky. He had close-cropped grey-and-brown stubble that aged him and made his grey eyes stand out to an almost startling degree, and a thicker triangle of salt and pepper whiskers beneath his lower lip. His left earlobe bore a small silver hoop.

I thought I could see fear in his eyes.

He rummaged in the stainless-steel fridge's pull-out freezer and brought out a box of frozen patties. "What are you good for, Gabriel? Probably two? I don't have much in the way of sides."

"Two would be good, thank you," I said. At twenty-two I still spoke to elders like I was ten years old.

He went out a pair of French doors into the small garden to light his green egg-shaped barbeque. As it heated up, he came back inside and went to the fridge to take out a head of lettuce and a big, round tomato. He paused and said, "Beers now?"

Rhonda and I were sitting at the small, square glass-topped kitchen table. She was leaning forward and holding my hand. We must have appeared conspiratorial. I looked at her to get our answer.

"We'll wait," she said.

"Yeah, I'm good," I said.

"Okay," said Tom.

He nudged the fridge's tall, thin double doors shut with his elbows and put the lettuce and tomato down on the thick butcher-block counter. Then he reached over to a magnetic strip mounted on the wall next to the stove and plucked from it a long, tapered chef's knife. I could tell by watching him wield it that it had a nice weight and balance. He held the tomato still with his left hand as the knife sliced cleanly into the red skin, and a thick roundel toppled soundlessly over onto the smooth, oiled wood. It was beautiful and hypnotic. I could have watched him using his perfect knife to dissect that full, ripe tomato on that gorgeous countertop all night and all day. He finished cutting it into glistening, uniform slabs, and then he tore a few pieces from the head of lettuce and laid them next to the tomato. He opened the box of frozen burgers and removed six, put them on a white dish. He opened a drawer and took out a large wood-and-steel barbecue flipper, which he tucked under his arm. He opened the French doors, and the cold air came in, fogging the window glass. The door shut with a suck against thick weather stripping. Rhonda and I were alone.

She exhaled dramatically. "Get me away, I'm dying," she said, and lay her head down on the table, her ponytail flopping over, expired.

"He doesn't seem that bad," I said unhelpfully.

"You're not qualified to comment," she said.

"That's fair to say."

"I don't need your understanding right now. I need your anger."

"I'll see what I can do."

"I'm going to get my stuff together so we can get out of here as soon as we're done eating."

"Okay," I said. "Should I go outside and talk to him, or—"

"He's fine. Just sit tight here."

I picked up my phone to see if it had anything interesting to offer. The voice mail icon hovered in the upper left corner of the screen, and when I swiped my thumb down I saw that I'd missed a call from my landlord. I didn't have to guess what that was about. Plus the phone—I—whoever—was out of data, a notification bubble said.

"Think I can get on the network?" I asked.

Rhonda, who'd been making her way down the hall, spun around dramatically and raced back to me. "Yeah, but do *not* ask him. He's weird about it. He used to take my laptop and type it in himself until I made him tell me what the password was. I was like, *Hi, I live here too.*"

I brought up a list of available networks. "Which one is it?"

"Skynet," she said. "Get it? He thinks it's hilarious."

"No."

"*The Terminator*? The movie? It's his favourite thing ever. It's from that. The AI that destroys humanity is called Skynet."

"Never seen it."

"Consider yourself lucky. Do not under any circumstances ask him about it, or tell him it's funny that he named his network that, or you'll get a lecture about its brilliance and how the whole saga fits together, and his ranking of all the movies. I can give you the short version later, if you're really curious."

"I'm good," I said. "What's the password?"

"*J-D-A-Y*-zero-eight-two-nine-one-nine-nine-seven."

I typed it in and joined the network, which accepted me and rewarded me with a flood of buzzing notifications.

You are now connected to Skynet. Is this a trusted network?

The temperature will fall to -5 tonight, with a chance of flurries. Open app for details.

The Leafs and Jets face off in fifteen minutes. Tap to watch.

PM Freeland says Canada willing to send aid, doctors to help southwest US resettlement effort.

Rhonda slouched down the hall and ducked into what I assumed was her old bedroom. I swept the notifications away, deleted the voice mail without listening to it, and read some entertainment headlines. The gloom outside the window to my left had become full darkness, through which I could just see the glow of Tom's barbecue, and a bit of his shape. He appeared to be hopping back and forth from socked foot to socked foot. I scrolled mindlessly until Rhonda came back with an olive-green backpack stuffed with clothes and a small, clear plastic storage container, cosmetics rattling like bones within. She piled it all on the floor in the foyer, then opened the mirrored sliding door of the closet near the front door, took out a pink wool coat and a dark grey nylon parka, and laid them atop her pile.

"We can leave anytime now," she said, turning to me.

Before I could speak, the French doors opened again. Tom walked in and placed the plate full of burgers and the flipper on the counter. Then he placed his hands down flat, looked out the window. A spacey look inched across his face. "Jeez but it gets late really early these days."

"Almost winter," I said.

Tom turned and looked at me and said nothing. His expression suggested he didn't understand what I'd said. He studied my face so intently that I felt uneasy.

"December soon," I added.

"Soon, soon," he said, finally. "Well, I guess we should eat. Buns are in the cupboard. Can you dig 'em out, Ron?"

We each stood at the counter dressing our burgers. The only mustard Tom had was the kind you need a spoon to apply. I prefer plain yellow mustard. Fancy mustard feels to me like the province of people who are missing the point. A burger is a burger, eaten by bringing your hands to your face. It is not a steak. To fancify any component is to obscure the truth of the thing: that it's grub, not cuisine. Fancy mustard seemed like a decent summation of where everything sat with us at that moment, in that room.

I said none of this, of course. I wasn't sure how one would navigate the competing forces at work: Rhonda's insistence that I should hate Tom, on top of her own simmering feelings toward him, which were obviously based on the parts of an iceberg I couldn't see; my own conflict regarding Tom, who as the father of the woman I was defiling nightly I was naturally opposed to, but who I really didn't see much wrong with, aside from the too-broad markers of his generation which he seemed unable to recognize for their ubiquity; and Tom's mooniness, which surfaced at odd times in his otherwise placid, even gregarious behaviour. Thankfully, I had decided quite early in our visit that my only path through was to deal with each moment discretely, survive it, and move on to the next.

"Computer," Tom said between mouthfuls, "play me something good."

"Okay," chirped the house's AI, its flat, standardized, region-free, vaguely female voice rising from points unseen, speakers concealed or disguised. There was a pause, a nanosecond's silence before it said, "Here's something you might like," whereupon huge twin columns of electric guitar revealed themselves on several sides of us and then collapsed into one another before obliterating the floor beneath us. I jumped a bit, while Rhonda, used to this, just touched her forehead.

"Oh, shit," yelled Tom. "Sorry! Computer! Volume: three!" The music hushed slightly while he spoke, and then continued at a level that allowed us to speak without yelling. "Do you know the Pixies?" Tom asked me.

"I mean, a bit. Not really, no," I said. "Sorry."

Someone yowled ferally over my shoulder.

"The best. The fucking best."

We ate and listened to Tom's music, conversing very little. Tom rose and raced to the fridge and brought us each a bottle of beer. "Glass?" he asked me.

"I'm good," I said, and twisted the top off. Rhonda put down her burger, opened her beer, and downed half of it in a single draft.

"Someone's thirsty," Tom said.

"Dad, Gabe played me this amazing song," said Rhonda, wiping her lips with the back of her hand.

"Oh, yeah?"

"What song?" I said. "Which one do you mean?"

"The one song," she said. "You have to hear this."

Tom looked intrigued. He asked, "Do you have it on your phone?"

"Well, no," I said, "but it's on YouTube."

"Call it up," he said. "Computer, stop." The Pixies were silenced abruptly. "Tell her what you want to hear," he said to me.

"Computer," I said, "uh, Aretha, um, Franklin, performing—"

"Wait," Tom said, "is there video? Let's see it. Computer: put YouTube on the dining room screen, please." There was a large painting over the sideboard, a night scene of a beach and a placid ocean, and a full moon splashing its brilliance over all of it. The image flickered and dissolved, became

150

the YouTube logo and a search bar. "Okay," Tom said to me. "Tell it."

"Aretha Franklin, 'Amazing Grace' live performance," I said.

A list of selections appeared, one atop the other. The first option, New Temple Baptist Church, was the one.

"See it there?"

"First result," I said.

"Computer, play the top choice."

The AI obeyed, and without any ads (Tom must have paid for the premium sub), Aretha appeared, and the choir, and the enraptured audience.

"Damn, Computer, turn it up," said Tom. "Aretha? Oh, man. Oh, man!" He leaned forward on his elbows, toward the screen.

Young Aretha, with her perfect hair, dangling earrings, white robe with silver sequins, smiled and sang into the mic, a wooden lectern before her. The piano plinked along, then the organ purred to life. She worked and reworked every word. Tom's discreet speaker array hummed while Aretha climbed to heaven and members of the choir rose from their seated positions to shout and applaud her testimony.

Tom began shaking his head. "Mm," he said, closing his eyes. "Mm!"

Rhonda looked across me toward her father. A tiny smile came to her mouth, which she quickly quashed. It seemed to me that we three were experiencing a moment of fellowship, music forming a conduit between our hearts, facilitating the frictionless passage of warmth in a triangular pattern. At one point Aretha had to sit down, so overcome was she with the spirit. Audience members wept openly. If there was a performance built to dissolve petty animosities, surely this was it.

Aretha sounded the last note, and the song was over. The preacher ushered her away from the lectern while those in the audience—the congregation—stood holding their hands in the air, their souls inflated to accommodate the presence of God. Then the video ended, and we were offered other videos to watch: another clip from the same performance; Aretha, older, performing for the Obamas.

I looked at Tom and saw that his face was streaked with tears. "Oh, hey," I said.

He wasn't just moved. Something in him had been scraped raw. He opened his mouth to speak, but nothing came out. Moisture tracked viscously from his nose to his upper lip. He tilted his head like a dog and squinted.

"We're gonna get going," Rhonda said then, even as Tom's tears fell onto his empty dinner plate.

I said, "We are?" I looked theatrically down at the uncleared table. Surely she'd been raised to help clear the table, I pantomimed with my face.

"Yup. Thanks for the burgers, Dad. Super good." She was already on her way to the door, and then she was putting on her shoes and looking back at me, still sitting at the table, Tom still weeping. "Come on, Gabe. Let's hit the road."

"Right," I said. "Yeah. Gotta get. Uh. Gotta go."

Even in this moment of obvious cruelty, I was absolutely allied with her, obsessed with her. Her craziness, her hair, the timing of her arrival in my life, her demonstrated willingness to disrobe for me. I rose, folded my paper napkin neatly, and placed it on my plate, which was dotted with crumbs and a bright, garish smear of fancy mustard. "Thanks for dinner, Mr. Glaske. That was, uh. Super good. Great to meet you."

He closed his wet eyes and waved his hand in lieu of words. And then we left.

About a week or ten days later we were naked, watching *The Office.* We were trying to be as still as possible because we didn't like the way we felt. A cook at the restaurant had given Rhonda some homemade edibles and professed their quality, but we took them when she got home and the effects were discomfiting. So we lay still, waiting for them to evaporate out of our blood.

An episode ended, and while the credits rolled, I said without moving my head, "What time do you work?"

"Four," she said, "but I was going to quit tonight, so maybe I'll just call and not bother showing up."

"You're what? You're going to what?" She had not disclosed this plan to me.

"I don't think my future is in restaurant management," she said, giggled sharply, then grew solemn. "Definitely not at Montana's Steakhouse. And my plan to save the money I need doesn't seem to be working."

"What are you saving money for?"

"For life? And for the people who expect me to pay back the money they gave me. Loaned me."

I sat with that for a few minutes. My blood wasn't leaping anymore, which was a positive development. Then I connected some dots and realized Rhonda's plan might involve fleeing, which made my cells start spiking again. "What are you going to do?"

"We," she said. "What are *we* going to do?"

"I don't know," I said. "I'm new to this plan. I just got here."

"If we found some money quickly, that would give us some space. Then we could leave."

"Leave to where?"

"Where do you want to go?"

"I... don't know."

"I think we should go to Montreal."

"*Je ne parle pas* French, remember."

"You'll be fine. Anyway, I think our best bet is to go to my dad."

"He'd lend it to you?"

"Dad keeps a wad of cash in his closet. It was about ten thousand bucks the last time I checked."

"Like, actual cash? Bills?"

"Yeah, remember those? He has a bit of a prepper streak. You know, grid's down, no credit, no internet, whatever, we all die."

I wondered if, like my father, Tom Glaske had found the experience of that first lockdown a challenge to his preparedness, his role within the family unit as he perceived it. Had he too been changed by it, and spent every moment thereafter weighing his readiness for collapse?

"When did you see the money last?" I asked.

"When we were there. Last week? Whenever that was."

"You want to ask him if you can have it?"

"Oh, I'm cut off," she laughed. "We'll just take it. He won't know it's missing for a while."

"Oh, shit."

"He's good for it. He'll just replace it. While cursing my name. Or, ha, fuck, he might think you took it. Ha!"

I laughed with her for a moment without thinking it the least bit funny, then fell silent. I didn't like the idea of being thought capable of that, by anyone, though by any reasonable measure I'd done much worse. My stomach flopped and lurched as I momentarily caught a glimpse of myself as I might appear to another.

That night, Rhonda—still naked, between episodes, while I was in the kitchen spreading margarine on a bagel— quit over the phone, as she'd threatened to do.

Two days later, my resolve conspicuous for its absence, I drove her back out to her father's house. The weather had turned from freezing to roasting, temperatures reaching highs we'd have called freakish at one point in time, but such things had become numbingly commonplace. This particular afternoon the city was blanketed by sluggish flat clouds and air that felt like a hot, wet blanket. My inclination, if theft wasn't on our agenda, would have been to sit motionless and naked and watch more TV while drinking beer. But I'd spent my last legitimate money, and the credit cards had run dry. I wouldn't have been able to afford the beer. So here we were.

It was a Tuesday—a normal Tuesday!—so Rhonda expected that Tom would be at work. Still, she said I shouldn't just roll right on up to the driveway. Park the next street over, she said, so I did. She was always beautiful, but something about the subterfuge with which we were operating made her almost Helen-like. As in I'd have gone to war if she'd so much as hinted that it was her will.

The plan, such as it was, was to go there and just walk in. If Tom was for some reason home, Rhonda would say we were just in the area, en route to somewhere else, when she recalled this thing she'd forgotten on our last visit but that she desperately needed. Then I would engage him in conversation, maybe about music, per Rhonda's suggestion. Meanwhile Rhonda would walk down the hall to

Tom's bedroom, duck into the walk-in closet, open the sock drawer, and remove the envelope of cash. It would fit comfortably into the pocket of her flowy boho skirt. She would re-emerge, say she'd love to stick around—maybe for more of those delicious burgers!—but she had to get to work. Sorry, sorry. But let's plan another evening, the last one was so good. We'll bring beer, dessert, chips. Anything. Let's have a wonderful, healthy, mature father-daughter relationship. It's within reach!

If Tom wasn't home, which was what she expected, we'd saunter in, take the cash, check the bathroom for any prescription meds worth nicking, take a quick tour through the liquor cabinet, maybe fuck on the living room floor if she was feeling kittenish (her word), and then leave again.

She spelled all this out for me again for the fifth or sixth time as we walked toward the house.

"I got it. No problem."

The door was locked, but she knew the four-digit code. Tom hadn't changed it since she'd left. Why would he? She'd be back, and he loved her. His daughter and only child. She had her mother's eyes and alluring-slash-maddening flippancy.

The air was eerily still, though that might be something I've superimposed atop the memory. The fridge hummed, then fell silent. The heat pump purred almost undetectably, a steady exhalation. A strong gust of wind outside made the house pulse audibly, and my nerves twitched. The ambient air pressure felt uneasy.

"Do we take off our shoes?" I whispered.

"Might as well," she said, but then, I think, began to run through scenarios, and since some of them involved flight, she quickly turned back to me and said, "No, keep them on."

I pulled my partially removed boot back on as she began to scope out the living room and kitchen. No sign of life. My pocket buzzed with a weather warning. Its buzz was longer than other notifications, which always produced a zip in my nerve endings, giving me a half second or so of belief—of hope—that something large and obliterating was coming my way.

"Turn that off," she said in a stage whisper. "Stealthy, remember? You're fucking terrible at this!"

"Yeah, right, sorry," I said, no longer whispering, confident we had the place to ourselves. I pulled the phone out of my pocket and thumbed the *Do Not Disturb* icon. But before I stuffed it back into my pants I jabbed the weather app icon, adorned with the little supplemental dot that indicated a notification. *SEVERE THUNDERSTORM WARNING*, read the text in a red ribbon strung across the screen. Normally this would send me into a deliciously agitated state, but I had no room for that just now. Rhonda would be unimpressed.

Still, I couldn't help myself. As she crept down the hall, I opened the satellite data to see the view from above of whatever was about to hit us. The radar bloomed suddenly from nothingness to fullness, a red irruption of locusts on our city's southern end, moving globularly, resembling in its elasticity a hunk of airborne taffy, stretched and pulled, squashed and balled. It stopped suddenly at the latest reading, then looped back to the beginning. It was a big one, and my stomach danced. It was practically on top of us.

All at once the light from every window was extinguished, candle-snuffed, poof. Another gust, followed by a noticeable contraction. The first flash lit up my eye sockets a billionth of a second before the boom. Down the hall I heard Rhonda, startled, say, "Oh, fuck!"

The house stopped breathing and everything sat so perfectly motionless that I realized the power had gone out. I stood in the middle of the kitchen raised up on my toes, waiting for something to happen. I don't know why. I thought whatever terrible fate that awaited me, whether it be animal or machine, had motion-triggered vision like the old movies suggested was true of Tyrannosaurus rex and the velociraptor. A heartbeat later there was a blip, a disturbance in my nerve endings, and the house came back online.

In the corner of my vision, through an archway into the dining room, the painting screen reignited, flashing white, then red, then a deep purple, and finally green to signify its good health, and the shimmery moonlight reappeared on the water and the sand. Distantly, other non-organic life forms reawakened. The microwave beeped, the heat pump gasped and then began to hum, the fridge trembled.

Rhonda stepped into the kitchen holding in front of her mouth an old, worn envelope. "Got it," she said, her eyes big and shining.

"Hello, Tom," the AI said. "Power has been restored after a weather-related interruption. Your phone's battery is at nine percent. Would you like to charge it now?"

Rhonda and I looked at each other.

"Is he here?" I whispered. All my muscles seemed to have stopped working.

"No," she said. "He can't be. I've been everywhere." Her assertion was undercut somewhat by the fact that she was whispering again, too.

"Okay. But maybe we should just go?" I was still up on my toes, as I'd been since the thunder and lightning's call and response.

"I don't know," she hissed. "Gimme a fucking minute." Just in case, she slipped the envelope, so full it looked ripe, into her skirt's pocket. I eased down to my heels. "Okay," she said after a moment, "let me just take a quick look around and then we can go. He probably just forgot his phone."

Thunder continued to skip across the sky, lightning strobing every window and reflective surface. It interrupted my thoughts and heightened my anxiety. Heading into this I lied to myself, rationalized that Tom would, when all was said and done, be okay with anything that helped his daughter. But it became suddenly clear to me, between electrostatic discharges, that this was theft. We were committing a very personal crime.

Rhonda didn't make it far in her exploration. The first door down the hall, on the left, was the bathroom. She turned on the light, then said, "Oh, shit, no."

Her voice sounded like she'd just discovered a bird with a broken wing, like, *Oh, poor thing.*

I walked quickly to her side and looked in. On one side was the vanity, an ovoid mirror over it, topped by three globe lights hanging on the wall. On the other side, to our left as we stood in the doorway, was the combination shower-tub. Beyond that, in a recess, was the toilet, and on the toilet, Elvis-style, was Tom Glaske.

All we could see of him were his bare, bluish, scarred shins and his wool-socked feet, and on the floor near them, his phone, its screen black. I put my hands on Rhonda's shoulders, felt them rise and fall as she took a deep breath.

"Oh, shit, shit. Oh, wow."

"Oh, Ron," I said. "Come here, don't look."

"No, I'm chill. I'm a bit zapped. Mushrooms."

"You're high."

"I microdosed. I always do it before I see him."

"Is he...?"

"He sure as fuck is. I mean, I think he is? Dad?"

She shuffled sideways into the dark room, and I put my hand out to suggest she slow down, or reconsider.

"No, let me see him," she said.

She took three small steps, her hands clasped at her throat. She stopped, leaned a little closer, then leaned back. "Damn," she said. "Fucking damn. Had to be his heart, right? It had to be."

She turned away from him, looked at me, seemed to be inventorying something. Our options, I guessed. She looked back at him.

There was no way I was getting any closer. I knew myself incapable of looking directly at what was in that room. And I didn't have the aid of numbing agents in my blood like she did. I could look at Rhonda, though.

Tears were in her eyes, reflected in the dull light from the shaded window.

"Okay," she said, turning to me. "We should go."

"Go? Like, leave?"

"Yes. Did you touch anything?"

She was disconcertingly calm now, her tears dried. Not devoid of emotion, but not subservient to it. Motherly. She might have been trying to protect me. She might also have simply been blissed out on weapons-grade mushrooms. Macrodosed, despite her claim.

"No," I said. "I don't know. Fuck. Maybe? Yes?"

"Okay, it's okay. Gabe? It's okay. But we need to go."

"Okay. Okay? What are we doing?"

"We're going to pretend we weren't here. I don't know what happens next, but it's much, much simpler if we just weren't here."

"The money?"

"Don't worry about that. Nobody's going to have any idea. Just drive me out of here. Let's go now."

We strode down the hall and out the door into a warm, thudding rain. There was the merest interval of stillness when Rhonda pressed the button on the front door's keypad to slide the bolt back into place. She could only have done this as a matter of habit or residual concern—what would it matter if the dead man's possessions were left vulnerable?

While waiting for the follow-up beep that would affirm the door had locked, she glanced up at me, and as our eyes met, I noted her look of sheepishness, almost believable but without sincere contrition. We got what we'd come for, after all.

This made me a co-conspirator, and I understood instantly how one could be implicated in something they hadn't steered, how a stooge becomes an accomplice, how even if they believe in the mission, the far-off goal, they might be enlisted in deeds they consider beyond the pale, swept into an act by momentum and loyalty and dumb faith. Planet-spanning structures were predicated on this— I saw all this in a flutter of my eyelid—a mesh draped across the plane of civilization, shaping its development, restricting its growth.

In moments like these, I was perhaps overly prone to such thinking. It wouldn't be quite accurate to say that my father planted the seeds—only that our soil had the same pH level and density of nutrients, and in it things readily took root.

Rhonda always spoke of escape. What I'd envisioned upon hearing that word was an ensconcing, a scenario wherein we found a pocket of safety, beyond plots and movements, outside catastrophe. The crumple and buckle of liberal democracies moving against shareholders' expectations, the climate's terminal spasms; I wanted the nearness of our bodies to blot out the ramifications of our epoch. How could the world be ending if her hair smelled the way it did? If her skin was as soft as it was? I felt the sexual charge of mere tenderness. Intimacy. I wanted the ultimate luxury: security, or its mythical approximation. The ability to ignore.

But in her eyes I saw something different: a tumult, a hissing cataract. Her carriage during this escapade—not practised, yet level-headed despite the circumstances clearly calling for extreme emotion—had thrown light on the distance between us. Though we'd lived similar lives, bobbed on the same waves, the experience had produced divergent results. Escape for her meant flight, always. An itinerance, unending and skittish, an eye on the door, antennae probing shifting air patterns for a go signal. She had no affiliation, wanted none, whereas I needed to latch onto something. She jettisoned cargo, battened down her hatches, whereas I looked for safe harbour.

I saw in her eyes a mirroring realization: We'd never find equanimity. I would pledge myself too completely to this pairing, and she too little. I wouldn't be able to keep up with her indefinitely. My momentum would peter out, and then I'd become unwelcome ballast.

In that single moment, we'd learned more about each other than we had in weeks of confession and physical intimacy.

We covered our heads and race-walked the block back to my car, got inside. I pressed the ignition button, it started without hesitation, and we drove away. We merged into traffic on the highway, and I gunned the engine, bringing us smoothly up to 130 kilometres per hour.

"I'll call him a few times," she said. "Then I'll text him, then call the cops and say I'm worried because I can't reach him."

"You think that's the best way to handle it?"

"We didn't kill him. He was gone before we got there. Probably the night before, at least. Did you see him? He was so, *so* dead. There was no life left in him."

"Shouldn't you stay to see that everything is settled? The estate, or whatever?"

"He has a guy. His lawyer, Stephane something. He'll take care of everything. Dad was prepared, I promise you that."

"Right."

"Right."

"Are you okay? Like, this is a lot."

"It *is* a lot. But I'll be okay." She paused then, looking out her window. "I'll miss him."

"Of course. He was your dad."

"I'm also mad, if I'm honest. Because look at what he and all his friends left us. Did I need to wait for you to die, Dad, to get a nice house and my own car? Because that's fucked up."

"Rhonda."

"All emotions are valid, Gabe. Baby. Anger is real and legitimate."

The next morning Rhonda was calm, almost beatific, when she said we had to go to Montreal. "I have friends we can stay with until we get on our feet, find our own place. Maggie and Guy. You'll love them."

I told her that I thought I should work a bit more to rustle up some money, because we'd need it. She agreed, so after coffee I took my car out to charge it. I sat in the plugged-in sedan and stewed. I thought about what Rhonda looked like naked, the rise of her hips, her belly, the concavities above her collarbones. Then I thought about her dead father's legs, mottled blue and grey in the main bathroom of his comfortable bungalow.

I realized then that the days I'd been living since meeting Rhonda didn't feel like my life. They felt like an episode, a temporary aberration.

The storm had passed, and the air was cooler in its wake. When my car was topped up, I opened the app and took every order that came over the wire. I worked until after midnight, then drove back to the apartment.

I found Rhonda eating crackers on my bed, bent over her phone. She greeted me without looking up. Crumbs everywhere.

"Good day? You make a lot?"

"Not bad."

"Ready to flee?"

"No, I don't think I am."

She grinned, then grimaced, her face a diagraph. "You think I'm terrible," she finally said.

"I think we both have some things to work on."

"You're not coming with me."

"I don't think I can. No."

"That's honestly where I figured this was going."

"You're not all that broken up about it."

"Gabe?" She looked at me with soft eyes and paused, as though weighing whether or not to continue. "I don't think I can be who you need me to be. Not right now, anyway."

I just let that sit, looked away, out the window.

"Do you have anything to say to that?" she asked.

I honestly didn't. I'd never felt so defeated in a conversation before.

"No, I guess I don't," I said, my lower lip quivering uncontrollably. I could feel her disappointment settle over my shoulders.

"Okay, then. Can you drive me to the train station tomorrow?"

"Of course," I said, though my car was almost dead again, and I thought she probably owed me some of the pilfered money so I could charge it. But that was of little importance to me then, low even among the innumerable sublunary concerns that threatened to blind me from seeing the actual tides of my life. The high and the low.

We embraced, which was a relief because it meant she hadn't yet begun to hate me. We got high that night and had sex one more time. We slept late the next morning, and then she packed what few things she had into a gym bag of mine that I'd never see again. I drove her to the train station while she used her phone to buy a ticket to Montreal. I pulled up curbside in the drop-off area and put the car into park. We both tried to load as much emotional punch into our goodbyes as possible, as well as some non-binding suggestions that we'd one day find one another again, when the timing was better, when we were better, more complete people. But the specifics pale in importance to the overall fact of our saying goodbye, and our moving apart: her on a high-speed train, and me in a car in need of a charge, always.

II

AT TWENTY-SEVEN I went north to work in a mine.

This followed several lost years of no traction, no direction, no relationships. I delivered food orders before that job became fully automated. Then I was on assistance for some time, until that dried up, at which point things became somewhat desperate. I found myself at the end of several expiring revenue streams, my schemes running on fumes, when someone told me that cobalt and lithium mining were the new gold rush—Northeastern Ontario the new Fort McMoney. I was drawn to the idea—the darkness, the cold embrace of tight spaces. I wanted to go underground.

The training program's entry requirements were minimal, as were those of the related financial aid, as long as you completed the courses, found work quickly, and stuck with it.

I had nothing to lose.

Lake Temiskaming, four hundred kilometres north of Toronto, is surrounded on three sides by textbook Canadian Shield: muskeg, bogs and lakes, trees, and frequent outcroppings of Precambrian rock—four billion years old, give or take—scoured clean by glaciation. Beneath the surface we have aerated the rock with shafts and tunnels,

Swiss-cheesing it in search of minerals that are of use to us.

From the top end of Temiskaming, though, if you travel north out of New Liskeard you'll find yourself in the middle of a startlingly flat and fertile landscape: the Lesser Clay Belt, which is the pie-shaped southern incursion of the Great Clay Belt, an incongruous oasis that looks like a chunk of archetypal Kansas had been casually discarded exactly where it wasn't meant to be. This unique topography resulted from the presence of an enormous ancient lake that stretched from the Manitoba–Saskatchewan border in the west to roughly the middle point of the province of Quebec in the east, hemmed to the north by the Laurentide Ice Sheet, an unbroken expanse of water describing a draping arc that echoed the current shape of Hudson Bay like a loose necklace. Its outflow was via what we now call the Ottawa River Valley.

At the end of the most recent ice age, about eight thousand years ago, the glaciers which both fed and contained this gargantuan body of water weakened and then gave way, leading to the sudden and catastrophic draining of an unimaginable amount of water, leaving behind rich, concentrated silt and sediment—a flat expanse of ideal farmland bordered by granitic outcroppings like supertankers moored at the horizon, and the musky stink of beaver-dammed bogs.

The region sat unexploited—and so without a European name—for eight millennia, scarce as it was with easily accessed mineral deposits, unlike the territory to all sides of it, until the end of the nineteenth century when someone suggested the land's apparent fertility be put to the test. Early results indicated the whole place was one giant basin of potting soil. Legislation was later drawn up facilitating the transfer of tracts of this land to men returning from the muddy, bloody fields of Europe.

That first generation of farmers quickly learned that while the life-giving properties of the Lesser Clay Belt's earth were not exaggerated, the frosts left too late and returned too early to make anything of it. The farmers diversified—sorghum, hemp, canola, oats, carrots, peas, different varieties of feed corn—but the growing season proved too unreliable. The only thing you could count on was the presence of blackflies from thaw until freeze-up. The most workable solution seemed to be to quit and move back down south, as most of those original soldier-farmers did, or to shift from crop farming into dairy.

With the twenty-first century's breakneck warming, though, came change. The frost line crept north summer by summer, and it became clear that the area would very soon be perfect for those crops that hadn't held on only a few years earlier, so long as there was enough water. By the early 2030s the calendar had morphed such that large-scale cultivation was economically viable, and the ag corps descended, setting up on land they'd quietly bought up a decade earlier in anticipation.

Things are great when the rains come, but about every second summer is too dry, so the few independent farmers left have found themselves edged out of access to water. Water theft and illegal irrigation set-ups have become routine, and the prosecution of these is now the prime means by which the big concerns squeeze out the little guys, including the handful of families that trace their ownership all the way back to the original land grants. The roads—now well maintained, after many years of neglect—are thronged with million-dollar pieces of heavy machinery, the kind no family farm can afford, and bank loans for such things are subject to predatory terms. There's little need for old agricultural supply stores or tractor repair businesses, as the companies all take care of that in-house. Hastily built micro-communities have sprung up to host workers and execs. The old arena in New Liskeard got an overhaul, and now it's a modern palace, hosting rec leagues and kids' teams at all hours. I'm told that trying to get ice time there is nearly impossible. It's like living in Toronto.

The mining towns have similarly rebounded. For decades the economic prospects in Cobalt, Gillies, and several small crossroads hugging the lake had been dim, swinging from poor to nil depending on whether or not Tim Hortons was hiring. Members of parliament and cadres of entrepreneurial dinguses long insisted the area was on the verge of finding itself on the leading edge of a wave of northern tourism— *tourism!*—that would see people from the south rush up en masse to take in all that area had to offer in the way of scenery, history, outdoor recreation, and possibly even adventure.

The crowds didn't materialize. But on the heels of that disappointment, the locals were courted with the prospect of a return of the mining companies.

Cobalt is a heavy element produced in the furnace of mature stars before being shot out into the void, where it tends to bind to other elements, thus making its extraction a bit of a chore. You have to smelt the stuff. For most of the twentieth century, it was seen as nothing more than a by-product of the business of silver extraction, but its value jumped when we realized we needed it for our smart phone and electric car batteries. Enthusiastic community leaders insisted Northern Ontario was perfectly positioned to wrestle a large share of the market away from the Congo River basin.

Locals lined up to sign on and don their helmets to descend a hundred metres into the Laurentia craton to pull out the blue stuff and ship it to the smelters, who then passed it to the battery-assembly plants in Southern Ontario. When there weren't enough locals to do the digging, the search expanded.

◆

I signed up online and did eight months of training at a college in North Bay, living in an old motel with two other men in the same program. At the end of it, we attended a job fair in a gymnasium, filled out forms, chatted with a recruiter, laughed at appropriate intervals. I got a message the next morning inviting me to Canada Cobalt Corporation's intake centre, which turned out to be a storefront in an old mall. After two weeks of VR training modules six hours a day, I was given a laminated employee card and an address in Button's Corners, Ontario. The unsmiling woman who'd overseen my VR sessions and given me more forms to sign said, "There's an employee bus that leaves at six each morning, or you can get yourself there. Whatever works."

"You're going *where?*" Mom said from back in Peterborough.

I passed through North Bay and left it behind, driving north on Highway 11, the Sea-Doo dealerships and lakeside condo developments thinning out and giving way to upcountry outfitters and oddly spaced locations of fast food chain restaurants attached to gas stations that were also hardware stores and agency liquor stores, as well as stops on the Ontario Northland bus line, where autonomous coaches let off those looking for work and those returning home. The country scrolled by: Archean igneous material gathered and folded, once the tallest mountains this planet has ever seen, reduced by a half a billion years' worth of erosion to rounded nubs topped with a thin stratum of humus where pin-straight conifers grow.

Coming out of Marten River I found myself held at fifteen kilometres below the limit by an ancient RV, unconverted and sputtering thick blue exhaust. I passed it just before pulling into Temagami, where to my left a couple of updated Twin Otters sat moored to the dock, waiting to ferry wealthy Americans to still remoter lodges where they'd try their luck at shooting repopulated moose that they'd have taxidermied into trophies and butchered into steaks to be frozen, shipped back home, and consumed in lavish homes overlooking valleys of obscene beauty unseen by the poor.

At Cobalt I stopped for a beer in a miners' tavern that hadn't been updated in forty years. Wood panelling, a cigarette vending machine presumably kept as a museum piece. The place was empty—just me and the bartender, a young woman who seemed resentful of her captivity. I said hello; she said hello. I walked to the bar and ordered a Canadian. She reached beneath the bar, opened a short fridge, retrieved the bottle of brown glass, its muddy colour an anchor to the past. She uncapped the bottle.

"Glass?" she asked.

"I'm good," I said, achingly grateful to her for not pushing for more conversation.

I tapped my phone as payment, took the bottle, and sat at a dark booth. The table was topped with glass, beneath which were faded, poorly copied photos and other small-town ephemera—hockey team portraits, newspaper profiles of local business people, old coasters advertising long-defunct beer brands. Tucked among them was the papery husk of a wasp. It might have been there a decade, possibly three. It was on its side, wings pinned to its abdomen, its colour drained.

I sipped and brooded until the bottle was empty. It took some effort to keep myself to one beer—restraint being a muscle I have perhaps under-exercised in my lifetime—but I managed to do it. I stood, said thank you to the bartender. She replied with a curt "Have a good one," bless her, and I walked out into the warm late-September afternoon air, the light gone nostalgia-coloured.

My car unlocked as I neared where it was parked, curb-side. I got in, blew a 0.03 into the little tube attached to the ignition on the steering column, and the machine perked awake, its dash displays sensing the level of ambient light and adjusting themselves accordingly.

Twenty minutes north and west along a highway that offered more of the same and I was outside the gate of CCC. I produced my shiny employee card, and the guard waved me in. There was a low administrative building of cream-coloured aluminum siding. Atop it rose three flagpoles: the CCC logo on a blue field, Ontario's ensign, the maple leaf. Well behind all this stood sentinel the very tall, very imposing tower of the headframe, boxy and clad in shining corrugated aluminum. Beyond, obscured from my view, sprawled the shed, housing the hoist machinery.

Razor-wired fencing stretched along both sides of the administrative building. A second gate to my right, and beyond that a flat, stony expanse with nothing but trucks and machinery evident. I parked, went through sliding doors to a bright, glassy reception area, and was directed down a long corridor.

The housing office contained three empty chairs, a screen showing weather updates, a second displaying the current fire risk level in the area (moderate), and a light blue counter topped with a clear shield, behind which sat a woman wearing light blue.

"Name," she said.

"Gabriel Ward, *W-A-R-D*."

She tapped the letters into an interface of some variety, invisible to me below the counter. "Ah, okay," she said, still looking down. "Starting tomorrow?"

"I am, yeah."

"You'll be fine," she added ominously. "You're in the Haileybury dorm. Hang on."

She stood and walked over to a filing cabinet, took a key from the pocket of her shapeless black pants, and unlocked the topmost of five drawers. It made a terrible grinding noise. She took a green plastic box the size of a shoebox from the drawer and placed it on top of the cabinet. She removed the box's top and took out a white plastic card, put it aside, then closed the box, put it back in the drawer, closed the drawer, turned the key, and slipped it back into her pants pocket. She walked back toward me, turned sideways, eased herself onto the seat, and spun back to face me, docking herself once more into the light blue counter.

"This is your key," she said, sliding the card into an aperture out of my view. She tapped some more on her device down there, programming the key. "Room 118. It's yours for a maximum of twenty-one days, then you're expected to find your own accommodations. There are housing listings on the employee comms board. Start there. The others will also know some places, so talk to them." She continued to tap away, then retrieved the card and put it on the counter, slipping it through a small opening in the Plexiglas. "Just one copy, so don't lose it. Ninety-three bucks for a replacement."

"Jeez."

"Yeah, they really ding you, so keep it safe. Laundry on site. No cooking in your room. There's a common kitchen, but most people grab dinner in the commissary here before going back to their rooms. There's restaurants too, though not many. No alcohol, no drugs, no visitors. Anything else?"

"I don't think so."

"You drive here?"

"I did."

"When you go outta here turn right, and take West straight east. West Road. That's 558. Go past the sawmill. Cross the Trans-Canada and keep going until you're in town. The dorm's on your left. You see a statue of a man with a dog you've gone too far. You get to the lake you've really gone too far."

❦

The dormitory was an old retirement residence, three storeys of brick in a rust colour so rich it appeared to glow in the late-day sun. It was on the western edge of town, situated on the point where the land tilted and began to slope toward Lake Temiskaming. I parked in the small lot around back, entered the echoey lobby—large square tiles of pale tan polished travertine—and moved with my single bag down the indicated corridor to my room.

My key card opened the door with a small, satisfying click. Inside, the air was still and smelled of rubbing alcohol and disinfectant with a faint hint of socks. The walls were cream, the carpet caramel, and the bedspread chocolate brown. I dropped my bag on the bed—something Mom had told me never to do (bedbugs)—and went back out to find a sandwich.

As I stood in the hallway testing the door handle to see that it was locked, a man came down the hallway. He was wearing layers of plaid, polyester fleece, and denim, a camo ball cap on his head. Scraggly grey-brown hair shot at strange angles from beneath. He held a six-pack by the crook of one finger, and he flashed me an incomplete grin. His stubble was grey, his eyes were drained of colour, and his remaining teeth were yellow.

"Another fuckin' newbie, right?"

"Yeah," I said. "Gabe."

He had stopped at the door immediately opposite mine, and as he stood looking me up and down, he slid his key out of his back pocket with his free hand and blindly fit it into his door's slot. I heard the small click even as he was sliding his tongue through the vacancy where his upper-left incisor must once have been.

"Fuck, they go through so many of you. Every time I turn around there's another guy in here. My advice to you is be careful," he said. "And follow their rules. They'll kick you outta here so fast. Justine ran down the rules for you?"

"Justine?"

"Lady at the housing office."

"Right, yeah, she did."

"No fuck-ups," he said. "Zero tolerance." He swung his six-pack by its collar.

"Got it." I couldn't tell what he was daring me to say.

"I'm Gil," he said, and we paused for the interval that at one point in time would have featured a handshake. "This is my hall. Watch out. You're in Gil's hall."

"Okay. Got it. Thanks, Gil."

I didn't understand whether he meant that he was a representative of CCC, or just that he was the meanest fucker on the floor and that my well-being depended on avoiding his wrath.

"I was here before you and I'll still be here when you're gone. Respect that, bud."

So it was the latter.

"Will do," I said.

He turned quickly though a little imprecisely and disappeared inside his door, leaving only the unmistakable airborne residue of weed smoke and fried onions.

Outside, the sting was out of the day's heat. There was a Subway within walking distance. I got a foot-long lab-grown teriyaki chicken and an iced tea, sat on a park bench, and ate while shooing pigeons. As the sun dipped over my left shoulder, the lake—visible distantly to my right, over the roofs of houses and shops and churches—turned a meaner blue before going dazzlingly dark. Nearby, men drank from plastic bottles while straddling scooters and bicycles, their feet planted on the ground, their laughter ugly and cruel. Street lights flared. I stood, sorted my recyclables into separate bins, and made for my room.

From the lobby I could hear Gil's crowd, their rhubarbing and laughter, and as I moved down the hallway toward my room, they came into view. Five men spilling out of Gil's room: two standing, one squatting on a plastic crate, and one sitting on the floor, his legs splayed out like the blades of scissors, his back leaning against my door. Gil watched over his acolytes from a chair positioned to prop open his own door. The men ranged, if I were to guess, from their twenties to their fifties, with Gil, hard looking and ragged, the oldest of them. They all had open quart bottles of cheap beer, and none of them were on their first. They wavered like bowling pins.

I walked slowly toward my room. "Hey, guys," I said almost inaudibly. They were talking in exaggeratedly loud voices, laughing.

"New guy," Gil said from his chair. "Guys, here's a new guy. New guy, these are the guys." They all laughed far too enthusiastically at this.

"Some of the guys," one of them said.

"Hey," I said again, then waded right into the middle of them, pretending to search for my room key though I knew it was in my left hip pocket, hoping the show of looking for it while approaching my door would suggest to the man slumped there that he might perhaps move aside, at least until I got inside my room. Finally, having feigned the search for what felt like an uncomfortably long time, I produced it, holding it straight up between my middle and index fingers. "Maybe I can just," I said, "like, get in?"

"Fuckin' Roscoe," said Gil, or something that sounded like Roscoe, "you're in new guy's way."

"Aw, fuck, alright," said Roscoe, or Russell, or Rusty. He rolled over onto his shoulder, pulling his hips with him, giving me just enough room to shuffle by, open my door, slip inside, and shut it quickly, worried that an arm or head might become lodged in the frame and keep me from closing it.

Standing inside, my hand still on the handle, I heard Gil shout "Goodnight, new guy," and then all five men laughed again.

I lay flat on the bed and scrolled on my phone for a time, tried to close my eyes. I thought about calling my mother, but I didn't feel up to faking enthusiasm, so I texted her instead: *Here safe. Long day. Got a room. Start tomorrow. Wish me luck!*

The hallway crew continued to laugh and drink. There are few things I find as distressing as raised voices in hallways, especially when I am trying to sleep on the other side of a door. Around eleven my phone buzzed, its vibration amplified by the cheap chipboard nightstand on which it rested.

Mom: *Glad ur safe + sound. Good luck tomorrow. XO.*

I rose, still wearing my clothes but wanting very badly to sleep, and opened the door slowly. No one was leaning against it, but there were now seven men in the hallway. The party was ramping up, the laughter sloppier.

I poked my head out the cracked door. "When do you guys think you might wrap it up?" I said.

"New guy," said Gil, by way of greeting. "Fuck, don't know. Hard to say, really." He was still sitting on the chair in his doorway, like a posted sentry. He leaned backwards and twisted his head to speak to someone inside the room. "Shelly, we winding down?"

Shelly was a big man in black jeans and dingy white socks who was sitting on the corner of the bed, just visible from the hallway. He had long hair of light brown, blond, and white that blended with his beard, and he was pitched forward, head down, elbows on his knees, both hands in front of him cupping a bottle. He looked up slowly, scanning the walls until he turned to Gil in the doorway.

"Doesn't feel like it," he said.

"We keeping you up, new guy?" asked Gil, turning back to me.

"Oh, no," I said, instantly regretful. "No, just wondering."

"Just wondering."

"Right."

"Any answer would be a wild guess, so how about I don't guess?" he said, raising his bottle to his lips.

I laughed unconvincingly. "Sounds good, Gil," I said, and ducked back inside my door, locking it as quietly as I could.

They dispersed around 12:30. I slept only intermittently after that, bouncing between shame and regret. I was wounded by men's callousness, by their willingness to damage one another, and I worried that my opinion of the events of the evening would have been different if they'd only invited me to drink and laugh with them.

But I'd come north to deny myself connections. I wanted to sequester, to be cloistered within a small space, living a small life, doing the unpleasant work of resource extraction, helping to provide things people wished not to need, but needed all the same. I yearned toward supplication, anonymous service, devotion to things generally left in the dark or unconsidered. I wanted to work by low light in tight spaces. I wanted to disappear behind that which was being dug from the earth and presented to the world.

There were still other ways to go about this. Actual monasteries, for example, where men pledged themselves to God and made ale and trained dogs while waiting for the end of the world. But I wanted only to do that which required belief in tangible things. Stone, mineral, electricity, progress in the face of peril. A collapse, a cave-in, a gas leak. Men still died in mines, and I wanted to exist in the face of that possibility.

The first day was all medical: swabs, blood tests, scans, the recording of biometrics on discrete systems, internal, fire-walled. Cold white rooms with tiled floors, harsh lighting, occupational health and safety posters. Beyond the housing office, further down the long corridor, was a warren of rooms peopled with masked employees in pastel scrubs, electronic eyes arranged in overlapping coverage. I shivered in the corner of one of those rooms in a paper gown—my uniform of white short-sleeved shirt, dark blue slacks, and matching dark blue zippered nylon shell folded neatly on a stool in the corner—while a doctor in CCC's employ ran down a list of questions that I answered to the best of my ability. Medical history, family history, mental health indicators, comfort with tight spaces. At no point was I invited to ask questions of my own.

Once reclothed I found myself in something like a classroom with eleven other uniformed people, male and female, twenties to forties, all nerves a-jangle. The screen before us, where once there might have been a blackboard, and then a whiteboard, displayed the CCC logo. The door opened behind us.

"Hello, everybody," a man in a light blue jumpsuit suddenly said. We all started, then watched in unison as he moved to the front of the room. "I'm Gurvaid. How's everybody doing today?"

Murmurs.

"Good. So, not much to say, except welcome, welcome to the Button's Corners–Moose Lake facility, and to most of you, welcome to Canada Cobalt Corporation. We're so pleased to have you on board. You'll find CCC is a great company to work for—I've been here nine years. Oh my! Wow. Nine years! It flies by."

Gurvaid stared for half a beat at a point above our heads, moving his lower jaw in and out. He was lean and handsome, smooth brown skin and black stubble, large hazel eyes, black hair apparently short beneath his dark blue CCC-branded cap. There was something reassuring about him. He projected capability and trustworthiness, his large-toothed smile convincingly sincere. He smelled warm, too. I caught it as he walked by. Despite my desire to remain free of attachment, I felt the hope bloom in my chest that he might be my supervisor, that he would direct me, take an interest in me. In a few short moments he became for me the human face of the Canada Cobalt Corporation, and indeed of this whole adventure, replacing Gil's catcher's-mitt mug, the impassive glare of Justine in housing, and the soft, round face of Deborah Mulaney, who'd taught me crystal composition for six weeks in North Bay.

"I'm just here to press play on the orientation video," said Gurvaid, "which will run for about ninety minutes, but we'll take a break about halfway through, and then at the end I'll be here for any questions you might have. Sound good?"

More murmurs.

"Okay, good."

With his right index finger Gurvaid navigated expertly and speedily through a menu on the screen, producing a big title card that read *Button's Corners–Moose Lake*. "Okay," he said, hands clasped. "Enjoy."

He began walking toward the door, but was stopped by the woman sitting at the desk immediately to my left. She looked to be perhaps a little older than me, and had a wide face with beautiful cheekbones, long brown hair tied back tightly, the glimpse of an elaborate tattoo snaking down her right arm and ending at the wrist just visible below the cuff of her stiff new company-issued nylon shell. She waved her hand toward him, looking uncertain.

"Sorry," she said, whispering, waving her phone at him, "but should we take notes, or...? Do we need to remember all this?"

Though she spoke quietly, she was asking on behalf of us all, so everyone leaned ever so slightly toward them to hear the response.

"No, oh, no," he reassured her, and so all of us, with his winning smile. Her shoulders softened, and she placed her phone face down on the desk. "All this information is available to you on the employee comms app. Don't worry." He raised his voice to be heard by everyone. "There won't be a test. Just sit back and watch."

He smiled broadly, hands clasped, and strode out the door, closing it softly behind him. We focused on the screen.

"Canada Cobalt Corporation welcomes you to its Button's Corners–Moose Lake facility," said a relentlessly cheery AI voice-over, nearly convincing but with hints of its synthetic nature evident at the corners of its speech, clipped word endings, transitions a half note off, a telltale too-perfect cadence. This had all become routine, of course. At some point we'd stopped caring that most of the voices we heard emanating from machines were not originally human, though I don't remember precisely when that was. So many such milestones have passed unremarked that you just get used to ducking your head and joining the slipstream.

The first half-hour was fairly benign corporate propaganda, edging into the history of the mine site. Just before the forty-five-minute mark, when we were scheduled to take our break, the video began to feature scenes from inside the control centre, where most of us would be working, a hundred metres below our feet. At these images I perked up, leaned forward on my elbows. This was what I wanted to see. The room pictured looked more brightly lit than I'd been anticipating, and didn't much suggest its underground nature. Technicians—"miners"—sat at individual consoles with a large array of controls before them, remotely manoeuvring the machinery actually engaged in extraction of the ore dozens of metres below them. I knew I wasn't going to be swinging a pickaxe, but I thought I'd be closer to the vein than this.

Gurvaid re-entered on cue. He lay his palm flat against the screen, and the images and narration paused. "How's it going so far?" he asked. "Any concerns?"

No one spoke.

"Okay," he said, "let's take ten minutes. Bathrooms are down the hall to your right."

Four or five people slid themselves out of their school desks and made for the door, while those of us who remained referred to our phones. The woman next to me turned hers over, picked it up, tapped out a message, and began swiping through photos of a young girl with blonde braids, a large smile studded with small teeth. When the woman looked up from her phone, she seemed removed. She exhaled loudly, put her phone face down on the desk once more.

She leaned a bit toward me and asked, "Was that a dumb question?" There was a hint of an accent that I hadn't heard when she'd spoken to Gurvaid. Southern US, though I was not versed well enough in the regional particulars to guess just where.

I said, "Sorry?"

"When I asked about a test earlier. I'm worried it sounded stupid."

"No, not a bit. I think everyone was wondering the same thing."

"I mean, this isn't school. They're paying us! But I didn't know for sure, and I didn't want to miss anything we'd need to know."

"Totally normal question," I said as casually as possible.

Now that she was looking at me, I could see her eyes, which were unnaturally blue, set below high-arched, finely shaped brown brows.

"I'm Nicole."

"I'm Gabe," I said

"Hi, Gabe. This your first mining job?"

"It is," I said. "Is it yours?"

"Yeah. I've filled sandbags and dug ditches, but never been down a mine."

"Scared?"

"No. You?"

"Nervous. I'll admit that."

"Sure, new job jitters. We'll be fine. Some of us are gonna grab a beer later, have a debrief. You wanna come along?"

"Sure I do," I said. Camaraderie, I reasoned, didn't have to mean connection.

"Great. Do you know the King George?"

"Nope."

"Look it up. Meet us there." Her phone shivered, and she broke my gaze, turned it over, bit her lip. I looked away to grant her a modicum of privacy. She tapped something out, put her phone down again, and tipped her head back to look at the ceiling.

The door filled then with Gurvaid's presence, and he swept into the room. "Just about everybody back? Great. Let's jump back in."

He placed his large, well-kept hand on the screen, and the video resumed where we had left off.

—

I immediately had misgivings about driving to the King George, which turned out to be about twenty minutes north of the dorm, in New Liskeard, but my options were limited. I'd tried to think my way around it for the duration of the afternoon's session, which meant I didn't take in much of what the second half of the video had to say, and when Gurvaid returned for a Q and A session, I couldn't think of anything to ask and didn't absorb any of the additional info being proffered.

One beer, I reasoned.

We wrapped at four o'clock. I hurried to my car, drove back to the dorm, and went quickly to my room. There was no sign of Gil, nor of Gil's attendants and hangers-on, though his door did appear to be slightly ajar. I ducked quickly into my own room, took off my shoes and jacket, hung my company-issued shirt in the closet, and lay down on the bed, trying to recover some of the sleep I'd lost the night before. I dozed off and on, got up about six, then had a shower and got dressed in street clothes.

I decided to take my time and see some of the environs. I zipped up into New Liskeard and drove around in ever tighter circles, zeroing in on the King George as the hour approached. I'd need a charge in a day or two, but filed it under things to worry about later.

The land opened and flattened in the slumping light. It had been a grey day, and the evening was close, damp seeming, and promised rain. The fields sprang up all around me in shades of green ranging from timid to voluptuous, intercut with golden stalks of wheat, all bordered by ten- or twelve-foot-high fencing, monitors spaced out every couple hundred metres, small signs emblazoned with the logos of global ag concerns over stern, all-caps warnings. I drove with my windows down, through the fields, breathing the rich air.

Since we'd tipped over all the conservative thresholds and begun spiralling into utter climate instability, I'd assumed that agriculture was a doomed enterprise, but here it was clearly thriving. Food had to come from somewhere, and the wholly lab-grown products that had flooded the market over the past decade still only achieved niche status. That figured to change over time, but as things stood we still pulled crops out of the ground, and as a result things in the Lesser Clay Belt were good. Good for some, anyway.

I drove long straight roads that intersected at right angles, obeying stop signs with flashing red lights though I saw few other vehicles. At one intersection I was afforded an expansive view south, to the place where the fertile land narrowed to its point and the town rose from the fields, and beyond it, in haze and blur, the long, blue lake.

I narrowed in on my target slowly, stopping in the large parking lot of what had clearly once been a Walmart—an imposing sand-coloured concrete box perched on a rise, facing west. It had been repurposed as an employment services centre with innovation incubation office space available for short-term rental. In the far corner of the lot there was a chip wagon that I was astonishingly grateful to see was still open. I sat in my car with the windows down and picked fries doused in vinegar out of a splotched paper bag, washed them down with a Coke. I sat looking out over the edge of the parking lot where the land dropped away ten metres to the highway, and beyond that, another step down, golden fields of hay, spotlighted in stray beams of sunlight punching through the blanket of cloud. The most recent cut of hay lay bundled and stacked in an impressive wall running east to west. In the middle of the field lay a loose array of goose decoys, and in the lee of that wall of bales, near where they'd parked their trucks, four men with rifles waited for the next airborne raft to wheel overhead, wings outstretched, bellies exposed.

At 7:15 I pulled up a half a block from the King George, which was a neighbourhood bar on a street of old two-storey houses. If it weren't for its sign in vivid green letters on red, I'd have driven right by, assuming it a residence. For a solid minute I sat in silence, all systems extinguished, steeling myself to meet, to talk, to perform myself.

Pulling open the bar's door, which stuck in the frame at the bottom, I was met with stale air. Old beer signs, imitation neon, a painting of Marie-Philip Poulin looking stoic and legendary in her maroon Montreal jersey, hoisting the Walter Cup—a reminder that we were in Ontario, but very near the Quebec border.

The King George had seen better days, but that made it the perfect spot to hide, have a drink, and conspire. It was underlit, all but empty save our party, and music wafted from an unseen source, loud but not too loud. It was of a volume which ensured that if Nicole were to spill her secrets to me, she'd have to lean right into my ear.

Seven newbie miners had already gathered around a long table in the middle of the room. Nicole sat facing the door and saw me first. She waved me over, and as luck or design would have it, there was an empty seat immediately opposite her.

"Have you met everybody?" she asked me.

"Just you," I said, milking a moment of eye contact.

She pointed to the woman sitting to her left, a small, dark-skinned woman with a black bob and an ear-to-ear smile. "Sheena," Nicole said, and then continued counter-clockwise around the table. "Tom, Wil, Ketanji, Fionna, and Sylvain."

"Hi," I said, adding a broad wave.

"Everybody, this is Gabe."

Light flickered behind me as something drove by. I stood an awkward moment, unsure of what to say. Nicole nodded toward the empty chair, and I pulled it out, sat, inched in toward the table.

We were eight people with nothing in common. The tone was light, cordial, a bit stilted. A server came to the table, I ordered a beer, a couple of people ordered a second. Nicole drank Coke. After three quarters of an hour we'd broken into discrete conversational units, groups of two or three getting to know one another, to turn occupational acquaintance into some manner of a support unit.

Sylvain, just to my right, was telling me in his heavy Québécois accent about his volunteer work, about how his environmental interests had led him into mining. It seemed like circuitous logic, though I wasn't trying too awfully hard to follow it. I was biding my time until I could edge into conversation with Nicole.

Eventually, a moment: she looked at me during a lull between her and Sheena.

"Why'd you come here?" she asked me.

"To the bar?"

"To this job. Here. The mine."

She was wearing a loose long-sleeved shirt, and in that instant I wanted very badly to see the rest of her tattoo—up her forearm to her elbow, maybe all the way to her shoulder—but it was far too intimate a thing to request. I leaned forward, wrapped my hands around my nearly empty bottle.

"New opportunity, I guess," I said. Seemed like a good bet."

"What were you doing before?"

"This and that. Existing. It was pretty clear I needed something to do. A new chapter."

"This guy is mysterious," Sylvain said. I hadn't realized he or anyone else had been listening. I was only trying to engage Nicole.

"No," I said, "just uninteresting." I nodded toward her. "What about you?"

"US Army," she said.

"I thought you had that accent," Sylvain said excitedly, as though it hadn't been readily apparent. "Where are you from?"

"Baton Rouge. Louisiana. My mom was from New Orleans before it went under. Met my father there. He was Canadian. From Montreal."

"Ah, Montreal," said Sylvain, pronouncing it properly, rolling the r so slightly and casually that I felt a stab of jealousy.

"What were you doing in the army?" I asked.

"Enlisted thinking I'd go to Europe, probably serve on the Eastern Line. But I never got there. Didn't even get shipped to the Mideast. Spent most of my time deployed to resettlement camps. Flood 'n fire duty, we called it. Florida, Mississippi, Oregon. Did eight years. Got pregnant, got out." She jiggled the ice in her glass.

"Oh, you're a mother," Sheena said.

"Yeah. Kaitlyn. She's six." She picked up her phone and flashed us a few photos of a young girl, the same ones I'd seen her flipping through in the classroom.

"So sweet," said Sheena.

"This seemed like a good, stable thing. I can send money home to her."

"She's still down there?"

"Yeah, she's in California with my mom."

I pictured crashing waves, picturesque curving highways, palm trees—the old California, in the old America. Before the Forever War had shifted to Eastern Europe, before the American Economic Collapse. Before the federal government had defaulted, and the worst of the domestic unrest began. Before pressure on the southern border had resulted in the creation of a twenty-five-mile-wide buffer strip, a dead zone routinely carpet-bombed by drones to ensure no living thing might successfully traverse it. Before the DOD broke from the executive branch, the judiciary dissolved, storms claimed several prominent low-lying cities, and the Pacific Northwest lost its forests to year-round conflagrations. Before the great exodus, of which Nicole was herself a participant. From the sound of things, her mother and daughter were ensconced in one of the safe districts. Parts of California had made out pretty well, considering.

"Will you go back?" I asked, feeling guilty, worried I was betraying a hint of self-interest.

"I'd like to bring her up here eventually, if I can get settled. It's just safer."

Sheena nodded solemnly in agreement, and I found myself doing the same. A hush descended. What was there to say?

There was a gravity settling on the evening. Night had come. If I'd earlier hoped to lure Nicole into mischief of some variety, I was now disinclined. She was too formidable, too layered and consequential, for anything less than total connection. Anything fast and fun would interfere with getting close to her, and I didn't want to make that trade. I waved to the server—who was leaning over the bar scrolling on his phone—indicating I'd be settling up for my single drink.

"You're going?" Nicole asked with a pleasingly disappointed tone.

I quickly explained my living situation, my terrible neighbour, my poor night's sleep. "Tomorrow's a big day," I said, "and I should get some rest."

Everyone seemed to accept this, though it deflated the mood in the room, and for that I felt some regret. I didn't mean to bring them down.

I stood, apologized, and waved to each person in turn, lingering, I'll admit, in Nicole's gaze a beat longer than anyone else's. Then, feeling excessively self-conscious, I walked to the door and out into the dusky evening.

Gil's cronies were choking the hallway when I returned to the dorm. Something had been spilled on the carpet just outside my room, and Gil's door was once again open. From inside, light flickered intermittently. I smelled smoke, and something uneasy crackled in the air. I glanced in, and a man lay prostrate at Gil's feet. Gil, in a wheeled office chair, was laughing at something, flashing his sickly teeth. I stood a moment too long looking in, trying to determine just what was going on with Gil, and with the motionless man on the floor below him.

"The fuck you looking at?" Gil spat at me, and fixed me with an unsteady glare.

"He okay?" I asked.

"What do you care? He's alive."

"But does he need help?"

"Don't worry about it! Go to bed, fucking newbie. Not your business."

Laughter from somewhere unseen; it sounded like several people. Men, mostly, but possibly a woman, too.

I looked down, my hand on my door handle. My left shoe rested in the tacky spot, an orangey island on a low-pile caramel sea. An archipelago of smaller islands arrayed off down the hall.

"Should I call to have whatever this is cleaned up?" I asked, lifting the toe of my boot up and down.

"Fuck off, kid. Mind your own."

I inserted my card in the door's key slot and heard it unlock. I slipped inside.

In the early morning, on my way to the bathroom to shower, I found a note had been slipped under my door. In red pen, with a childlike scrawl, was a message:

FUCKING NEW GIY, ITS POEPLE LIKE YOU WHO DONT KNOW THEIR OWN BUSNESS THAT MAKE THINGS BAD FOR THE REST OF US. REMEMBER THIS IS <u>MY HALLWAY</u> AND NOT YOURS SO KEEP THAT IN MIND AND DO <u>NOT</u> REPORT ANYTHING TO MGT OR YOU WILL BE VERY UNCOMFORTABLE
—GIL (ACROSS THE HALL)

I folded Gil's note carefully and tucked it under my phone on the dresser and then went about my morning.

Gil's parties continued, and he continued to treat me as though I'd done him some harm, but things at the mine were on the whole positive. By the beginning of my second week, I had begun to feel somewhat skilled at piloting my mining drone—we called them diggers—though I had much to learn. I was on a team of six, supervised by Gurvaid. Once we'd done ninety days under his watchful eye, some of us would be switched from the day shift, seven to three, to nights, eleven to seven.

Not that you'd know, once you were seated at your terminal, whether it was day or night. From the ground-level building, a large elevator carried you down one level to a long passageway leading back toward the headframe, where it opened into a larger space with a bank of three more elevators. Those descended about sixty metres further into the ground and let out onto a long corridor built from sequestered carbon blocks and lined with maintenance and storage rooms, the commissary, and at its end the control room, naturally cool and constantly humming. This was our workplace. Inside, in carefully calibrated three-quarter light, twelve workstations lined the walls, with six more up the middle of the room. A large video display took up the end wall, with a ticker running conditions across the bottom, as well as a box for employee communication, several rectangles showing CCTV camera feeds from throughout the facility, and a running count of the tonnage of cobalt being extracted at the site (an estimate, Gurvaid told me, though a pretty good one).

Each workstation contained a seat that looked like it belonged in the cockpit of a strategic bomber: a set of joysticks and manual controls on either side, one main joystick in the middle, wraparound screens, and a wireless headset.

A smaller screen, closer to the miner's face than the main display, held a readout of the digger's vitals. We'd been told what some of the acronyms and numbers there meant—the important ones, presumably—but most were completely unintelligible to me. All of this was linked by massive braids of wire to the actual shafts and tunnels, where the braids terminated in wireless relays that beamed commands and messages to and from the wheeled drones. In modern mining, very few humans touched any rock.

Experienced operators piloted the diggers working the face, using their trained eyes to discern what rock should be sent on for processing, and what was merely waste. As new hires we were mostly tasked with the removal of the empty waste rock, using our drones' shovels and pincers to feed it into autonomous carts that ferried it back to a lift in the central shaft.

Before much time had passed, it became impossible not to understand that our employers placed more value on the multi-million-dollar machines we controlled than they did on us. That made some financial sense, of course.

I found the shifts passed fairly quickly, likely owing to their novelty. I was still mastering the finer points of my digger's controls and trying to map the totality of the mine in my head. There was some aspect of slow-motion adventure to it all that kept me engaged.

Nicole was on my shift, too, stationed three spots away from me. Two or three times a week we'd get lunch together in the commissary. They did a good vegan club sandwich, though the coffee was unspeakably bad. How it was possible, in 2037, to produce a bad cup of coffee was a mystery that seemed to elude all concerned. Seventy-five percent of the global coffee market was controlled by the Saudis, who grew consistently excellent beans in massive vertical farms where the pests and diseases that had decimated the South American industry were assiduously kept at bay.

Being cradled in the depths of the earth, beneath and amid all that frozen time, induced in me a great sense of safety. The terrible world carried on above us, but we crawled down into rock that predated all life on our planet, and what we did down there was unknown to virtually all the actors topside. Above us the land thronged with human error and pulsed with the remnants of the Cambrian period, when plant life first gained its terrestrial foothold; the Ordovician's great explosion of bivalves; the Mesozoic, Age of Reptiles; the Cenozoic, and all the periods, stages, and ages therein. We grew our food in soils deposited in our neighbouring period, the Wisconsinan, so ridiculously proximate to us in real terms, though it predated human civilization. Being down there within the cold rock pushed at the boundaries of my comfort, but also introduced a happy clarity to my thoughts. I never woke to my alarm dreading another workday.

◆

As I came to feel at ease in all those subterranean rooms, I grew perhaps overly comfortable with Gurvaid.

One day, I saw him passing through the commissary, walking to the counter and selecting from a basket a single banana—I'd never seen Gurvaid eat anything but fruit, nor drink anything other than water.

As he passed by, I called to him: "Gurvaid, do you know Gil?"

"Gil?"

"In the dorms. Older guy. Where does he work?"

"Oh-ho," he said, "you mean Gil McCandless. You must be in the Haileybury unit, are you?"

"I am, yeah. Is that his name?"

Gurvaid stopped midstride and came to stand with his chest square to me, his feet planted shoulder width apart, the banana cupped gently in both hands in front of him. Everything Gurvaid did seemed head-on, direct, sure. He appeared to have cracked the code. He was the most successfully human person I'd ever met. You could model a civilization on him.

"Gil was a front-line technician. He worked at the face. This was a few years back. Five? Six? He doesn't work here anymore." Gurvaid's soft brown eyes smiled independently of his mouth, though it smiled, too. "He was injured. I believe a bit of waste dislodged from a passing clearance drone and caught him unaware. In the back. I can't say much more; I wasn't there. But he was injured in such a way that left him unable to do the job. When he recovered, he was offered administrative positions but fought the company every step of the way. Very aggressive. Eventually he reached a settlement, and part of that included housing. Nominally he has a role, a sort of a residence don."

"He lives across the hall from me."

"My sincere condolences. But it's a temporary arrangement, right?"

"Oh, for sure."

"Many have complained, but there's a certain fear that he'll make such trouble for the company if they try to persuade him to leave that it won't be worth it. The people who stay there are, after all, just passing through."

"True."

"Think of him as a sort of rite of initiation. It will pass." At this Gurvaid chuckled.

"Right," I said.

"If you're speaking to Gil, give him my regards. He'll love that. Actually don't. I wouldn't want to make any more trouble for you. Have you had luck finding a place of your own? They're always ready to help in the housing office."

"I think I'm close to securing a place," I said, "but thanks."

"Very good. I won't take up any more of your break. Enjoy your lunch, Gabe."

—

Perhaps ten days later I sat at one of the commissary's round tables with Nicole and Sheena. They'd recently moved into an apartment together and were both eating food they'd brought from home, while I was working on the second half of my club.

I'd been giving them regular updates about Gil, portraying my patience and restraint in mildly heroic dimensions and eliciting from them the appropriate amount of sympathy. Since my exchange with Gurvaid, they'd taken an interest in helping me secure a place to live. They'd already tipped me off about an apartment in their building, a nice three-storey block with a view of the lake, but I'd narrowly missed out on it by calling the management company about five minutes too late. Disappointed, Nicole and Sheena began giving me near daily reports on what was available in the area. Their concern felt warm and maternal—I'd found myself enmeshed in a network of care.

"We'll find you the right place," Nicole said matter-of-factly.

Up to that point I'd been operating under the assumption that I was romantically interested in Nicole. It seemed natural. I was there to find or shape something new, and Nicole—tough, beautiful, kind, smart, and stranded, in a way, far from where she belonged, like me—seemed the human embodiment of that. So I wanted her. It was the only way my lizard brain knew to accommodate all these stimuli.

But when she'd said that—that *we* would find me the *right place*—I was struck by Nicole's kindness and openness. It seemed to reference my own continuing effort to line up the person I was with the person I wanted to be. Things began shifting within me. Getting way ahead of myself, it became obvious that Kaitlyn, down there in California, fatherless, staying with her grandmother, deserved someone steadier than me. In all likelihood I would only prove in the long run to be a void, like my father, and I wanted no part of that scenario.

And I had become so comfortable with Nicole so quickly that romantic and sexual entanglement would be both risky and akin to backtracking: we'd have to reintroduce ourselves, and there was no guarantee the newly introduced versions of ourselves would be as comfortable with one another. I didn't want to lose Nicole due to my own romantic ineptitude. It occurred to me for the first time in my adult life that there were more ways to keep a person close—even a desirable woman like Nicole—than sexual possession. To my twenty-seven-year-old mind, this was a revelation.

What was more, it was very, very clear that Nicole didn't need me, whether as a partner or a fling. She was whole and coping just fine. All she needed was her little girl.

I eventually secured a nice room on the top floor of an old house. It had two beautiful dormer windows that looked south toward the lake and the lights of Haileybury, such as they were. It was an old attic, adequately upgraded, with strange, random bulkheads and protrusions from the walls, and a platform for the bed raised six inches off the floor. The kitchen and bathroom were brand new, and I was assured the downstairs neighbours were very quiet.

It was a Saturday, and I was carrying my few things out of the dorm. When I closed my door, Gil's shot open as though there'd been a great disturbance in the hallway. Gil stood in a ratty bathrobe and a pair of notably new-seeming black high-top sneakers, swaying just a bit, his hand still on the door. In semi-daylight he looked even more haggard than I'd known, a face exposed to too much sun and too few vegetables. He smelled awful.

"Going, are you?"

"Got a place. My three weeks are up."

"Good riddance. I hope they fire you."

"Thanks, Gil. Take care of yourself."

"Bye, fuckface."

That was the last thing Gil ever said to me.

He died a few months later, when we were in the iron grip of winter. The snow was deep, the wind relentless, and the nights were mercilessly cold. The slanted roof over my head as I slept was rocked by frequent cryoseism, and my car was laminated in mud, salt, and sand. I'd had to buy a coat and gloves, a warm pair of boots.

I was in the commissary when Gurvaid asked me, in a

mock whisper, "Did you hear about Gil?"

"What about him?"

"Died in his sleep. Took a couple of days for anyone to find him."

"Aw, no," I said, unexpectedly moved. "What of?"

"Rot, I guess. The way he lived."

"Alone."

"In every sense of the word," Gurvaid said.

◆

They waited until spring to bury him.

I didn't go to the funeral, but I heard it was sparsely attended. No family had travelled to see him off. But one afternoon in April, I woke in the early afternoon, well ahead of my overnight shift, and drove to the cemetery on the south end of Cobalt. It was a lonely and desolate churchyard with a decrepit fence. In the spring sunshine it was doing its best to appear pretty, small bluebonnets and dandelions in the thick grass among the listing stones. In a new quarter of the yard, where a dozen recent graves stood in a perfect grid, was a patch of new grass, thin and wispy.

His stone was a simple slab of dark grey Quebec limestone, polished on its face but left rough on its edges and back. It read: *Here lies Gill McCandless, a child of God, March 1, 1983–February 22, 2038.*

It shocked me that he was my parents' age. He'd looked ancient, like a feature of the landscape. And it made me chuckle at first that his name had been rendered with a spelling mistake, though that gave way to sadness, and then in the ensuing days to a burr-like irritation that clung to me and that I couldn't shake.

In the end, lying in bed one night, traces of artificial light and a faint boreal aroma drifting through the open dormers, I decided I'd call the cemetery, and the monument works, and possibly even CCC, to see if anything could be done about fixing it.

III

WHEN I WAS FORTY-ONE and living on the forty-second floor of a converted business tower in Toronto's New Lakeshore district, I was contacted by a woman named Anna who claimed to be my father's widow. This was a week before my birthday. I had forsaken the disorder and slapdash character of my twenties and thirties in favour of simplicity, stability, and routine. I gave up chasing sex, highs, and novel forms of terror. I no longer liked to be surprised by things.

So I was quite shaken when she messaged me.

"I know this is likely a shock," she'd said, and "Maybe it would be best if we had a call."

Without thinking, I punched in the number she provided. My orange tabby, Willie, lay purring on my lap, while my heart hammered like a knock in the pipes. I should have paused and asked myself what I wanted, but I was so surprised, and in the moment felt quite worried that I would disappoint her if I refused. I asked my watch to contact the number and specified voice only, so I would hear her, and her me, but we would not see each other. Just electric-blue squiggles representing sound waves on the screen in front of me, as it woke from blankness when the call connected. Just her name in the lower left corner, confirming her identity.

"Hello, Gabriel," she said. I had to admit that her voice was warm, friendly. "I'm so glad to hear your voice."

"Hello, Anna. Do I call you Anna?"

"Anna, yes. Anna Gerson."

"I'm sorry," I said after a beat. "I don't know what to say. I didn't know he had a widow. I didn't know he was dead. I didn't know he was still alive."

"He was, though I must say the last few years have not been easy. This must be a lot. I'm sorry to spring it on you."

"It is. It is a lot."

"He left you a letter. It's sealed; I haven't read it. But listen, I suspect it would fill in a lot for you. He wanted me to give it to you."

"A letter."

"Can we meet?"

"In person?"

"I'd like to give it to you. It's what he wanted."

Mail it, I should have said, *to save us both the trouble.* I knew immediately that I'd never read it. But some corner of me must have thought I owed him at least the ceremonial act of taking possession of it, if only to comfort Anna, to allow her to feel she'd done her part.

"Okay," I said. "Where?"

"There's a little place he liked, the Imperial. Do you know it? Used to be a bar."

My watch, listening, shook softly on my wrist and flashed a map with a red pin on the likeliest hit. "On Dundas?"

"That's it. Tomorrow night?"

"Okay. How's eight?"

"Oh, I'll be out past my bedtime, but why not?" said Anna with a small chuckle, which she clipped apologetically.

"Okay," I said.

"Okay," she said.

After a moment of silence, we both stammered, and I said, "Well, until tomorrow, then," said goodbye, and disconnected.

Then I asked my watch to turn off all the lights in my apartment, and I stood at the window watching the torrential rain smear the city's lights into streaks and arterial courses.

At that point we'd had four days of rain and already the Don Valley had filled, loosening the river's banks, which moved in a diluvial ooze toward the lake. The insoluble footings of the great Bloor Street bridge were intact but had slipped just a little on their substrate and would need repair. Braids of water thick as trains ran down sidewalks and streets, downspouts gushed or blew open, businesses in older buildings had their basements flooded. During intervals of lighter rain a heavy fog pushed in from the lake and obscured everything.

During the Carnian Pluvial Episode it rained non-stop for about two million years, from 234 to 232 million years ago. It's also sometimes called, somewhat more poetically, the Wet Intermezzo. I imagine that sometimes: the pre-mammalian Earth like a sandbox, an experimental laboratory, the unseen hand of seeming randomness toying with atmospheric and geologic factors just to see what might happen to successive waves of flora and fauna, all manner of them. A million billion factors had to break just right to make the world we know, the horses and forests, the upright hominids and hot fudge sundaes. I get a sense of dislocation when I think of that. It rained for twenty thousand centuries.

This was like that, but less. A massive Pacific tropical low, its size and intensity the result of the oceans' rapid extreme warming, had blown in over Oregon, stretched all the way to the Great Lakes and parked itself there, where it would dump warm rain from Cascadia to Southern Ontario for two weeks. When things like this happened—and they happened quite often now—they no longer stuck to the old seasonal progressions. Since the Gulf Stream had gone haywire about ten years earlier, the old markers of spring, summer, fall, winter had begun to mean less and less. What you got on a daily basis became a crapshoot. It was all very disorienting.

Things were worse elsewhere, of course. Coastal flooding on Vancouver Island, Halifax ceding its old waterfront to the waves. There was a population boom up north, along the now-viable Arctic sea routes. And the EU had just begun the extremely complex job of building the North Sea Enclosure Wall in the hopes of saving the Low Countries.

Standing in the darkness after the call with Anna, I almost felt that if I could open my windows, I could reach across to the building opposite and wipe the rain off its gleaming glass face.

At ground level my building was nearly featureless—windowless, blank sand-hued concrete facades cladding the building's power plant and pumping facilities. From the third floor up to where the building topped out at the fiftieth, a semi-tasteful mix of glass and composite wood panelling added an inoffensive feature to the skyline, with blunted finials at each corner meant to evoke ornamentation without being quite as ostentatious as ornamentation. At night the south- and east-facing windows from the tenth through the thirtieth floor lit up with ads, though you could not see the moving images from inside. But it was a common arrangement, and it helped keep rent down a bit, at least in theory, as the public advertising firms kicked money to the property management companies. It had become common to include "ad-rev bldg" as an enticement in rental listings.

It was surrounded by newer supertalls, several of them also looping bright ads on their faces. I could see the top of one tower, a warning light flashing rhythmically from its highest point, and in the screenless surface of another I could just make out the reflection of the CN Tower and its dancing coloured lights. The red strobe atop its spire had long ago been surpassed on the skyline, but despite the recent completion of its years-long tornado-proofing retrofit, the building's iconic shape remained. My mind's eye swooped beyond its perch on the water's edge, out over the black water of Lake Ontario where floating wind farms bobbed.

Then I went to bed. I lay awake all night with the questions I'd had for so long but that I'd eventually packed away, certain they'd remain unanswered.

I had never stopped thinking about my father, but in the years since I'd last seen him, he'd become a void. Memory and shadow. I never spoke about him. Mom would reference him sometimes when I was growing up—*Your dad used to do this*, or *say that*, or *One time your father and I*, that sort of thing—but that had stopped at some point I could not now name. I hadn't heard her talk about him in decades. Mom and I had learned, eventually and with great effort, that we hadn't needed him, and it was important to both of us that we not pay undue honour to the role he'd once occupied by speaking fondly of him—even if I thought back happily to so much of the time I spent with him, and I'm sure she did too.

As I lay in the darkness with Willie, still purring and tucked into the crook of my arm, I wondered if my inability to cut Anna off, to thank her but tell her I was not interested, meant that I now found myself in need of answers. I had lived so many years without them, and yet one short conversation was forcing me to confront my own assumptions, my inability to conceive of the simple notion that he continued to exist whether or not I thought about him, sought answers, went looking for him. He had lived a life. Slept, woke, ate, maybe had a dog, maybe learned to play guitar. Loved, possibly, and ached. Maybe reproduced again. Worried about his health. Read news articles, novels. Lusted and feared.

And chose, every single day, not to see me.

I still remember the warm, ruddy scent of him as he bent over to tie my skates, my foot in between his knees, his cold knuckles looking dry and cracked, the slight pinch at my ankle as he tugged hard on the laces' slack. Did he remember me in skates, struggling to keep up, the sun bright and the air cold? Or me overcoming my fear and leaping out over the water, the smell of July, of rich plant life and hot stone, my pale limbs, the dark green water?

He'd shown me the constellations, and he'd given me wolves. He helped me swim, and read, and before our unit shattered he'd been one half of my universe. For the first decade of my life, as curiosity and uncertainty billowed within me, he was one of the twin anchors of my existence. He stood next to me in a thick dusk, redolent of pollens, streaked in peach and lavender, and he put his arm around me, and he said, "You're safe, Gabe." When I was ten years old, that was everything I needed to hear.

In the years since, it has not once occurred to me to wonder what I might have done then to calm whatever troubled the wild green expanse of his heart. But that's not a child's responsibility. And I didn't believe his letter would have told me anything about that, anyway.

Near dawn—with the rain still falling but the sky's darkness beginning to soften, and with Willie having moved to the sill so that I could see him quite clearly in silhouette, sitting and looking out at the same lights, his ears alert, twitching—I resolved that Mom would never hear of any of this. Not of his death, nor of Anna, nor of any letter. She was in the very early stages of her illness, and to tell her any of this would agitate her. I couldn't stomach the idea of doing that.

Exhausted and achy, I had only coffee for breakfast and then put in a sorry day's work at my desk. I reheated some lab-grown salmon and rice for dinner. Then I showered, dressed, fed Willie, put on my impermeable and boots, and stepped out to meet my father's widow.

The streets were deserted. The largest city in Canada by a safe margin, the second largest in North America, and still this desolate scene. A police airship loomed a block down, nearer the lake. A wheeled maintenance drone the size of a beagle, its small lights blinking and water pouring off its sides, crept down the opposite sidewalk and hoovered up a piece of trash. But not a living soul in view.

Such public solitude had been rare for most of my life. Twenty years earlier the global population had topped out at 9.2 billion before going into steady decline. Our family unit handily demonstrated this: my parents had only me, and I was, and remain, childless. I liked to say that I had chosen not to procreate when I pictured myself telling my progeny that ice had once been a naturally occurring phenomenon. But the truth is that it was never far from my mind that my own father had likely never considered himself capable of abandoning his family right up until the moment that he did, and I had never been sure that I was better—stronger, more honest, more loyal—than him. It would be easier, I decided, to avoid the question altogether.

Years earlier, when I was leaving the vasectomy clinic, the nurse asked me if I had anyone to take me home. The question sounded pointed to me. She just wanted to know if I had arranged for anyone to help me home, my underpants stuffed with gauze and a potent painkiller slinking through my veins, but in the moment I had interpreted it as a rebuke. "No, nobody," I'd said. She summoned a car for me, and I went back to my apartment and slept for the better part of the next three days.

I cinched my hood against the rain and darted off the sidewalk, leapt the curbside river and into the empty street, unnoticed by human eyes but captured by several of the myriad cameras trained on every inch of downtown Toronto. Somewhere, something undoubtedly registered my presence, but I saw no evidence of that. Half a block up, feeling already that the rain was beginning to saturate my waterproof coat, I pulled on the left handle of a set of double doors, next to which was posted an almost obliterated sign for the city's PATH network of underground pedestrian passageways.

The system had once been extensive, an ant farm of tunnels lined with shops and eateries that would shelter on-foot commuters or wanderers, offering warmth, dryness, and car-free passage throughout the downtown core, allowing them to emerge into the lobbies of business towers, shopping malls, and transit stations. Over the years the map had become patchwork, some sections sealed off by property owners, others flooding or falling into disrepair. When pulling on these door handles a person could no longer be certain they'd gain entrance to PATH, whether they'd be able to reach their intended destination, or what they'd find along the way.

But the rain drove me underground in the hope that I'd be able to make it most, if not all of the way to Yonge and Dundas, near where the Imperial was located. I'd given myself lots of time—forty-five minutes for what was usually a twenty-minute walk—thinking that the rain might slow me down.

The door opened rustily, grudgingly, and a row of motion-triggered lights blinked on, revealing a concrete staircase bisected by a yellow rail that leaned somewhat off true. A bit of trash littered the stairs, but all in all it didn't look too bad, though for the moment it led down into darkness. I lowered my hood, shook the water off my shoulders and arms, and descended.

At the bottom of the staircase, where the next bank of lights popped to life, the concrete gave way to cracked beige-brown tile, from which sprouted, a short distance away to my right, a fenced-in corral containing rows of delivery and maintenance bots sitting in silence, nestled into charging docks. There were several rows of them, and as I walked by the pen I saw, at the far end, the small cat door–like access point where they wheeled themselves back home at regular intervals, found a vacant station, and put themselves to sleep. There was nothing else happening, just my steps and the ambient hum of the fresh air exchanger lending the cavern an almost country kind of silence.

More lights flared on ahead, and out of the gloom zipped a security unit, about four feet tall, a screen on its front side, and atop it a dome that housed cameras. The screen said *SECURITALL* in a steel-plate typeface that kept crawling up and disappearing near the dome, only to reappear at the bottom, just over the bot's fat tires. It caught sight of me, paused, then accelerated toward me. I kept walking, and the unit performed an arc around me before it assumed a pace about five steps ahead of me. Behind the dark dome, its highest-res camera was almost certainly focused on my face, which it captured and beamed off to a server for a facial recognition scan, tapping border control and police databases to make sure I wasn't someone who wasn't supposed to be there. It probably also calculated the likelihood that I was inebriated, and did a quick air test to gauge whether or not I carried anything infectious.

I hadn't ingested anything, and all indications suggested I was free of pathogens. As for my record, I'd miraculously avoided the law despite my flirtations with criminality. That didn't stop me from experiencing low-level dread in these sorts of moments. You'd hear from time to time of the rediscovery of decades-lost security footage implicating someone who'd lived a full and otherwise clean life believing they'd beaten a rap. Part of me assumed that this would one day prove my fate.

But not this evening, apparently. The unit slowed, fell back as I kept walking, and zoomed off to investigate another area of the PATH system.

I passed permanently shuttered fast food outlets, and tech maintenance shops that were closed for the night, their metal roll-down gates dented, plastered with ads. The lights flared on ahead of me and shut off behind me. At a crossroads—an intersection studded with bolted-down tables and chairs—another security drone raced down the perpendicular corridor without stopping, my unthreatening presence having already been recorded and sorted into whatever they labelled the file for unremarkable persons and non-offenders.

The last time I'd been underground, the passage to the south of where I now walked had been blocked, so I swung north, hoping. In an atrium roughly under Richmond Street, I encountered another drone corral. This one apparently was not functioning—its docking ports were mostly empty, and among those occupied no lights blinked, and no telltale subaudible hum emanated. Further along the corridor, still heading north, a section of lighting failed to come on, and I quickened my pace while shining my watch's torch ahead. A wall of screens mutely reported the day's news—another self-driving car lawsuit winding through the courts, and a spate of drownings in flooded underground survival shelters—in text and still photographs, though one of the dozen panels blinked and cut out. A boarded-up storefront vibrated with machine intent that I felt on the skin of my face.

As I continued, the general air of disrepair and disregard escalated. A bank of lighting panels fizzed to life over my head, but the next group remained dark. A steady trickle of water fell from a tangle of pipes and onto the side of an overturned bucket. When the tunnel forked, I headed east again, but began scanning for a functioning exit.

A double door, unmarked but promisingly unlocked, relented to my shoves, and the spectral shape of an unlit staircase materialized. I started up. Before the second set of doors at the top, I was required to pass through some type of scanner. It was feebly lit, almost certainly non-functioning, and I could only guess at its original intended purpose.

The rain fell just as hard on Queen Street, but a handful of people milled before Old City Hall. A streetcar floated by, its interior lights revealing a half a dozen blank faces. Hooded again, I turned right. The Aquarium—what used to be the Eaton Centre shopping mall, but had since been converted to a giant server farm and quantum computing hub—appeared to buzz, brightly lit. It had earned its nickname from a photo someone had posted somewhere of an array of its QCs looking like octopuses suspended from hooks. A few dozen people were coming out of its many doors, and more stood about waiting for rides.

I turned north again at Yonge, walked on through waves of rain. A transport drone overhead tilted, and water spilled off its curved flank, hitting me like a tidal wave. At Dundas Square I waited for the light to change, though traffic was extremely light. Surrounded on all sides by massive flashing, chattering screens and shrill holoprojections, I felt harassed. I missed the tunnels' relative silence.

The Imperial Ex-Bar sat just off the square, huddled beneath monstrous towers—a toadstool at the feet of redwoods. Its brick corner looked improbable and lost amid the made-over city, a relic without any particular charm except its relic-ness, a famous bar that, like a lot of others, was no longer a bar. In the run-up to the federal prohibition plebiscite which narrowly upheld the legality of alcohol in 2035, a lot of licensed establishments—assuming they were getting out ahead of the shift—remade themselves as booze-free social houses and thereby found new clientele by serving coffee, smart teas, light snacks, or cannabinoid cocktails. When liquor remained available, these old bars simply never reapplied for licences, and a new category, the ex-bar, was born. They remain popular, as do good old-fashioned bars, though there's the trace suspicion that one or the other of them will prove to be a fad, set to fade one day sooner or later.

It hit me as I came through the Imperial's door and into its dark, woody, underlit main room that I wouldn't know

how to recognize Anna if she were already there—but that
didn't end up being a problem. The place was quiet, and
sitting at one of the first tables I saw was a well-preserved
woman in her sixties or early seventies. When I turned my
face toward her, I saw her jaw drop a detectable distance.

"God, oh, god, I didn't think you'd look so much like
him," she said.

"Anna?"

"Gabriel," she said, rising from her wooden chair.

As I approached her, I quickly developed the sense that
she was what Mom once called a cable-knit feminist: the
type of well-off woman who didn't think of herself as wealthy,
but who bought the expensive sweater because quality lasts
longer; who paired the sweater—cream or navy blue, generally—with inherited pearls but no gold; who had long ago
cross-country skied on ravine trails on snowy January weekends; who streamed public radio, attended book club meetings and abstract dance performances; who raised money
for women's shelters and the public library; who had one
child, if any, and taught them about sustainability, and
that history was the story of the overclass's oppression of
marginalized populations, but whose daily life was largely
devoid of contact with those very people. In all, a relatively
benign presence, even a force for some good, and not at all
that dissimilar from my mother's own person, the excep-
tion being that Mom would've been more likely to buy her
sweaters from a thrift shop.

Mom had begun sharing these sorts of snide comments
and unvarnished opinions with me once I was sixteen or
seventeen, a tacit admission that the motherly persona
I'd known as a child had been a bit theatrical or, to be fair
about it, restrained. But as I neared adulthood, she started

to treat me as a social equal, a friend, as though life was a jog around a track and I'd come abreast of her, so we could continue on together. I found this to be one of the great pleasures of aging: this frankness, this openness that she and I shared. I enjoyed that right up until her mind began to slip. Then it became a crapshoot—sometimes I was a child (hers or someone else's), sometimes a confidant, and sometimes her elder, scolding her for not finishing her dinner.

I glanced at my watch, and Anna hesitated a moment, probably also waiting for a reading. Neither device apparently picked up a detectable rise in airborne pathogens, so we got close to one another. She opened her arms in a gesture of embrace while I held my right hand out at belt height. She stepped back and took my hand and said, "It's just so great to meet you."

"You too," I said, somewhat coldly, because I still didn't know what I was doing there, or what I hoped to take from the meeting. To balance things out, I offered a half smile, meant to recognize the awkwardness of our situation. I wasn't sure Anna saw it.

She seemed genuine—kind, well-meaning. She had cool green eyes and white hair pulled back in a loose ponytail; she was wearing the aforementioned expensive sweater in a kind of oatmeal shade, a bit worn. Her face was round and inviting, colour in her cheeks. She was shorter than Mom, and wore display-enabled glasses.

I took off my dripping coat and draped it over the back of the chair opposite her, then sat. We stared at each other, trying to size one another up. I couldn't be certain what her interest in me might be, which is to say part of me suspected there was a financial consideration. Had he done well for himself and in a moment of late-life guilt decided to leave me everything? Was Anna trying to place herself between me and my father's wealth?

"Well," she said, hands folded on the table before her. "Should we order something?"

I tensed. Ordering would complicate the process of a quick departure, if that's what I decided to do.

"My treat," she said, "please," and turned the menu screen toward me. I tapped for a cup of mid-grade decaf and rotated the screen toward her. She browsed before settling on something, and then we talked about the rain for ten minutes until our order wheeled over to us on a bot cart. Hers was a carrot cupcake with white frosting and a white mug of herbal tea with honey.

She held her mug up and said, "Well, here's to connecting."

I held my mug up but did not clink hers. "That's an interesting way to put it," I said.

She blew on her tea, took a sip, and put the mug down on the table. "Look, listen, I don't have a hidden agenda," she said.

"You're just delivering the letter. On his behalf."

"I just thought you'd want to have it. He wanted to communicate with you."

"Why'd he wait?"

"I wish you could have asked him yourself," she said, which I thought was a cute comment, given that the only thing preventing me from doing so when he was alive was his decision to excise himself from my life.

"I don't."

"Of course. I understand."

"I don't know how you could. I don't understand myself. I came here not knowing what I wanted, which is the wrong way to enter into anything."

My father's shadow loomed over things, even from the grave. It was perhaps beginning to dawn on Anna that several of her assumptions would have to be re-examined. About who my father had been, why he'd done what he'd done, and the nature of the falling out. About my interest in forming a relationship with her. She'd need to be coached through the process, though I didn't intend to be present that long.

She said, "I think it's natural for a child to yearn for any connection to their parent. Here he's offering it. Through me."

"I don't think there's anything natural about this situation."

"Were you hoping there'd be money? A will? Because we don't have much, I'm afraid."

I suspected her definition of *much* differed from mine, but it didn't matter.

"I wouldn't take it if there was. I've made it this far without his help."

"Of course." She took an envelope from an oversized tote bag resting on the floor near her chair and placed the pale rectangle on the table between us. "He loved you, Gabe. There were things that prevented him from reaching out to you. Maybe he explained some of it here."

She looked at me with an uncertain smile that hinted that she'd thought I'd be overjoyed in this moment, and was trying to nudge my mood in that direction. Then she looked around the room, perhaps feeling exposed. She broke a piece off her cupcake and popped it in her mouth.

It was a plain white envelope, not thick. Whatever he'd hoped to communicate was concisely expressed. *Gabe*, it said in black ink, written in a hand I recognized, the letters a bit wild, oversized. The envelope had been bent and re-flattened. Its corners were softened. It looked as though it had lived in a drawer for a few years.

"There it is," I said, not moving to pick it up.

"Yes. Please take it. Whether you read it or not, I won't know. But he wanted you to have it."

"You keep talking about what he wanted, as though his wishes should mean something to me." I said this calmly, then took a sip of coffee, placed my mug back on the table. "I hope I don't seem rude, but I think I'm permitted a little animosity. Some confusion, too."

I picked the mug back up and held it in both hands to feel its warmth. The rain continued outside. Anna picked another piece off her cupcake, brought it to her mouth slowly, watching it all the way.

"You're absolutely entitled to that. But try to remember who he was. You only have one father." She opened her mouth and took in the orange cake and its drift of icing.

"Had."

"Yes, had."

I put down the mug, picked up the envelope, turned it in my hand. There were no markings other than my name. Nothing to indicate who it was from other than the peculiar, slashing handwriting, and the barely subdued panic it suggested. I folded the paper in half and then in half again, and slid it into my shirt's breast pocket.

I picked up the coffee once more and downed what remained of it in one gulp. "Thank you for the coffee, Anna," I said. "It was good to meet you. I'm very sorry for your loss." Then I stood and put on my coat. Before turning to leave, I paused to give her a chance to speak.

"I hope you read it," she said. "It might help you to understand."

"Maybe. I doubt it. I expect it's just a list of justifications."

"Thank you for meeting me, Gabe. If there's anything you want to know, anything you want to talk about, you know how to reach me."

"Goodbye, Anna," I said, and left.

—◆—

I stayed above ground on the walk home, and the rain lulled a bit. I waded through a new pond on Dundas, and when I turned south on Yonge I found myself failing to keep pace with the debris being carried along with the gutters' current. I considered adding the letter, pulling it out of my pocket and letting it drop from my fingertips into the stream, watching it speed away, swept clear down to the lake, where it would disappear forever. I don't know why I didn't.

When I walked through the door and took off my wet coat, hanging it on a hook there, my watch noted my elevated heart rate and blood pressure as well as the late hour, and triangulated my mood and need for relaxation. It transmitted a command to the smartbox on the wall, which responded by softening the lighting, producing an intra-uterine red-orange slow pulse. It lowered the ambient air temperature a degree, and discreetly piped in a muted per-formance of Bach's cello concertos, almost inaudibly, from all sides. I made a cup of cinnamon tea, asked my watch to switch off all screens, and changed into warm, dry clothes. Willie slunk over to me and wove himself between my feet as I stood at the counter stirring honey into the mug.

I took the envelope containing the letter from my shirt pocket and placed it in a bowl I usually used for fruit. I handled it like a hand grenade. I brought my mug of cinnamon tea to bed, where I made a nesting space for Willie. Together we lounged until a fitful sleep overtook me, a sleep of off-kilter dreams and frequent bathroom trips.

＿＿

A week later, it was my birthday. The letter was still in the fruit bowl. I'd spent the intervening days working, sleeping, trying to read, running errands. I told myself nothing had changed, but of course something had. Such seismicity occurring so far below my feet was not so easily felt, but the dimensions of my life had shifted, unquestionably. My landscape had been altered, even if only by centimetres, and my brain was busy trying to assimilate the new measurements.

I decided to take myself to the movies. It was less about celebrating my birthday than it was capitulation to a desire: to bounce myself off of the world's reflective surfaces, to see if the person who came back to me was the same me I'd known, or if I'd changed in some way.

Runnels of rainwater poured off my hood and in front of my face as I trudged through ankle-deep puddles, two blocks north and then west along Queen. My destination, the Orpheum Theatre, sat squat and listing, joined on either side by similarly low-set buildings, a great uniform loaf of them occupying the entire block. Whole swaths of Toronto are still only two storeys tall, even today, the residue of WASPy early twentieth-century ordinances aimed at restricting the construction of high-rise apartment blocks that would quickly fill up with undesirables—immigrants, single women. The result, a century and a half later, is limited housing stock, sky-high rent, and a very strange skyline—the latter of which will continue to give the sense that

Toronto is a provincial city right up until all the remaining low-rises are razed and replaced with towers hundreds of metres tall, glistening and garishly illuminated, owned by absentee foreign parties, occupied by wealthy lessees, hedgers and VC parasites with multiple passports.

The Orpheum's marquee peaked out over the sidewalk and announced via analogue signage the evening's feature: *VERTIGO (Con-NonAI), 7:00 and 9:30.* Black letters and numerals on a yellowed field, glowing warmly in the hissing rain and soft-edged fog, the streetcar gliding by on Queen, a few faceless passersby. No director could have staged it better.

The bracketed stipulation was that the Orpheum's lone screen was a conventional one, a non-immersive viewing experience. You sat in a seat, and images made entirely by human beings played before you on a flat surface. There were no headsets, no n-links. Which, if I'm being honest, is how I still prefer it, especially for an old movie, though such showings are difficult to find now.

I had meant to make the early show, but became busy doing nothing in my apartment, so only just after nine did I stand before the box office, making my selection on the small screen. One ticket, one small popcorn (no Buttr), one natural-source water. My watch asked if I wanted to complete the transaction, I said yes, and it was done. I went through the rotating door into a hushed and desolate lobby with its missing or crooked fixtures, fraying carpet, and general air of mould and dissolution. On a screen over the counter to my left, a digitally rendered depiction of a handsome man in period costume—burgundy pillbox cap, matching vest over white shirt, black pants—welcomed me and indicated that my snack was ready, nodding down toward a kind of airlock portal. I opened the small, clear door at my end and took the bag of warm popcorn and the beverage carton. "Right that way, sir," said the man on the screen, indicating the very obvious entrance to the theatre itself.

Reddish half-light filled the auditorium, just enough for me to make out perhaps twenty rows of seats, nearly all empty but for five or six other patrons—one couple and the rest singles, like me. On the floor a strip of faint lighting traced my route like the aisle of an airplane. I descended a third of the way down and sidestepped my way into the middle seat. It was broken, sagging under my weight until roughly perpendicular to the sloped floor. The one next to it on the far side was solid, so I moved there, draping my damp coat on the broken chair.

Vertigo was a happy accident. I'd have been in that seat on that night no matter what was playing in that indie cinema. Anything would have done, really—anything old and big and bright, and offering much-needed escape. But when, earlier that day, I looked up the listings to see what the Orpheum had on offer and saw the entry—Vertigo *(1958) (con) (nonAI); dir. Hitchcock. Stewart and Novak. Newly restored transfer. 7:00 & 9:30. Closes Thurs 4/11*—it seemed to me the inevitable end point of several strands of energy. I knew instantly what shape my evening would take. I'd settle solo into a worn velvet seat, let the lights go down, and lose myself in the film. The thought of watching a ninety-four-year-old movie was dazzling. All its actors gone, the director, the grips, the dressers. The world it depicted, completely gone. How was it ever even possible?

I am a defender of twenty-first-century cinema. I believe great, timeless work has been done. I'd point to something like Bunny Yamagashi's masterpiece *The Mushroom Imagines*, filmed entirely on the backup camera of a 2026

Toyota bZ4X. But if pushed I'll admit that none of it will ever be as integral, as in the midst of it all, as movies were in the last century.

So I resolved that for my forty-second birthday I'd take myself out to see a picture, and when it was over I'd head a little further down the block for a drink at the Lute and Loon, dark and cloistered, and still licensed to sell actual cold, wet beer.

The popcorn was undersalted. Good for my heart, but not what I'd hoped for. I unscrewed the lid of the cardboard water carton and drank. The lights dimmed, and just as I was turning off my watch's notifications, the picture began.

❧

Vertigo opened, as it always has, into a great whirl of Bernard Herrmann's score, and a VistaVision close-up on a woman's face. I don't know who she was. Her lips first, where James Stewart's name appears, and then a pan upward to her eyes. Kim Novak. Then we shift over to her right eye, where Hitchcock's name materializes. Eyelashes and the gleam of bright studio lighting reflected in convexity. The eye fills the entire screen, which is suddenly bathed in red. The title appears. We are uncomfortably close. We are at the level of obsession—twentieth-century obsession, the lens trained on a woman whose permission is not sought.

Saul Bass's abstractions follow, concentrics, whorls.

And then the foot chase across San Francisco rooftops, the perpetrator of an unnamed crime, the uniformed cop, and Scottie Ferguson—Stewart—bringing up the rear. The cop falls to his death trying to help Scottie, who is hanging from a gutter, paralyzed by the titular affliction.

Someone in the front of the theatre chuckled as the cop fell, spiralling downward into an alley—the effect was admittedly dated, unrealistic.

Is everything that follows a death dream? The theory is popular. It suggests that Scottie fell, too, and that what we're shown in the ensuing two-plus hours is a swirl of memory, projection, supposition, and unrelated nonsense. I don't believe a bit of it, and I hope it's completely incorrect. It feels like a surface reading, too shallow for Hitchcock.

Retired, Scottie is pulled into a scheme by an old friend, Elster, to watch his wife, Madeleine, whom he says has been acting strangely. That's our set-up: a man monitoring a woman's behaviour.

And then Scottie sees Madeleine for the first time, in a restaurant, as orchestrated by Elster. The scene is marvellous. I'd seen the movie many times, and this scene had always bowled me over. The saturated colour, reds, Madeleine's green dress, so rich it seems to be photosynthetic. As she leaves with Elster, moving right past Scottie, she is captured in stunning profile against a pulsating red backdrop.

She moves out of frame—and out of the restaurant—but not before walking past a full-length mirror. A woman and a reflection of a woman. Hitchcock is obsessed with showing us Kim Novak in reflections.

Scottie follows Madeleine, clearly falling in love with her, despite or because of her strange behaviour. She buys flowers, visits a grave, an art museum, stares at the painting of Carlotta, reputedly Madeleine's great-grandmother.

Madeleine walks the seawall beneath the Golden Gate Bridge before throwing herself into the bay, whereupon Scottie rescues her, thereby binding himself to her, their lives locked together until some awful conclusion.

Scottie eventually witnesses Madeleine's ostensible death, a fall from the mission bell tower, where he could not follow her because of his fear of heights. This being Hitchcock, there is deception involved, and conspiracy. But Scottie believes he has watched the woman he loves leaping to her death, a death he could have prevented were it not for his shortcoming, and so he is destroyed, institutionalized.

Upon his release he encounters another woman uncannily similar in appearance, though altogether different in bearing. This is Novak's achievement, breathing life into both guises. But Scottie pursues this Judy furiously, and once he has her, he begins a campaign to complete her transformation into Madeleine. There is such terrific violence in his insistence that Judy get the right suit, identical to that which Madeleine wore the day she died—Madeleine, into whose image Judy must configure herself if she is to have Scottie's love. The clothing, the shoes, the colour of her hair. *Judy, please, it can't matter to you*, he says. Relenting, Judy asks, *If I let you change me, will that do it? If I do what you tell me, will you love me?*

Scottie's terrible desire is twofold: to bring back the object of his obsession, and to undo the death he believes he caused, thereby absolving himself.

And when Judy's transformation into Madeleine is at last revealed in gauzy green light, Scottie, who, to his credit, seems to understand how aggressive and ugly his compulsion is, finds himself caught in the memory of the bell tower, while Judy, now Madeleine, falls limp in his arms, for he has murdered Judy. And in transforming this woman into an idealized thing, beautiful but bereft of life, he sees that he has robbed himself of an authentic connection. But he can't help himself. Like the title sequence tells us unambiguously: it's in the gaze, and the gaze is disorienting.

They make their way to the very same bell tower, because like all narratives this one progresses deathward.

Keep me safe, Judy implores Scottie, minutes before the end.

It's too late, he says, but he goes in for one last kiss anyway. Judy is startled, and falls, and the bell tolls. Scottie stands on the very lip of the tower, peering down to a body we never see; he is no longer afraid of heights, or no longer afraid of his own death, understanding that though he has at last achieved self-improvement there is no one left for him to share it with.

And this: despite all our desire to return to the past, there is no repeating it, not really—and to immerse yourself in it risks death, be it psychic or physical.

The lights rose and I sat bewildered, a little resentful of suddenly finding myself back in this concrete world. I put on my coat, visited the washroom, and stood studying a poster for the movie I'd just seen, though it couldn't tell me anything I didn't already know. Then, seeing no way to delay it any longer, I went outside.

The rain was still falling, heavily and loudly. I walked west, the water forming a curtain in front of my eyes. There were few people, but a lot was happening. Autonomous delivery carts ferrying food and goods zipped by on the sidewalk, some dispatched from delivery trucks parked curbside. Sirens wailed distantly overhead, more than was typical, which suggested to me weather-related mayhem. A massive air scrubber drone hovered over Queen just to the east, slowly pivoting, its dozens of lights flashing, water cascading off its sides in sheets.

In the wake of experiencing *Vertigo* again, there rang inside me the idea of solitariness equalling loneliness—of moving about in the world with the sense that there is only one person who can rescue you, one person with whom you are matched, and thereby bound, and if you fail in your mission to find that person you are simply alone.

There were moments when I believed that myself—in those moments, the city was a very lonely place for me, because I suspected that if such a narrow definition of love had any validity, the person I was supposed to have found almost certainly did not live in Toronto. They lived wherever Rhonda had wound up, or in Thunder Bay, where Nicole had eventually settled.

But those were fleeting thoughts, because my life was full. Simple, but full. It might be true that Rhonda had been my truest match, but at twenty-two I could not envision a life with her, and in my forties I still couldn't. Matching doesn't yoke you to a person. It means you encountered someone significant, and your life is richer for it.

And Nicole remained in my life, but as a friend, a regular correspondent. She'd met a geologist named Will, fallen in love, and together with Kaitlyn they'd moved to Thunder Bay, where they still remained. I'd been there, slept in their guest room, eaten with them. And Kaitlyn, grown now, astonishingly, studied environmental science at U of T. It was their final year there. From time to time we'd meet for coffee, and they'd tell me about their life, about their mother. I think I felt toward them the way someone who'd chosen to have a family might feel about their own child.

And I still had my mother, who I spoke to a couple of times a week, and who was still capable of travel. She would come and visit me in the city, and we might go to a show, or just have dinner somewhere nice. On the tentpole holidays, I still made my way to Peterborough to stay in her old house and celebrate with her.

With all of this, I was full. My life had a pleasingly rounded shape to it. Living alone, I had discovered, didn't have to mean loneliness.

A couple of blocks on from the Orpheum, I came to the door of the Lute and Loon and pushed inside. I stomped the rain from my boots, unzipped my coat, and sat at a small table. The menu screen turned toward me and lit up. I tapped in an order for a stout and paid. In a moment a harried look-ing man, about university age, popped in through a door and placed the pint on my table without a word. "Thanks," I said to his back as he went back through the same door. The first sip was velvety and smooth. Its cream clung to my upper lip until I licked it off with the tip of my tongue.

A man who'd been sitting at the bar talking to a chatbot projection walked by on his way to the washroom, a little short, with thinning dark hair. He smiled timidly, and did so again when he returned a few moments later. I was sip-ping slowly—I didn't need to be anywhere anytime soon.

The man sat back down at the bar, but instead of taking back up with the bot he kept his body open to the rest of the small room. Three other tables were occupied by couples or small groups, and there were three or four more empty tables. A screen in the corner mutely displayed a scroll of news headlines, weather updates, sports scores, and cur-rency valuations. Washy, streaky light came in through the large window. Another streetcar slid almost noiselessly by, its flanks flashing images of gorgeous young people wearing the season's fashionable long coats, dancing.

The man at the bar, apparently bored with the AI's conversation (they can get a bit repetitive), looked about and settled his eyes on me, which I only knew because I'd been watching him. I don't know why, except that he was the only other solo person in the room. The unwritten rule demanded that I be aware of his actions.

"How are you doing?" he asked with a trace of a Southern accent. It seemed safe to assume that he was an American refugee.

"I'm okay. Yeah. How are you?"

"It's dry in here and they have beer, so I'm great."

"I'll drink to that," I said.

"Let's drink together," he said. "I'm Dean." He stood, picked up his glass, and moved toward me.

"Gabe," I said.

"Gabe. Good to meet you." He indicated with his eyes the empty chair across from me and said, "Mind?"

"No," I said, thinking we'd speak for a few minutes while I finished my beer, at which point I'd excuse myself. Nothing too strenuous.

"So what do you do?" he asked.

"Sales. I sell intermodal containers converted into compact homes, very basic but livable." He remained silent, and so I felt compelled to continue, though I'd already said more than I was comfortable saying. "Emergency housing. Disasters, conflicts. We deal in bulk orders from governments and NGOs."

"You're an activist."

"No, we don't give them away. I make a living. I do it all from home. A workstation below a tiny window, in a little warren. I have a small apartment. It's monastic. I'm two paces from my kitchen. I can open the fridge without standing up."

"So you're a profiteer," he said, smiling. I didn't believe the comment was meant maliciously. It was a joke.

"I have a job. What about you?"

"Used to work in the insurance world." He pronounced it *in*-surance, but however it was pronounced, the word had become shorthand for hardship since the economic convulsion of the 2030s had disrupted, then strained, then caused the collapse of the industry. Dean rolled his eyes in a gesture of *What was I thinking?*

"Oof, that's rough," I said.

"Yeah, well. That's life. We lick our wounds, move on. You insured?"

The question was not apolitical. He was asking if I had money—enough of it to be a little more than comfortable, enough to afford what had become a luxury for most people. I had wound up on the privileged end of the new caste system, but I liked to think I was not blind to the unfairness of the situation. Nor was I above participating in the grey economy, which generally required a willingness to keep silent about the status of a particular person or business— i.e., insured or uninsured. This was a tacit agreement—that is, to keep society moving while recognizing that one may find oneself in a situation where one assumes full liability and responsibility, no matter what has happened to person or property, or who or what might be practically or morally responsible. It was the only way things like, for example, a rundown conventional indie theatre could still operate.

"Home and health," I said.

"Auto?"

"Don't have one. I prefer trains anyway."

"I love cars," he said. "That makes me a bad person, I expect. But driving," he said, and closed his eyes for a second, lost in the memory of a hairpin turn, or a flat, open road. "People talk about disasters, and there shouldn't be so much money involved, and how can you reduce it like that. But it was the best possible system. How else do you deal with it?" He lifted his glass, paused a moment, took a sip. "I came up working for an older guy who told me Hurricane Andrew changed everything." Here he paused again and eyed me to see if the reference meant anything to me. When I said nothing, he continued. "That was 1992. Something like sixteen billion in damage, quadruple what anyone had ever seen. After that, insurance was on borrowed time."

"Right."

"Humans have managed to make superstorms. That's all on us. The scale means it isn't, *Oh, I'm your neighbour, I can help you.* Premiums go up, up, up, no stopping them. There's no ceiling. Whole communities gone. States. Governments all strapped. There's no money coming in. Whole thing falls apart."

"Florida," I said.

"Right. Louisiana. The people who used to pay for all this can't absorb it. The old model doesn't work. Not enough money to move around."

I was only partially following him and assumed Dean had had a few more beers than I had. I was also vaguely aware that there might be something else at work in this conversation, something subterranean. It wasn't mean-spirited—I got a good feeling from him. He was kind and well-meaning, if a bit lost or without certainty.

"So how do people get around that?" I asked. "Or has that ship sailed?"

"I mean, there are still willing parties. Those happy to underwrite things."

"Are you offering me wildcat insurance?"

"No, no, god, no." He chuckled. "I'm out of all that. I just remain interested in the idea of it. Like, what does risk cost? How do people manage their exposure to risk? It's such a human thing, to find a way to make danger a bit safer, and then to turn that into a business."

"And then that business falls apart because humans have fucked everything up."

"Everything," he said.

He smiled at me. Looked me in the eye for the first time, which made me squirm. His were warm and brown, like his hair, which had receded at the temples, leaving at the top of his forehead a rounded peninsula that would soon be an island. The dark skin of his face was creased in such a way that made smiling seem his natural resting expression. Worn jeans and a plain black T-shirt. Dean felt like a good soul.

"So, what do you do now?" I asked.

"I teach economics part-time," he said. "I need something else, but I haven't located it just yet. A second income stream."

"I wish you luck finding it."

"Thanks. I'll be fine."

"Where are you from?"

"Baltimore, Maryland."

"I thought I heard a bit of a—"

"Yeah, I can't hide it. Ran up here like all the others."

"No, you shouldn't hide it. No reason for that."

"If I thought there was a chance things could be fixed I'd go home. But. It was already bad, then the Big One knocked the whole country backwards."

We were only three years removed from the monumental Cascadia Subduction slippage event and the subsequent inundation of most of America's Pacific waterfront, and the West Coast hadn't yet recovered. Whole area codes from Puget Sound to Southern California still hadn't re-established basic infrastructure, and it was beginning to dawn on the populace that many never would.

"Did you lose anyone?"

"No one in my immediate circle. But everybody knows somebody."

"Sure. What a mess. I'm sorry."

"Not your fault," he said, and smiled, then raised his glass and drained it. "You need another?"

"I wouldn't say no," I said, surprising myself with my willingness to pass the rest of the evening with a stranger.

Dean said, "Menu," and the screen lit up, turned to him. He tapped in an order, and the same student came back with two more glasses before disappearing again. Dean and I raised the new pints and clinked them, and he said, "Here's to chance encounters with new people."

"Yeah," I said, "I'll drink to that."

"So you know where I'm from. What about you?"

"Not far from here."

"A local."

"I wouldn't say that, really. But I've been in the city long enough that it feels like where I'm from."

"A man of mystery," Dean said, and then smiled.

A lull fell over the table, a brief hush. He rolled his glass back and forth in his hands, staring at it.

"Listen," he said, his shoulders hunched, never looking away from the glass in his hands. "Would you be interested in coming home with me?"

"Oh," I said. "No. Thank you, but no."

"Okay, well, shit," he said, clearly humiliated. "Can't blame me for trying."

"Of course not. And really, thank you. But I don't. I mean, I wish."

"No, it's okay," he said, sitting back, waving his hands.

"Sorry."

"It's okay."

"Really, Dean."

"I've been sitting here trying to figure out, you know, how to get to that, but I never stopped to ask myself if you'd, you know. If you."

"I'm not, I don't, but I'm glad you asked. Is that weird to say? I am."

"That counts for something. I just wanted to. With you. And I thought."

"I appreciate that, Dean. Thank you. Sincerely."

"I should go."

"No," I said. "Let's finish our drinks. Come on. There's no reason to run off."

So we did. Dean finished his beer and then ordered a soda. I sipped my second stout slowly, and we talked some more, though it was clear that something had left our conversation—the edge it had held, the mystery I'd felt about what Dean's underlying intent might have been. I knew now, so the intrigue was gone.

When we were both done our drinks, he put on a long coat and we stood looking at one another, saying goodbye. He laughed a bit, which made me feel good about how we were leaving things. Then he scurried out into the rain, turned west, and was gone.

I made a trip to the washroom before putting on my own coat, mostly because I did not see that any good would come from moving our goodbye out to the deluged sidewalk. But then I too was out. I turned east and shouldered my way through the rain until I stood in the small lobby of my building, where I lowered my hood and confronted my own reflection in the stainless-steel elevator door.

I would never see Dean again. I would not turn back into the night, into the rain and the dark, to hunt him down. I was nearly back home, and that small, warm, softly lit space beckoned me. My cat, my books.

But I wanted to thank Dean for the way I was feeling. It was something I have felt infrequently, though memorably: a sense of being right up against the very trembling face of things. I had walked home shaking, pushed into some higher state by the extreme weather, by the realization that I needn't have answers to all my questions, and by the fact that I'd been desired, even cursorily, or as a matter of convenience. I was momentarily held in the regard of another. Seen.

I was too full of life—from feeling those feelings, being in those feelings, being outside and looking at those feelings. Of magnanimity. Of having forged and been forged by connections of chance and choosing. Of being here, pulse in my throat, rain on my face. For now, if not for long: *here.*

IV

I'M FIFTY YEARS OLD NOW, still living in Toronto, down-townish. Mom remains in Peterborough, but on the fourth floor of the Empress Gardens—in an *independent living* room, the term engineered to suggest that supervision is unobtrusive but attentive. Meals are provided, for example, but when it comes to taking her meds each day she's on her own. Every month, when the statement pops up, I worry that what it really means is that she's alone and unseen. But when I call for updates, the staff seem to know her, and some of them even appear to care about her. This isn't difficult to imagine, as even in the fog her mind is producing, amid the neural misfirings and dropped connections, she retains much of her personality, which has always been a little bit irresistible.

Her footing is firm when she's talking about the past. They always remind me of that when I call or visit, presenting it as a helpful tip, a winning strategy for dealing with a patient well into cognitive decline. Ask her about something from twenty or thirty or fifty years ago and she's sharp as a tack. Keep her there. The remembering returns her to who she was, and she carries that back into the present as a scrap of confidence, even if only briefly.

It's been too long since I came to see her, so with most of a weekend free I've taken the maglev up for a quick visit. Having already checked into my hotel just around the corner from the Empress, I walk the short distance on the dark street with my head down, my shoulders drawn up to my ears. In these moments, I fear nothing more than recognition. Even this brief exposure to the geography of my upbringing seems complicated and measurably more tiring for the mental energy of processing each face I pass and parsing it for a connection. Do I know them? Do I know their family? Do they know me and mine? Will I be required to stop and remember and fill years of absence with awkward and insincere conversation? But for the entirety of the journey—a block and a half, on an underlit sidewalk—I encounter no one. A small blessing.

At the two-stage entrance's outside door, the embedded tech in my earlobe receives the building's air report, the measurement of airborne particulates and pathogens present. My Lobe whispers to me that all are within acceptable limits, so I leave my respirator stowed safely in my coat pocket as I enter the glassy cube. The first door seals shut behind me; there is a palpitation, a pulse in air pressure, and then the second door opens in front of me.

A woman stands behind the desk in the lobby. "Hi," she says to me. "How are we doing?"

"Really good, thanks."

"Oh, good," she says, "and how can I help you today?"

I think I might recognize her voice as one I have spoken to earlier by Lobe, but I can't be sure. I make out her lapel-pinned ID as I near the desk. It reads *Dina*. Did I speak to a Dina? My inability to remember is a small indictment upon me.

"I think we spoke earlier," I venture. "I'm here to see Kat Reynolds."

"Oh, sure we did, hi, okay." Dina is in her mid to late twenties, dark haired, in casual clothing I wouldn't quite call medical scrubs, with neon running shoes. A Lobe booster, helpful when working inside a building like this all day, is visible when she tucks her hair over her ear. "Do you want me to call up to your mom's room in case she's indisposed?"

"No, I don't think that's necessary."

"Does she know you're coming today?"

"I've told her, but I doubt she remembers."

"Of course," Dina says, which I take to mean that she's familiar with the particulars of my mother's condition.

It's just as likely that so many people housed in the Empress Gardens' nine-storey independent living tower are in similar straits that it takes only a word or two for Dina to understand what's alluded to when the subject of memory arises. How many, and how often, I wonder, are residents moved from independent living to the adjacent fully staffed assisted living wing, with its twenty-four-hour nursing and in-house medical suite? In my experience the two related facilities exist almost exclusive of one another, and I expect this is done for the peace of mind of residents of the tower, as well as their families, who don't want to think of their loved ones being temporarily warehoused, waiting to be shipped to the hospital-like setting of the assisted living wing, itself just a waystation on the path to aquamation.

"Enjoy your visit," says Dina, with an authentic-seeming cheeriness. "She'll be thrilled to see you."

❥

The obverse to all that is good, the blight on what is otherwise a lovely surface, is this: my extreme trepidation at returning to Peterborough—not because of what my father did, and not because Mom failed to shelter me, but because as she continues to slip, I don't know from one visit to the next what I will find when I come here. It's become my habit to steel myself for something unpleasant. She may forget who I am. She may think I'm someone I'm not. I once found her alone in her room, legs bare, with a sweater tied around her waist. I later found her pants stuffed in a cabinet.

My trepidation breeds guilt. Shouldn't a son always be pleased to see his mother? Shouldn't he leap at each opportunity to spend time with her, his best friend, his protector, provider; the one who dreamed him into being and breathed life into his dreams?

I've read all the literature, and the prevailing wisdom is that I should look upon her disease as a new chance to come to know her, as a natural and interesting shift in her identity and in my relationship with her. But that's complete bullshit. My mother is disappearing before my eyes, leaving only a shell, which will itself diminish and wither and then die, and it is all awful to witness.

I am afraid. Afraid for her, and afraid for me, because I have known for two years now that I have a matched set of the APOE4 gene, one from Mom, one from Dad, which in tandem form the outline of a bullet I almost certainly won't dodge, though I have been preapproved for mesenchymal stem cell therapy, which might forestall the worst of it.

◆

The lift is an unmirrored box with thick brown carpeting and fake wood panelling. The lighting, screaming from chintzy faux antique sconces, should be warm and natural seeming, but is instead harsh and thin. It attacks the pain receptors behind my eyes.

The lift, having made contact with my Lobe and established my preferred language, asks in standard American English, "Floor?"

"Four, please and thank you," I say. I tell myself continually that I needn't be polite to bots, but I can't seem to shake the habit. It's a cut corner, a small act of relaxation practised several times a day—instead of trying to determine which of the many voices I hear are human and which are artificial, I treat them all kindly and thereby, I hope, avoid offending people. I've been chided for this. Kaitlyn ribs me; they say I'm trying to curry the machines' favour before the inevitable takeover.

"Yes, of course," says the lift as its doors quietly slide shut.

The doors part a moment later to reveal matching decor: similar panelling lines the walls, the same sconces, the same too-bright light, and carpet in a complementary tone. The overly cool air smells acridly of whatever solution the scurrying machines use to disinfect the rug. It hits the back of my throat with twin suggestions of floral and chemical.

I walk past six or seven apartment doors on the way to Mom's. Half of them are open, revealing people sitting in front of screens, their volume up to nearly unreasonable levels—the elderly, by and large, have not flocked to embedded tech the way the rest of us have—so that as I pass each I catch snippets of dialogue, music, someone talking to a videowall of squirming grandchildren who answer yes to a question in unison.

Mom's door is shut but unlocked. I knock, wait a beat, then enter. Her room is small and neat, with a bed, a table with two chairs, a single bookshelf with a few titles she hasn't touched in years, photo frames, mementoes. The bathroom has a walk-in tub. There is a kitchenette with an induction range, but that's unplugged because none of us are confident she won't burn the place down. There's a kettle, and she drinks tea all day long. There is a loveseat for visitors, and an armchair facing a large window. The window looks out over a rooftop garden on the building opposite, and beyond that a sliver of a view of the Otonabee River, or occasionally its dry bed, and still further East City, still mostly residential, but its urban canopy just a fraction of what it used to be. She spends much of her time sitting in that chair, and the staff tell me they often find her dozing there, as she is doing now. Night has fallen on this early evening in mid-November, and there is nothing to see through the glass but a few lights. Mostly it shows a pallid reflection of the room. I can see myself framed in the open door I've just come through.

"Hi, Mom," I say at a volume intended to wake without startling.

She perks up, snaps her face toward me, and says, "Oh, Artie, jeez. Where were you?"

"It's Gabe. How are you today, Mom?"

"Oh, Gabe. Right. Shit."

"Just me, Mom."

She turns away from me and looks back at the window, at the side of her own emaciated face. She looks to have lost weight since I was last here in August.

"This can't last forever," she says.

"What can't, Mom?"

"This darkness," she says, waving a shaky hand at the window and the night beyond it.

She's gesturing down toward my streets, or what used to be my streets, where I ran freely before I achieved exit velocity and willed myself out of Peterborough.

Like most people with a hometown, I have conflicting emotions about the place now. I should have all of this settled by now. Certainly for most of my adult life I assumed that there would eventually come a time, a point of transition, when I would have sorted out my emotions and thoughts—when the accumulation of experience ceased and I tipped into the back half of life, characterized by drawing on that experience to make confident decisions, to know my own mind, and to be at peace with my past, the people and places that shaped me. Freeing me to move forward, right on up to the end. But no. Emphatically: no.

This tension is the result of all the memories I have of the place. Most of them are good, though of course not all. But Mom has stayed here all this time, and she and I lived here together until I was nineteen. Grade school, high school, friends, my first job—a part-time gig driving the kiddie train at the Riverview Park and Zoo—my first beer, my first kiss. I played basketball and learned to drive. Storytime with drag queens at the library. Free summertime concerts in Del Crary Park. Christmases when, unbeknownst to me, Mom battled financial challenges and tough schedules to make something special happen. The warm glow of windows on snowy nights, when we still regularly got snow.

Mom had embedded herself in the community, burrowed in deep. She exhibited yarn art in local galleries. She volunteered, doing annual cleanups along Jackson Creek. She canvassed for a friend who ran for city council. She acted in amateur theatre, and with a troupe of other enthusiastic locals, she dressed in period costume and roamed Little Lake Cemetery each November, telling the stories of locals lost in the wars. She hosted big holiday gatherings full of friends. Sometimes she cooked everything; sometimes everyone pitched in, potluck style. It depended on her financial particulars at the time. Most of her jobs were part-time or fleeting, in the retail and service sectors, though she twice tried to return to school to train, once for nursing, once for heat pump maintenance and installation. In both instances the money ran out quickly, and she was back serving coffee or drinks, or ringing up purchases. She eventually got a foot in the door at the Costco on the south end of town near the highway, evenings and weekends at first while she held on to daytime shifts at a coffee shop, and after a year of that she started pulling full-time hours, which came with benefits. It was a retail job in a giant sterile cube, about as appealing as an airplane hangar, but it paid a decent hourly wage and they treated her well. *The people are good*, she'd tell me. She made a friend, Jen—a co-worker of the same age—and they became close, Jen soon a fixture at all those gatherings, birthdays, camping weekends.

Mom stayed at Costco for fourteen years. She was able to move out of rentals and into a two-bedroom wartime Victory House just north of downtown, locked into a good mortgage just before interest rates went screwy. The house, on Glengarry Avenue, had been updated once or twice but it showed its age through sticking windows and doors that scraped grooves into its original pine floors. She loved that house, on a street of identical houses, in a neighbourhood of identical streets, though the trees had matured and differentiated, and the houses had been painted, renovated, reshingled, converted to solar, their gardens planted, turned over, replanted, in the ninety plus years since it had all been built. It was a sweet neighbourhood, and in it she became a fixture, a sweet old woman, until she began to periodically forget what town she lived in, or what had happened to her husband, or that she'd had a son.

My telling of all this isn't fair to her. This is her story to tell, to change, or to conceal. I've pushed her aside and made her an accessory to my story. There are a lot of factors at play there, my selfishness being only one. The other inescapable one is her memory—the floor has fallen out from beneath her. The best she can do now is to assemble isolated memories, amassed but unconnected, pearls on a string. When she is done there are too many pearls missing for the string to be considered a necklace.

When I visited her at home three Easters ago, I stood in the doorway smiling, having said hi, and trying not to get too alarmed by her weight loss. I looked at her face, her rehearsed smile, and saw that she was trying to place me, her eyes suddenly slowly turning icons as she waited for a memory to load. After that, I quickly got her name on a wait-list for a room, and when her spot came up that fall I rushed back from Toronto to help her downsize in a hurry. I got to work boxing and labelling and listing items for sale or giveaway on various buy-and-sell apps, and it was clear most mornings she had no idea what was happening or where she would soon find herself.

In the end, I must shamefully admit, on the day I moved her from her own house to the small apartment up here on the fourth floor, I only told her that I was taking her to lunch. I put her in the passenger seat of her own car and drove downtown to the Empress, and we walked in, me nodding to the staff members whom I'd already enlisted in this plan, and into the dining room. I sat Mom down, and she was served a plate of peas, potatoes, and cod fillet with a white sauce. I remember the meal looking very sad and forlorn on her flat white plate. I excused myself to run up to her room and make the final preparations, arranging her most precious items, folding back her comforter the way she liked. Then I scurried back down to the dining room and made a show of taking my mother "back" to her room, as though she'd always been there, as though I hadn't been lying to her, stealing her independent life from under her. But I told myself it was for her own good, and I was doing it with everyone's approval—the staff and Mom's doctor, even Jen, who still visits her two or three times a week for tea.

Everyone entitled to an opinion told me it was the best thing for Mom. Why, then, do I still feel monumentally shitty for having done it? Why, if left unmedicated, does this memory have the power to rob me of sleep?

❧

"How was dinner?" I ask.

When I called earlier, they told me she was in the common dining room enjoying chicken, hot from the bioreactor, and genuine steamed carrots. The aroma still lingers around her, almost exactly like my memories of the real thing. My stomach groans. I'm starving and have been all afternoon, but I'll grab something later, maybe at one of the spots within walking distance. Oh god, maybe fries. And beer. But then there's the risk of recognition again, and there is nothing on this Earth worse than drunken recognition. But I have thought of fries now and my brain will not let go of that. Neither will my stomach, whose protests are so loud that I think even Mom might have heard.

My mother turns her head to me, and there is a moment of total confusion in her eyes before my face clicks into its proper slot. "Dinner was good, honey," she says in a reas-suring tone, as though I'm the one in need of help. She is and always will be my mother, no matter her frailty, her deterioration. "It was fine."

I consider asking what was on the menu, already know-ing—it would be a kind of memory test—but I know perfectly well how she'd do, and I don't want to do that to either of us just now.

But then she surprises me. "Actually it was mush. I couldn't even tell what I was eating. Mush."

Her memory is sponge, but her wit and her ingenuity when it comes to concealing her memory loss are formida-ble. Every single interaction with her breaks my heart anew, but she also impresses me with that defiance.

"And did you eat?" she asks, picking up the thread, se-cretly grateful for the hints I have provided about what time of day it is, where she finds herself.

She was so magnificent. I was ten years old, and she held the falling sky aloft to allow me the room to live. She skated beautifully. Her dives into that green-black water were so clean and graceful.

"I did. Couldn't touch another bite. I just popped in to see what the fun was tonight. Are we going dancing? Where's the *party*, Mom? Is there a floating craps game you want to hit up? I'll get a car if you just tell me where it is."

She laughs until she starts to cough. "Oh, yeah, where's my sequined dress?"

"Too many late nights lately, huh? We'll stay in. What's your pleasure? Cards? Watch some TV? Listen to music?"

I'm keeping it light, edging around the abyss, because I'm not sure I have the energy to dive in tonight. I don't have the stamina for revelations. Keep it breezy.

"Oh," she says, looking concerned, "I don't know."

She tries to avoid situations where she'll have to be on her toes to obscure her slide, but if it weren't for those situations we'd have no situation together at all.

"Any jobs for me? Anything you need done?"

"Probably," she says, and I know I have appealed to the practical side of her that, while typically dormant, will never be totally lost. It's who she is below memory.

"Cleaning? Moving? Fixing? Breaking?"

She points a trembling right hand toward the closet door. Not her index finger, but her whole arthritic claw.

"I have some things in there I keep meaning to get rid of. Maybe you could help with that." She's improvised this problem, created it from scraps of memories of old closets filled with long-gone junk, but I'm happy to play along.

"Sure I can." I open the louvred doors and stare in at racks of clothes she hasn't worn in twenty years, boxes, files, bags, stacking totes. "Oh, hey, wow. Where to start?"

She stands and walks shakily toward me. It took me years to see her physical decline. In my mind's eye she is still perched on a rock in her polka-dot bathing suit, preparing to leap, to arc her strong body down through the air, to cleanly pierce the surface of the lake. But she has been thin and unsteady on her feet for a long time now, her back bent, hands quaking, the skin on her face falling. She's still in there, though. The light is dimmed but not extinguished.

"What have you got hidden in here, Mom?" I ask, turning to her. "Contraband? A body?"

She meets this with a look, her very particular way of pairing knit eyebrows with pursed lips that aims to devastate me, and that never fails to meet its target. "Just... stuff," she says after a moment.

On the top shelf there is a case I recognize, a small hard-shelled American Tourister valise that had been her mother's. It might once have been used as an overnight bag, but it's held photos for longer than I've been alive.

"Oh, wow, the old photo box."

"Oh, yes," she says, "that old thing."

"Let's take a look." I pull it down and carry it over to the loveseat.

"Oh, there's nothing in there," she says with the tone of a student walking into a test they suspect they won't pass. "Just junk."

"Family photos," I reply, squeezing the tabs that release the latch, "are not junk, Mom."

She sits down next to me as I open it. The case emits a faint mustiness, exposed as it is to the first light and fresh air it's known in many years, and there's also a note of chemical sourness. Its quilted and pleated grey satin interior shines with the memory of an age of luxury, or the facsimile of one. I'm trying to remember air travel. Small plastic cocktail glasses with toothpicks, swizzle sticks, napkins with airline logos printed on them, business suits, the sight of clouds from above. I'm pulling these things from memories of videos and books, not memories of memories.

Piled inside are photographs in various sizes and formats, dating from the 1930s until about the time of my birth, or rather a few months after, as the most recent photo I uncover has me in diapers on a blanket spread on grass, dappled sunlight and shade falling on me from a tree overhead, unseen in the picture. It's near the top of the stack, and I remember it clearly, having seen it at intervals throughout my life, from my early childhood until sometime in my early adulthood. I hold the glossy four-by-six in my hand, tilting it so that Mom can see it.

"That's at the house in East City, just off Hunter," she says. "You'd be less than a year old there. Dad was working at a restaurant about a block away, he'd walk to work. He was doing a lunch shift that day, so I had you alone. It was hot. A heat wave."

"What was that house like?" I ask, trying to get her to exercise an atrophied muscle. She can't remember precisely where she is at this very moment, or what she had for dinner, but she can tell me in granular detail about an unremarkable afternoon in 2011. This disease is strange and cruel.

"Oh, it wasn't nice. We rented that place for two years. There was a couple who lived upstairs, a bit older than us. Tina and, oh, jeez, what was his name?"

"But it had a yard?"

"Little one. Some grass, a couple of trees. You're under the apple tree there. We had chairs back there, a little barbecue. We'd sit back there if the bugs weren't too bad, have some beers. It wasn't such a bad place, I guess. Drafty. Monty was his name. Tina and Monty." This is among the longest string of words I've heard Mom put together in several years.

"East City? I bet if it was still light out you could see it from your window."

This jars her, grounds her in the moment, exposes her to the fact that she isn't really sure just where she is sitting. "Could be," she says noncommittally.

It's also possible—even likely—that the house in question was torn down years ago to make room for something newer and far more expensive. I'm old enough to remember when Peterborough was its own city, marooned somewhere between Toronto and cottage country. For years now, though, it's functioned as the eastern end of the Greater Toronto Area. Maglevs zip in and out at a constant rate.

That's how I got here today. Those with money and lacking patience summon air taxis at all hours, zooming them to lakeshore homes or downtown glass towers.

I plunge my hand back into the mess of photos and sift around, pull out at random a black-and-white print of six people in sun hats, summer dresses or pressed trousers, sitting on a blanket. "Who's in this picture?"

"That's your grandmother, the little girl there. Just a baby."

"Oh, my god. That bonnet. What year would this be?"

"She was born in '45, so that's about '46."

"Nineteen forty-six. Just after the war."

"That's right. And that's my grandparents, Hanna and Richard. This is Dominion Day, I'm pretty sure. Do they have flags?"

"I don't see any."

"Mum must've told me that, because I'm sure that's when it is." With her bony left index finger she points to a man in a white short-sleeved shirt, top button undone, a straw hat pushed back to reveal his forehead, squinting eyes, a big smile. "I don't know who that is. Might be Uncle Harold. Sure it is."

"Richard's brother. They look alike."

"Sure it is. He died a couple of years later. Drowned."

"Oh, god. You never told me that."

"He was a drunk. Took a long walk off a short dock."

"That's awful."

"Yup. But that"—she's pointing to the woman next to Harold in a floral-print dress and broad, long-ribboned sun hat—"would be Jeanine. Harold's Jeanine."

"Where'd she end up?"

"Well, Harold's dying was about the best thing that ever happened to her. Last I heard she was in Montreal. Married again. Don't know when she died."

"Where was this photo taken?"

"Ottawa, I'd guess. Don't know where."

"A park, looks like."

"Might be Major's Hill," she says, holding her hand out in space, placing the photo's patch of grass into its original space in relation to the surroundings. "Sure it is. You can see where the canal is. Sussex would be over here, and the Château behind. That's where it is."

"That's downtown?"

"Yeah, Parliament Hill is over here, across the canal. The Château. They built the American embassy here, the art gallery down there. We used to go to concerts there during the Tulip Festival."

"Who'd you see there?"

"Oh, nobody you'd have heard of. Punk, folk. I remember a ska show."

"Ska?"

"The things you've missed, my boy," she says mischievously, a flicker in her ageless eyes, a wry upturn of the corner of her mouth, exactly the same as when she'd pretend to have forgotten that it was Christmas Eve.

The next photo is of her in mirrored sunglasses, with a straw hat cocked rakishly over one eye, her hair wind wild, a tank top revealing smooth browned shoulders. She looks to be in her twenties, her features defined, skin perfect.

"Oh, god," she says. "That's at Cavendish. Your dad took that." There comes a long pause.

"You on vacation there?"

"We drove down, got a campsite, spent a week on the beach. Art got so sunburned the second day we had to buy a little beach shelter so he could stay out of the sun. That was a good week. We saved up and went out for a lobster dinner. God, it was so good. We played minigolf, went to the drive-in movies. Perfect weather."

"What year would that have been?"

"Before you were born. That's probably 2006, 2007? In there."

"So you're..."

"Twenty-five, twenty-six, something like that."

"You look so young."

"And so hot!" Laughter, unexpected by both of us, bursts out of her.

"Mother."

"Sorry! But I look good!" Her laughter becomes too much for her, so she leans back and coughs, wheezes. Tears come to the corners of her eyes.

Here are the hidden corridors, the early morning skating lessons, the dance still latent in her body, even now. All the things about her I will never know. How do we reconcile the people who raise us with who they were before we even existed? How can the person who gave you life remain a stranger? Everything I know about her pales in comparison to all that I don't. That was true of both of them. And even as they raised me they had a second life, a secret life, which they knew and lived, but which was kept from me. I don't say this with bitterness. We all do this—dodge and conceal, show different aspects of ourselves. I don't think we'd be full people if we didn't. We must believe we're more than one thing. Parent, partner, lover, friend, employee. But the mystery of my very human parents baffles me. It tantalizes and thrills and bloodies me.

"You do look amazing there," I say. "I see why Dad fell for you."

"Yeah," she says.

She stops laughing, grows a bit distant. I worry that I've done damage by mentioning Art.

"What am I going to do with all these?" she asks, indicating the case and all its photos.

"Just hold on to them."

"Maybe you should take them," she says. "Go through them, keep the good ones, throw out the rest."

"Mom, these are your memories. I don't want to get rid of them."

Her eyes begin to go a bit swimmy, and then I recognize the space opening up between us. She has receded into her fog just as suddenly as the photos brought her out of it.

"Why'd you bring these? I don't need them."

She may even have forgotten who she is speaking to. I might be her son, or my father, or hers. Every room she occupies is a room full of ghosts.

"No, they were in your closet, Mom."

Why does this always surprise me?

"Of course they were," she says, pretending she remembers the last several minutes. "Well, get rid of them. Just junk. More crap I don't need."

"Sure, Mom," I say, intending to do nothing of the sort, and knowing she won't remember telling me to get rid of them. I place the photos back in the American Tourister, shut its lid, and secure the silver clasp. Then I pick it up by the handle and carry it over to the closet, then place it on the floor next to the closet door. "I'll put it here so I remember to take it with me."

She's sitting back in her chair with her eyes closed and doesn't reply to me. For a second I think she might be asleep.

"That okay, Mom?"

"Sure, yes, that's good," she says without opening her eyes.

"Why don't I leave you be," I say, sensing her fatigue, or projecting my own. "You could use some rest."

"Will you be back?" she asks, suddenly alert and looking worried.

"Of course. I'll be by in the morning. Why don't we go out and get some breakfast? I saw a place near here that looked good."

Her eyes scan the room, rest on the window, but the darkness and the reflection of this room give her no information. "Oh, I don't know," she says. "We could just eat here."

I don't know if she means in her apartment or in the common dining room. I doubt she knows which she means, to be honest. In either case, my internal reaction is revulsion. I want to get her out of here, but I also know that the further I take her from what she knows, the more uneasy she'll feel.

"It's just on the corner, Mom. I think you'll like it."

I take a pen from a cup and a sticky note from a pad near her screen, and I write *BREAKFAST WITH GABE IN THE MORNING*, then place the note on the back of her door. I'll also tell the woman at the desk, who I hope will spread word among the staff so that if Mom misses my note and shows up in the dining room for breakfast someone might mention me to her. These little strategies feel close to deceptive, but I've also found them completely necessary.

"Why don't you get a good night's sleep, Mom, and I'll do the same. I'll see you at nine."

"Are you not staying here?"

"I have a hotel room. I didn't want to put you out."

"Oh, right," she says. "That's right."

"Are you okay to get ready for bed yourself?"

"Gabriel, I do it every night. I think I can handle it."

"Of course. Sorry, Mom." I move over and stand in front of her, bend down, and kiss the top of her head. Her grey hair feels like straw and smells like flowers. It's good to know she's still bathing daily. "Goodnight, Mom."

"Goodnight."

"Nine, okay? I'll be back at nine."

Outside, the night has turned sharply cold, with a stinging rain. An air-quality drone buzzes overhead, red light blinking on its belly as it turns sentiently. I watch it until it draws my attention to the vertical wind turbines on the Empress's roof, humming and corkscrewing away. They'll be quaint soon, like handset phones, or polar bears. The Danes are about to bring fusion online, and eventually we'll follow suit. It'll likely take the Americans a while to muster the capital in what affluent, secure pockets remain of their country, but they'll get there. We're mired in anticipatory jurisdictional squabbling, provinces and the feds locked in their eternal dance, but that stuff will get straightened out, and the need for hyperlocal solar and wind plants will dwindle. Skylines will be remade. Incentives will make new energy start-ups temporarily rich. One way or another our screens will remain lit.

I turn up the collar of my mushroom-leather coat and make for the hotel, but then remember that I need to eat, so instead of turning left on George Street, I cross, heading further west, and begin to hunt around to see what's closed since my last visit and what's popped up in its place.

It takes only a glance south down George to trigger memories as thick and real as life: a summer night when I was sixteen and drunk for the first time, witnessing an act of random, horrific violence. Directly across the street from the hotel, where there is now an upscale restaurant and a fitness studio, there was once a bar called the Delta. My friend Aston was in a band—they were called Velouria—and they were playing their first or second show ever there, opening for a more established band of university students called Sympathetic Eyes.

The Eyes had a devoted following of older kids, even some grad students, all of whom displayed a much greater level of sophistication than we thought possible. They made the fit of our ragged jeans and the wear and tear of our Chucks look childish, while their jeans and Chucks seemed both accidental and runway worthy. But we outnumbered them, which bolstered our confidence. By the end of the night I think we'd successfully usurped their power, made them feel as though they'd been on the fringes of our good time, and not vice versa.

Many of us had gotten drunk beforehand because we knew we weren't likely to be served at the bar, though that turned out not to be a problem. It was mid-June. Twenty or twenty-five of us showed up already buzzed, and kept ducking outside to smoke, getting higher and higher as the evening went on. The show was loud and sweaty and wonderful, and I felt grateful and loving toward a good number of people I sensed I wouldn't be seeing anymore, but toward whom I harboured no malice. The evening had a distinctly valedictory air. I hoped everyone would find happiness.

Knots of us stood curbside at closing time, having spilled out of the bar, now taking up a sizable portion of the road. Traffic was limited to rideshares, most of them hailed by young people who'd been kicked out of clubs and bars and were now jockeying for sex or companionship or violence. I was with Aston and Hunter, two of the band members, both good friends of mine. We were sharing a joint. There was a lot of laughing. My shirt clung to my chest and back. The night was hot and close.

Who were we? Self-aware primates pinned by an invisible force to the face of a planet on the brink of ecological collapse, beholden to blind systems of waning efficacy. We were at the portal to a future we couldn't even begin to envision. All the stock images looked like our parents' lives, not our own. We didn't know what we were capable of or what would be required; we only intuited the coming of great change, schismatic, sudden. We just wanted the chance to catch our breath. Who would survive? What would we do? We'd already lived through a worldwide plague. Some of us had suffered, some had lost people. The experience had marked us, though not visibly. In a lot of ways we were still locked down, forever the children we'd been the day before the great interregnum.

A man walked down the sidewalk alone, parting those of us clustered there. He was gruff and dishevelled, with a thick beard, a faded black tee, and a tatty plaid shirt falling off his shoulders. Hunter was speaking and had to step aside to let this man pass. Half a block further on, near another bar that was also disgorging its patrons, a second man, bald, in shorts and a tank top, with tattoos the length of both arms and all the way up his neck, stood swinging his arms.

I thought for a moment this second man—the bald, or shaved-headed, man—might be Max, my childhood best friend, whom I still spotted around town from time to time, though we no longer acknowledged one another. Max had, two or three years previous to this, begun a sudden slide into anti-government, anti-science, white nationalist extremism. I don't know what precipitated it, other than the usual pathogens: boredom, online radicalization, disinterest in the usual patterns, the common path. We'd all bathed in the same waters, but most of us showed some degree of immunity, while Max, for whatever reason, proved susceptible, and succumbed. He was a fixture around Peterborough for a few more years after that night, after which I lost track of him, and I have no idea what's happened to him since.

The first man moved to avoid bald Possibly Max, who seemed to be talking to himself, or to no one. When the bearded man was two or three steps further along, Possibly Max lunged after him and knocked him down, riding his back as he fell. Once they were both on the sidewalk, the bald man punched the gruff man so hard in the back of the head that his face bounced off the pavement. We all watched this. We all stopped talking, but we did not move. I won't speak for the others, but I was afraid of the bald man, whether or not he was Max. He stood up and continued to speak, and then to yell, at the first man, who lay unmoving on the ground. The bald man stood astride him, swung his arms wildly, muttering, and then walked off, turned up the next side street toward a darkened parking lot, and was gone.

I saw a few people inch toward the prone man, and others were on their phones, but most of us stood where we were, uneasy, unsure. With each passing second our inaction became complicity. Word filtered into the group that police or an ambulance or both were on the way, and most of us scattered. I slunk off into the dark morning and walked home alone, and I did not speak about what I'd seen, even when I read that the gruff man had suffered brain injuries and that the police would like to speak to anyone who might have seen anything. I did not want to admit to being there, young, drunk, high, a bystander who'd made no move to help. It all created a sketch of a person I did not want to admit to being in the eyes of those who loved me.

—

The wind—gusty, fricative, lulling in vowelish intervals, only to return with percussive clamour—pulls me back into the moment, and I stand at the corner of George and Charlotte looking for a sign. I pick one out: *Dawson's*, it says, where another bar used to be. I cross diagonally against the light, go inside, pass my hands under the UV cleaner, get an all-clear air reading, remove my coat and hang it on a hook, and take a seat at the bar. It's quiet—three or four other patrons on this side of the bar, more on the other in a big room with larger tables, a few dartboards, and a dozen enormous screens all showing the Leafs game. Over here the feeling is downtempo, quiet—the seductive comfort of inebriation.

The woman behind the bar says to me, "What can I get-cha?"

"Pint of Guinness and a menu?"

"You got it," she says. "Just need you to sign off."

She pushes a screen across the surface of the bar. It displays the standard waiver listing the risks of alcohol consumption. Its reader finds my right eye, and with it I'm able to steer a cursor down to a checkbox. I tell it my full name and the screen flashes green. The server says, "Great," slides the screen away, and reaches her left hand below the bar, pulls out a physical menu, relic of a past age, that she throws down in front of me while simultaneously using her right hand to produce a pint glass that she holds up to the

Guinness tap, while her newly freed left pulls the handle. She's got the motions down—a vet.

"Meeting someone?" she asks me.

"Nope, just me."

"You live in town?" she asks, which I take to mean *I've never seen you here before.*

She almost reads as genuinely curious, but it's safer to assume she's only being polite, filling our interaction the way she expects I, a customer, would like her to. Protecting her tip. On a busy night she would have already moved on. This definitely isn't flirtation, though a younger me would have read it as such, and wouldn't have minded—she's lovely. Thirty-ish, loose ponytail, wearing a vintage black Kurt Vile T-shirt and leggings. But these days, on the scale of interactions I'd rather not have, an inquisitive stranger is only a half spot above someone who knew me long ago. I'm just here for a plate of fried food, enough beer to make my mind a little bubbly, followed by an unsteady walk back to the hotel and a night of deep, dreamless sleep. I'm worn out.

"Just visiting my mom. She lives over at Empress Gardens."

"Oh, nice. How does she like it there?"

"Hard to know. I think she's fine."

"My friend's aunt is there. I hear it's great. Is your mom from Peterborough?"

"Yeah. Well, not originally. But yeah, we lived here for a long time."

"But you got out," she says, smiling knowingly.

"Eventually."

She nods but doesn't pursue. I think she's finally gleaned my shortness, which I hope doesn't come across as rudeness, just an unwillingness to share. I'm not looking for a back-and-forth that skims the details of our lives. Just another beer.

"Well, let me know what else I can get you," she says.

She is about to step away when I surprise us both by saying, "Shot of whisky?"

She stops comically, wheels around. "Sure. What kind?"

"Crown Royal, if you have it."

"Sure we do."

She stands a shot glass on the bar, spins on her toes, grabs from the backbar a bottle plastered with warning labels, and turns back to me all in one smooth loop. The golden liquid runs in an unbroken arc from the nozzle into the glass.

"Bottoms up," she says.

I nod, pick up the glass, and throw it back. The rye smokes all the way down my throat and into my stomach, where it finds most of the first Guinness and not much else. The meeting is somewhat antagonistic.

"Do you know what you want to eat?"

I haven't looked at the menu yet, not even to glance at it, but I'm seized by the re-emergence of an earlier impulse. "A huge plate of fries."

"Just fries"

"Please."

"Sure thing," she says, and begins tapping on a screen.

When she places the plate in front of me, I'm halfway through the second Guinness and beginning to feel a little light. The plate is fairly spilling over with shoestring French fries, steaming hot, their colour a deep golden brown, flecked with some manner of seasoning. At first sniff I'd say onion powder, paprika, garlic, and salt. A lot of salt. My stomach does a somersault of excitement. The warm steam bathes the skin of my face as I lean over. They smell like nothing less than heaven—baseball games and summer nights and hungover mornings, the smell of rain on hot pavement.

I remember a chip truck across the street from a repertory movie theatre in Ottawa where we used to go to watch Bogart double bills, a girlfriend and I. Where the operator, a small, round man with a moustache, would step down out of the cramped kitchen in the back to drain a large plastic bucket full of potatoes and water into a sewer grate as we stood eating fries out of a grease-spotted paper bag, stuffing the hot potato wedges into our mouths as fast as we could so we could retake our seats before the second feature began.

Or standing in line for a tray of fries at a hockey game in Peterborough, then moving to the condiment station, pressing the pump to draw crimson lines across the pile with ketchup, a heavy snow falling outside, the smell of the fries filling my nose as I walk back out to the seating bowl, the Zamboni still painting its broad strokes across the surface of the ice, the Petes a period away from beating Oshawa.

Or Dad and Mom standing at the kitchen counter with a new deep fryer, Dad cutting and soaking the white potatoes, Mom dropping them into the hot oil, laying the newly golden spears out on paper towels, then shaking salt and pepper over them.

The first bite tells me that the crunch on these fries is perfect, a crisp resistance before the white, steaming pillowy insides are revealed. The spices strike the right balance between spiky and savoury. They're too hot, but I'm too hungry to wait. I've got a decent mouthful before the woman can even ask if I want ketchup. I hold a finger up and chew quickly, swallow before I'm ready.

"Maybe some, please," I say.

She places a single-use biodegradable squeeze bottle in front of me. I break the seal and squirt a small circle's worth, then spiral the nozzle to build the pile up. This isn't about the right portion size, but about achieving an aesthetic ideal, a full, round dome of ketchup, bright red and ridiculously, deliciously salty. I put the bottle down and select a long, slender fry with which to prod the oversized dollop. The fry comes away with its garish red smear, a theatrical wound, and the image is so perfect it could be an advertiser's confection, projected in stunning resolution on the side of a thirty-storey building. I put the whole fry in my mouth and close my eyes. Has there ever been a more perfect food?

I finish the plate, shovelling every last nub and fragment into my maw, and the second Guinness, and then order another half plate of fries and a third beer. I feel an overwhelming sense of well-being, as though I've been dipped in a broth of warmth and affection. The world seems properly aligned, and I'm not in the least bit worried about Mom. Soon—later tonight, or tomorrow morning—I'll almost certainly regret these decisions, but these moments feel like a secret pocket, insulated, my actions divorced from daylight's shame and repercussions. Such moments, I have come to recognize, grow increasingly rare the older I get.

The room goes a bit blurry at the corners, and all the sounds begin to slur in my ear. Finally overcome with the fatigue that's been lurking all evening, I ask for the bill, then lower my glasses to pay by retscan, including an irresponsible tip for the talkative woman behind the bar. She smiles once more, says, "Have a good night," as I spill off the stool and totter toward the door.

Outside the rain has turned to sloppy flurries, and snowflakes land with splats on my face and neck, though I don't feel anything but a buzzy sort of pleasure as I float the short distance to the hotel. The lobby is bright and warm, the elevator comes quickly, and I fall asleep lying horizontal across the bed with my clothes on.

◆

Morning finds me a bit rudely. Daylight spills into the window where I failed to pull the heavy curtains last night before collapsing. My Lobe is issuing a soft alarm into my ear; it knew I'd made plans for nine, so it rouses me at eight. My window faces west over downtown Peterborough, but the sun is clanging off a facade of mirrored glass across George Street, some kind of cheap printed five-storey box that went up in a matter of weeks, retail at grade, residential above. My conventional glass window frames me standing ragged in yesterday's clothes, my mouth dry, my head echoing. I close the curtains and say, "Weather, please."

A forecast graphic appears in the corner of my vision, and my Lobe speaks: "Sunny and cool this morning, clouds moving in around noon. High of twelve degrees Celsius. You have breakfast at nine o'clock with your mother. Your TopSpeed Rail reservation is for 2:15 this afternoon. Would you like me to confirm the reservation?"

"Yes, please."

"Okay, I've confirmed your TopSpeed Rail reservation. Will you need transportation to the station? I can arrange that for you."

"Not yet."

"Okay, I'll ask again later."

I shower and dress, pack yesterday's clothes into my small bag and set it on the foot of the bed. I pick up my coat, which looks like I tried to hang it over the back of a chair near the door but it fell to the floor instead. I put it on and stand looking at myself in the mirror.

I'm very much my mother, her nose and eyes, but there's a lot of Arthur Ward in me, too. His mouth and cheeks, my thinning hair closer in colour to his brown than her auburn, though I'm grey on the sides now, and my beard, when I let it grow, is flecked with white. I'm much older than I ever saw him, but I expect my body aged like his would have—thickening at the shoulders and chest, trouble with stairs, the redness below the eyes after a few drinks.

With my bag on my shoulder, I take the elevator down and breeze through the lobby. On my way out the door, the Lobe in my ear coos, "Will you be checking out?" and I answer in the affirmative.

The air gleams in the morning sun. I round the corner. Beyond Empress Gardens there is a sandstone building with greenish accents that used to be offices belonging to the provincial government, but which has since been re-purposed as housing. The sun has just crested its modest peak and shines through the trees on the building's rooftop, spearing me in the eye at the very instant a cool gust meets my face. The net effect is to wake me up about as well as the cup of coffee—that I'm very much looking forward to having soon—otherwise would have.

Mom is a little agitated when I arrive. I was worried she might be. I should have dated my note, or been clearer; my failing to do so has her confused, worried she's missed me, sitting on the end of her bed twisting her hands dryly together.

"Good morning," I say as cheerily as I can.

"There you are. Did you bring Anna? Is she waiting in the car?"

"Did I bring who?"

A line of questioning arranges itself in my head, but I know Mom will shut down if I push it. What does she know, and when did she know it? I don't want to press her now, though. She's upset enough.

"No, no, it's me. Mom? It's Gabe."

"I know that," she says, pretending to be annoyed.

"How are you this morning?"

"Fine. How else would I be? I'm fine. But you're going to be mad when you see what I've done."

"What have you done?"

"I trampled your rhubarb," she says. I don't know who had a patch of rhubarb—her mother? Her grandmother? Someone other than me, anyway.

This might not be a good morning to leave her apartment. For a moment I consider calling off our breakfast date, but I need coffee and a light breakfast, and I would do anything to avoid eating the selections on offer in the unspeakably depressing dining room of the Empress Gardens. I'll risk it.

"It always grows back," I say, and this seems to reassure her. "Ready for breakfast?"

"I've eaten."

"No, you haven't, Mom. The staff told me you were waiting for me to pick you up and take you out."

A thousand questions descend on her poor mind, including *What staff? Who are you talking about?* It's possible I lack the strength to be as gentle as she needs me to be this morning.

"Really? Oh." She relents, admits defeat. Mom glances at me, and I see that she's scared. She can still deliver to me enormous packets of information—whole terabytes of it—with a single glance. She's terrified.

"It's okay, Mom. I'm taking you to breakfast, right around the corner. It'll be nice. Don't worry. I'm here."

"Where?"

"Little place on the corner," I repeat, placing my bag on the floor and walking over to help her up to her feet.

She raises her right elbow to me and I take it as she heaves herself up from the rock-hard mattress. She leans into me a bit, not for balance but as a sort of armless embrace, a way to thank me and tell me she is glad I am here.

We make for the door where her coat is hanging on a hook, but she stops suddenly and looks down at the American Tourister case sitting on the floor next to the closet.

"Where did that come from?" she asks. "Did I leave it out?"

"Nope, I did."

"Is it empty?"

"It's full of photos."

A few years ago, when all this was new to me—to both of us—I might have said, *We looked at them last night, don't you remember? You told me all about them, all the people in them and where they were taken and when. We had a lovely time, you and I, looking at old photographs and reminiscing.* But I know better now—she wouldn't believe me if I told her that, and no cajoling on my part can bring her back to a place of remembering.

"Well, it's in the way there," she says. "We should get rid of it, or put it away or something."

"We can do that when we get back," I say, and she nods.

Arms locked together, we walk slowly down the hall to the elevator, which delivers us into the lobby. Dina is at her post again. "Good morning, Ms. Reynolds," Dina says. "Is that handsome young man taking you on a date? I'm jealous!" She's overselling it, but part of Mom loves it, even as she waves her hand dismissively.

———

I hold Mom up as we walk slowly toward the diner I'd seen on the corner. We'll be seated at a table in the window, but Mom will complain about a draft, so we'll be reseated further back, where the light is dimmer. I'll read the menu to her, and she'll have scrambled eggs, no toast, and a cup of tea. She'll forget that I'm leaving today when I tell her, and I'll make vague but emphatic promises about returning for a visit soon. I'll ask her about the time when I was seven and I was stung by seven wasps. I'll ask her who taught her to fish. She'll take a slow, careful sip of tea and then tell me about the first cup she ever had, loaded with sugar, when she was nine. I will not ask her about Art, or Anna, and she won't offer anything.

When we're back in her apartment she'll say, *Tea races right through me*, as she has always said, and she'll duck into the washroom. While she's in there I'll tuck the case of photos back into her closet, and consider for a second that virtually all the photos that would ever be taken of her have already been taken, and try to guess how many more will be taken of me.

By lunchtime she'll be a bit tired so she'll sit in her chair by the window and doze off. I'll slip out, and shortly thereafter I'll be zipping back to Toronto on the maglev, hovering millimetres above the earth, smooth and silent, an audiobook whispering into my ear. I'll wonder to myself if Mom will remember that I was even there, or if the staff will tell her, and whether or not she'll believe them, their voices drowned out by the whispers of those dead and lost.

Eventually the Japanese medication she's on, which has held her relatively stable for about five years, will lose its purchase, and she'll begin to slip. She'll become more paranoid, more confused. She'll lash out at anyone around her, even me, possibly with physical violence, certainly with cutting words. She'll suspect people of all manner of nefarious doings. When she can guess who I am, she'll accuse me of stealing her money, or trying to poison her. She'll begin to forego all personal hygiene. In time she'll be unable to feed herself, which will trigger a move to the full-care wing of the Empress. Sometime after that there will be an event—a fall, a choking episode—that will put her in a hospital bed, and she'll never leave it. I'll rush to be by her side, and I hope—I pray—that I'll get there in time.

PART 3: DAUER

I TRULY DO BELIEVE we'd have left the cabin no matter what. That whether or not my father got it into his head to try to shoot a deer, Mom had already made up her mind. That she understood there were no good options before us, and that taking me back to Peterborough—and to school and masks and hand sanitizer and the company of people—was, for all its risks, the better of two poor choices. That keeping me there at the lake, with no outside contact and with a father who was tilting off balance, was the more dangerous option. That she owed it to me to make the hard choice.

We didn't leave right away. I don't think there was a conversation between them, really. My father must only have understood that Mom was taking me back, and that—given his fear of her formidable character, and the dynamics of their relationship—he was powerless to avoid it. And I have to guess that he knew, at some level, that he really was not capable of caring for me alone, certainly not under those circumstances. The nights were growing cooler, the darkness coming noticeably sooner. The cold would come. The snow would come, and the lake would freeze. We would be without water in an under-insulated cabin at the end of an unplowed road. That was no place for me. It was no place for him.

A few nights after he grazed the deer—with what I still believe was the only bullet he'd ever fired—Dad woke me. He climbed partway up my ladder and shook my foot, and when my eyes opened and I made him out by the shape of his head in the feeble light, he jerked his head toward the door, meaning *Come on.* Meaning *There's one more thing I want to show you.*

I shook off my covers and climbed down, and we slipped our feet into our shoes by the door. Then we went out into the night.

He walked ahead of me but kept turning his head back to see that I was keeping up. In his gestures—the manner in which he abstained from putting his hand on my shoulder or back, or taking my hand—I understood he was relinquishing his claim on me. He was only pointing the way for me. He was no longer carrying me, because I was no longer his to carry.

We walked to the clearing at the road and stood next to the elder, which was dark and plain now but had exploded in white, fragrant bloom earlier in the summer.

"Look," Dad said, and pointed his face up to the sky.

The Milky Way cut across our vision, thick and bright and fuzzy. The longer I looked, the more of it emerged: constellations for which I knew no names. I knew only the Big Dipper, and there it was, larger and brighter than I'd ever seen it. The darkness shimmered and waved, the points of light in fuller colour than I'd known them to possess, blues and whites and reds. There was not a cloud to be found, and the stars were alive.

"Watch," he whispered, because there was no sound.

The night was still and silent and cool. I wrapped my arms around myself, while my father dared not touch me.

I know now that it is called the Perseids meteor shower, and that it is an annual event, coming each August to decorate late summer's nights, regular and dependable, and that it had been blazing long before we rose and developed language and named the eighth month *August* and built our cities, and that it will continue long after we and every name we have invented are forgotten. But I didn't know it that night. I didn't have a word for the wonder I experienced when a brilliant white dot flared into existence and then drew a sharp, curving line across the sky before vanishing, its tail swallowed by the darkness. Though I suddenly understood that the world of myth was real, lying out there, beyond, I could only say, "Oh!"

And then it happened again. And again. Dozens of foreign objects entering our atmosphere and exploding soundlessly into colour and light, streaking across the overhead dome, and then disappearing. They were coming in succession, two or three a minute, and on just a few occasions coinciding, differing and wayward trajectories catching the corners of my eyes.

I can't say with certainty, but I think we were there an hour, watching the heavens leak their dying radiance. After a time Dad lay down on the hard road while I crouched, my knees bent over my feet, and continued to hug myself for warmth while looking up and trying to guess where the next explosion would occur. I was never right, and my inability to predict it thrilled me.

"Okay," he finally said.

I followed him back inside and slid off my shoes and climbed back up into my loft, and was asleep so quickly that I nearly forgot the whole experience.

━◆━

The next morning, I woke to my parents arguing about the car—who should keep it, and what the other would do. They were standing in the kitchen, Mom holding a coffee cup and facing Dad, him leaning against the counter, his body angled away from her, as though he might simply push himself forward and slip out.

"I'm not gonna survive out here without transportation," Dad said. "I'll have to go get my own supplies, and I can't carry everything."

"Jesus. That's great. How do we get home?"

"I guess you don't. I guess you stay here with me and we do this together."

"Do what, kill ourselves?"

"You're in more danger there. I wonder how long before you realize that?"

"How long before you realize how stupid you're being and come with us?" she said. "Maybe when it starts snowing?"

Dad tilted his chin down into his chest and let a long, expressive breath out through his lips. Then he walked toward the screen door and looked out through the porch, toward the lake, and said something he'd said before. "Look at that," he whispered. "What more could you want?"

"Fine, Art," she finally said, and put down the coffee cup she'd been holding. "We'll find a ride. We'll be okay. Gabe," she said, raising her voice, "get up. We've got to go."

"Okay," I said, because in a flash of bone-deep child wisdom, I realized I had expected all of this. I knew that I was making a momentous decision, choosing one over the other. It didn't take me a second—I would go with the one who made me feel safest.

The humiliation my father experienced as a result is the likeliest reason I can conjure as to why he never reached out to me.

She made me a peanut butter sandwich and packed a bag while I sat at the table eating. Dad went out into the screened porch, where he sat staring at the lake, not once turning his head to look back inside.

The door banged shut behind us, and we began walking. Dad didn't say goodbye, or even leave the porch. We walked into the bright, golden morning, the air fresh and cool, smelling of pine needles and the lake's mineral, metallic taste. The breeze had a new snap to it. I'd need a coat soon.

Mom walked with the green nylon pack slung over her shoulder, and she held my hand. The cabin disappeared.

"It'll be good to get back, won't it?" she said.

"I guess," I said.

We walked up the dusty road, past the trail to the old Vauxhall, past where we had seen the shape of a bear, past the fetid wetlands and the dry washes. We must have walked past Daniel's land, too—though I never knew exactly where that was, and saw no sign of people anywhere near us that morning, at least not until we reached the highway.

"What is he thinking?" she said, more to herself than to me.

"He loves you," I said. I didn't know what might give her comfort in that moment. She gave a small laugh at that. "He calls you beautiful a lot."

"Beautiful and stupid, maybe," she said, which was nearly the harshest thing I'd ever heard her say, so I said nothing. We walked on in silence.

My parents had loved each other and were for the most part happy right up until their dissolution. I suppose it's possible that she believed he'd spend a few sullen days alone before deciding that she was right and driving back into the city to be with us. She might even have believed that he'd come roaring up the road in the Honda and apologize, and that we'd then go back and properly close up the cabin before returning to our life in town as a family. That could explain why she didn't seem terribly emotional as we walked away from him, to a new life that featured only the two of us, and the virus's threat, and the terrifying possibility of me returning to school in just a few short weeks.

Or maybe my mother kept her head because she prioritized my well-being. I was her only child, and when forced to choose between her husband and her son, she did what she'd always known she would do.

We continued up the dry road until I could smell the pavement and see the flashes of cars speeding by. The world spinning on, the world we'd soon rejoin. Its bump and jostle, its crises and consolations. Our lives waiting to be lived, however they might look.

When we got out near the highway, where the pine abruptly stopped at the edge of a ditch and a thatch of phragmites and tall grass crowded the gravel shoulder, she stopped walking and slid the pack off her shoulders. From a zipped pocket on top she took out a green bandana.

"We'll need these," she said. She folded it into a triangle and then placed it over my nose and mouth, binding it in a tight knot behind my head. "Best I've got right now. We'll get you some that fit."

"It's tight," I said, scrunching up my face and feeling the fabric press against the bridge of my nose, and the dampness my breath made inside.

"Nobody loves them, but you'll get used to it," she said, and then she took from the bag her own mask, a black cotton one with loops that she pulled over her ears. I could see by her eyes that she was smiling, but I couldn't see her mouth or her nose, and she looked strange to me.

ACKNOWLEDGEMENTS

The creation of this book was greatly aided by a Recommender Grant from the Ontario Arts Council. I'm grateful for the support they provide to artists and creators in this province.

This book quite simply wouldn't exist without the collaboration of my editor, Bryan Ibeas. His vision of this story's possibilities—and my ability to pull it off—changed it completely, for the better. Thanks, friend, for the trust and confidence. Looking forward to working with you again.

Norm Nehmetallah, publisher of Invisible, is a tireless champion of writers, independent presses, and booksellers. Thanks, Norm, for your belief in me and in this book.

The entire Invisible team is an incredible group, each member exceptional at what they do, and collectively unstoppable. Jules, Kim, Megan: thank you.

Thanks to Take Cover Books in Peterborough for their support, and thanks to independent booksellers everywhere.

Thanks to ADF, COF, and TJF for understanding and love.

CC: from you, all possibilities flow. Thank you.

This book is dedicated to the memory of Denee MacKinnon. Love you, Mom.

Invisible Publishing produces fine Canadian literature for those who enjoy such things. As an independent, not-for-profit publisher, we work to build communities that sustain and encourage engaging, literary, and current writing.

Invisible Publishing has been in operation for over a decade. We released our first fiction titles in the spring of 2007, and our catalogue has come to include works of graphic fiction and nonfiction, pop culture biographies, experimental poetry, and prose.

We are committed to publishing writers with diverse perspectives. In acknowledging historical and systemic barriers, and the limits of our existing catalogue, we emphatically encourage writers from LGBTQ2SIA+ communities, Indigenous writers, and writers of colour to submit their work.

Invisible Publishing is also home to the Bibliophonic series of music books and the Throwback series of CanLit reissues.